SPECI   ᴇᴅꜱ

THE ULVERSCROFT F
(registered UK charity nι
was established in 1972 to p
res¹⁻⁻⁻⁻⁻ ᵈⁱ⁻⁻⁻⁻⁻⁻ ⁻⁻⁻ ᵗ⁻⁻⁻⁻⁻⁻⁻⁻ ⁻⁻ ⁻⁻⁻ ᵈⁱ⁻⁻⁻⁻es.

Tel: (0116) 236 4325

website: www.foundation.ulverscroft.com

Nicola Slade was brought up in Poole, Dorset. She wrote children's stories when her three children were growing up, later moving on to adult fiction. Winning a story competition in *Family Circle* galvanised her into writing seriously, and since then her stories and articles have been commissioned regularly by several national magazines. *Scuba Dancing* was her first published novel. As well as writing, Nicola has been a Brown Owl and an antiques dealer. She currently lives in Hampshire with her husband; her three grown children live nearby.

A CROWDED COFFIN

It is late summer in Hampshire and former headmistress Harriet Quigley is enjoying life. Her cousin Sam is moving next door and the only cloud on the horizon is the continual village gossip. But suddenly, it's all going pear-shaped — and sensible, practical Harriet has only herself to blame. Sam has warned her not to play Miss Marple, but Harriet is suspicious about several newcomers and she can't help herself from asking discreet questions. With a sudden death in Winchester Cathedral, a hunt for ancient treasure attracting unwelcome attention, and history that looms uncomfortably close, Harriet finds herself trapped somewhere very nasty . . .

NICOLA SLADE

A CROWDED COFFIN

Complete and Unabridged

ULVERSCROFT
Leicester

First published in Great Britain in 2013 by
Robert Hale Limited
London

First Large Print Edition
published 2013
by arrangement with
Robert Hale Limited
London

A catalogue record for this book is available
from the British Library.

ISBN 978–1–4448–1753–9

Published by
F. A. Thorpe (Publishing)
Anstey, Leicestershire

Set by Words & Graphics Ltd.
Anstey, Leicestershire
Printed and bound in Great Britain by
T. J. International Ltd., Padstow, Cornwall

This book is printed on acid-free paper

Dedication

My mother and grandmother taught me that if you can read you can do anything. I wish they had known about my books, they'd have been my fiercest critics but my staunchest supporters.

Acknowledgements

A *Crowded Coffin* is a work of fiction so all the people in it are products of my imagination, as is the village of Locksley. Winchester Cathedral, however, is exactly as described — apart from the corpse — and is a must-see on every visitor's itinerary. The history is as accurate as I can make it but, sadly, I forgot to keep a record of the dozens of books and websites I consulted when doing research. However, I'm enormously grateful to everyone whose brains I picked, whether they knew it or not! Finally, thanks to my brilliant first readers, Olivia Barnes, Linda Gruchy and Joanne Thomson, who did their usual thing by spotting typos, idiotic mistakes and gaping plot holes.

Principal Characters

Harriet Quigley	A recently retired headmistress who finds herself down in the dumps
Rev'd Sam Hathaway	Her cousin, a canon who wants a career change
Rory	An artist with a painful past
Edith	A returning exile, beset by ancestors
Walter and Penelope Attlin	Two of Edith's ancestors, both alive and kicking
Rev'd John Forrester	A popular parson
Brendan Whittaker	A handsome henchman
Mike Goldstein	A tantalizing Texan
Gordon Dean	A man who makes money
Lara Dean	His daughter, who spends money
Karen	A housekeeper who was at school with Edith

Elveece	A Polish plumber
Dr Oliver	He only sat down
Sutherland	for a few minutes'
	rest . . .
Margaret	A watchful witness
Mackenzie	

Assorted cats, dogs, art historians, ghosts and villagers

A CROWDED COFFIN

Murder is easy. It's disposing of the body that throws up a few problems.

You might think a piggery would provide the perfect solution but you'd be wrong.

'Dispose of a body?' The pig farmer's roar of laughter bodes ill when, oh so casually, you pose the question. 'Oh dear, oh dear, that old chestnut does crop up. You wouldn't believe how many times I get asked that.' He shakes his head and takes the trouble to explain. 'You can't just throw a body to the pigs, you see. You'd need to dismember it first and who has that kind of equipment handy in their kitchen?'

Who indeed?

So why, with the pig farm only one of a dozen discarded avenues, scarcely remembered for ages, should you suddenly find yourself, of all things, unable to face bacon or roast pork?

LOCKSLEY BULLETIN: VILLAGE NEWS

Foul Play? Cathedral Worker Still Missing after Six Months — Police Concerned

1

Police are anxious to contact Colin John Price, a junior researcher at the Stanton Resingham archive, associated with the Diocese of Winchester. Mr Price, a single man, aged thirty-four, was last seen on the fifth of January this year, when he had had two pints of beer at Locksley's pub. Tom Draper, landlord of The Angel, said he had served the missing man. 'He was very interested in the history of the village,' Tom told *The Locksley Bulletin*. ''Specially about Locksley Farm Place. He also asked about the people hereabouts, up at the farm and in the village, and about the vicar and the history of the church.'

Inquiries locally have so far drawn a blank. Mr Price's car, a 2008 reg. Honda, was found vandalized in Locksley two days later. A police spokesman told *The Bulletin*: 'We do have some concerns as Mr Price's credit cards and bank account have not been touched and he has not been seen since the date in question.'

In answer to a question put by *The Bulletin*, the police spokesman said: 'Local residents can rest assured we are doing all we can to find Mr Price. At the present time we cannot comment on whether there is any suspicion of foul play.'

1

He cowers there, flattening himself into the mud, waiting for the enemy to strike again, slipping in and out of consciousness until memory reminds him that this isn't Korea and he isn't a young soldier any more.

So why is he lying in the cold and dark, hurting, injured, knowing he is in mortal danger? He tries to move, his old bones grinding, one arm slack and useless. He feels inside his sodden shirt with his good hand. Collarbone broken, most likely. But how? What has happened? Why is he lying out here? The last thing he remembers clearly is leaning on a five-barred gate, surveying the farm and thinking there was rain in the air.

He winces as he tries to move, sure he is in a puddle; plenty of rain now. How long has he been out of it, then? Thinking is a huge effort but he has a vague memory of a noise just before it happened. Thunder? No, not thunder. Despite the pain, the fog in his mind is clearing. He'd thought it was thunder, that's it, but his hearing isn't too good nowadays (not that he'd ever admit it to his wife) and he'd been distracted by something on the other side of the field. Something that couldn't possibly be there.

The rumble of a car approaching along the track had startled him from his reverie, the sudden hard revving of the engine his only warning as he'd leaped out of its way.

'Someone drove at me deliberately,' he whispers now.

And there it is again, the low growl of an engine approaching. Coming to finish him off.

★ ★ ★

Harriet Quigley glanced at the Arrivals board at Southampton Airport. Twenty minutes until her cousin Sam's flight landed gave her time for a coffee and a welcome pause for thought, even though she was desperate to discuss the awful news with him. A good deal had happened in the two days since she had dropped Sam off on his outward journey. Their parting conversation had seemed almost trivial at the time but had now acquired a sinister significance.

'Did I tell you I had lunch with old Walter Attlin? From your village?' Sam had asked as they left the M3.

She'd been intrigued. 'My cousin Walter? I didn't realize you were on lunching terms with him.'

4

'I'm not really,' he'd said. 'But I bumped into him the other day in Winchester High Street and he buttonholed me. Said he had a problem and I was just the man to help, so we had lunch in the cathedral refectory. He's a great character, isn't he?'

She nodded. 'So what was his problem? And did you solve it for him?'

'Not really.' His grin was mildly apologetic. 'Sorry, Harriet, he swore me to secrecy but I think it did help him to thrash it out with someone from outside, as a sort of sounding board. He said the trouble with getting to your eighties is that the friends you always trusted are either dead or demented, and he's been worrying himself silly. It's a pretty tenuous link between us, but the fact that he's related to you through your father, and that you and I are first cousins on the other side, seemed to make him feel more comfortable about talking to me, even though we've never really known each other well.'

★   ★   ★

Now, as she spooned froth off her cappuccino, and waited for Sam's arrival, she shivered. Her elderly relative, Walter Attlin, was foremost in her thoughts. His misadventure the other night had shocked everyone in

5

the close-knit village, and she had a lot to discuss with Sam, who was not just her cousin, but her closest friend. Things were happening and Harriet was worried.

'Penny for them, Harriet?' The tall, silver-haired clergyman was standing in front of her now with an amused expression on his long, pleasant face. 'You were miles away. Are you all right?' Concern replaced affection as he asked, 'How are you? And what's the latest on Walter?'

'I'm fine, Sam.' She rose — very like him in looks; tall and slim, with a smile never far away, though her own hair was firmly kept to a natural-looking honey colour — and gave him a brief but affectionate hug. 'Got all your stuff? Great, let's get going. Walter's — '

She was interrupted by a shout. 'Miss Q? Oh my God. Grandpa? You . . . ' she stammered, her face ashen. 'He's not . . . you haven't come to tell me . . . ?'

Harriet turned in surprise to see a petite twenty-something girl steaming towards her, face puckered with anxiety.

'Edith? What on earth are you doing here? I thought you were in America.'

'But Grandpa. Is he . . . is he . . . ?' The girl fell into Harriet's welcoming arms.

'He's fine, honestly, Edith. As fine as an

eighty-something man with a broken collarbone can be. And better than most, tough old
devil that he is.'

'Oh, thank God. You're sure?' the pretty
blonde said as she emerged from Harriet's
affectionate hug, still pale though some of the
tension had clearly drained away. 'But if
you're not here to tell me bad news, then
what are you doing here?'

'I've come to meet Sam. Do you know my
cousin, Sam Hathaway? He's a canon at the
cathedral. Sam, this is Edith Attlin, my very
distant relative and erstwhile pupil. Of
course,' she added with a grin, 'that was
before I retired and found myself busier with
village life than ever I was as a headmistress.
I'm sure you must have met her a long time
ago because Edith's grandfather is Walter,
from Locksley Farm Place.'

Sam Hathaway looked relieved at Harriet's
news about Walter, but he made no comment
as he shook hands with the new arrival.

Edith gave Sam's hand a perfunctory
pump. 'This is going to be very cheeky but
could I hitch a lift, please? I have to get home
straight away. I was going to get a taxi, never
mind the expense, but if you're heading my
way . . .'

'Of course you can have a lift, but what on
earth are you doing here?' Harriet was

leading the way to the car park. 'Your grandfather is doing remarkably well, in the circumstances, so do stop panicking.'

Her expression lightened and, blue eyes twinkling, she added, 'I rang your grandmother first thing and she said that, according to the hospital, he's recovering in leaps and bounds and is anxious to get home. I think she translated that as meaning he was driving them mad. Now, where did you spring from? Nobody said anything about expecting you.'

They reached the car, an immaculate, original Mini. 'My VW Golf died so I thought I would put my mother's car back on the road. She had it from new and it's still going strong,' Harriet explained as Edith clambered into the back seat and Harriet tucked assorted bags around her.

Sam, with a rueful look at the leg room, folded up his long body like a penknife and slotted himself into the front passenger seat. Harriet ignored his grunts as he settled himself, and as she drove back towards the motorway, returned to her question. 'Where have you sprung from anyway, Edith? You weren't on Sam's flight from Belfast, surely?'

'No, I came home via Amsterdam. It was the quickest way I could get back from the States. We landed earlier but there was a problem with picking up the luggage.' She leaned forward. 'You're really sure Grandpa's all right? The message I got was that he'd been run over and rushed to hospital. Gran insisted he wasn't in danger and that I was to stay put, but I couldn't. I just had a few loose ends to sort out, which took a day or so, and after that I got the first possible plane out.'

Sam twisted round to look at Edith, his eyes showing his concern. He opened his mouth to ask questions, but as Harriet tanked over him, he sat back, knowing he wouldn't be able to get a word in edgeways.

'Your grandmother was quite right; he's shaken and uncomfortable but he's going to be fine, honestly. How long can you stay?'

'I'm home for good,' Edith said briefly, her face still taut with anxiety.

'Really?' Harriet glanced back at her. 'I thought you were happy earning shed-loads of dollars in Hollywood as the very upmarket English governess to the brats of the rich and famous. Film stars and directors and so forth.'

'I was, until my latest employer suggested I might like to consider becoming his fourth wife, even though he was still apparently happily married to his third one. Unfortunately she overheard him proposing and things got a bit out of hand, to say the least.'

Harriet looked surprised and Edith shrugged. 'Like I said, it was awkward, so I packed my bags and camped at a friend's house while I said my goodbyes. I'd actually handed in my notice anyway, which is probably what prompted his suggestion, and packed up ready to leave, so I was able, pretty much, to hop on a plane when I got the phone call about Grandpa. Anyway, I haven't been home since Christmas and I do worry about them, so it seemed a good time to make a break.'

'Yes, well . . . ' Harriet took a sharp corner at a risky gallop ignoring Sam's sharply indrawn breath as she did so. 'About your grandfather, Edith. As I told you, nobody's worried about him long-term, but a broken collarbone and bruising at his age is always tricky so they decided to keep him in hospital for a day or so, purely for observation.'

Sam nodded, concern furrowing his brow, while Edith looked pale and anxious as she asked, 'Are you *sure* that's all, Miss Q? What happened? I never got the whole story from Gran.'

'Quite sure, I promise you. As I keep saying, he's said to be recovering well. Apparently he went for a stroll round the garden then decided to walk down the lane to the Burial Field but he claims he was distracted by a noise just when he reached the gate to the big paddock. He thought it was thunder — it was a muggy night — so he just carried on pottering. This is where it gets a bit hard to swallow . . . He says he'd just reached the rise when he thought he saw something at the edge of the copse. He stopped to look and that's when he realized it wasn't thunder he'd heard at all.' Harriet concentrated on the traffic for a moment then continued. 'He says the car drove straight at him. God knows how he managed to leap aside but he says the car didn't actually hit him. It was when he fell that he broke his collarbone.'

Sam and Edith both looked appalled and Edith exclaimed, 'But, but that's . . . that's . . . Is he sure?'

Harriet glanced at her cousin who shook his head slightly. Walter Attlin might be in his eighties but he was an astute old man with a logical, practical intelligence and a calm temperament. If he said that a car had been driven straight at him, then that was what had happened, unless . . .

'He's, he's all right, is he, Miss Q?' Edith faltered. 'He's not — not getting — '

'You mean, is he getting senile?' Harriet snorted. 'Of course he's not. He told the police what had happened and someone came out to take a look but there was a

11

terrific downpour later that night and the place was like the Somme so any evidence, tyre tracks and so forth, was washed away. Besides, even though it was a failure to stop after an accident, there wasn't much they could do except put it into the system. I don't think they took seriously his assertion that he was deliberately targeted; after all, they don't know him the way we do. And anyway, what action could they actually take? The car and driver were long gone.' She concentrated on overtaking a car-transporter. 'I gather he's backpedalling now,' she continued. 'I suspect it's because he doesn't want to upset your grandmother.'

Sam Hathaway digested this information then returned to something that had caught his interest. 'What's this about a burial field?' he asked. 'I've only been to the house a couple of times, a long while ago, when we were kids, remember, Harriet? It's not my side of the family, though I do know the old boy slightly. Who have you got buried in there? Family graveyard?'

'It's where the original Roman villa is said to have been built.' Edith sounded glad to take her mind off her grandfather's accident. 'Did you know that story?' Sam nodded and she carried on. 'Well, there's a stone there, in the middle of a little copse. Oh, you really must come and see it, Canon Hathaway, it's difficult to describe. And Grandpa would love to show it to you.'

She looked anxiously at Harriet. 'Is that all, Miss Q? I got the impression when I phoned a couple of weeks ago that Grandpa was worrying about something. That's another thing that had already prompted me to come home, really.'

'You might as well know,' sighed Harriet, taking the turning off the roundabout and heading towards Hursley and Locksley village. 'There's been something rather odd going on. The tenant of Walter's other farm died recently, old Misselbrook, and practically the minute he died, not quite three weeks ago, Walter received an offer for the smaller farm to include the Burial Field and the big paddock that both border on to it. A very good offer, and all done properly through an agent, but he turned it down, of course. Walter's sold land in the past but, not this particular parcel. They would never let the Burial Field go, even without all the history. It's much too close to the house.'

Edith looked puzzled as she nodded agreement, then Harriet changed the subject. 'And while I think about it, Edith, it really is time you stopped calling me Miss Q and called me Harriet. It's years since I was your headmistress and we're related after all. Besides, if even your grandparents' aged retainers can call me Harriet, it's silly of you to be so formal.'

'Aged retainers?' Edith's puzzled frown deepened as Sam Hathaway joined in Harriet's laughter. 'What do you mean?'

'That's my fault, Edith,' he assured her. 'A few days ago Harriet said something about the staff at Locksley Farm Place and I made some crack about how feudal it sounded, having aged retainers around in this day and age. That's when she put me right.'

'Well? Who *have* they got at the moment? The first message I got came from the doctor and I only managed to snatch a brief word with Gran and that was all about Grandpa. I know the couple they got through an advert didn't work out but I never met them. They were due to start in the New Year, after I'd already flown back to Los Angeles. I heard they'd got someone new but I thought they were still using that agency.'

'Fingers crossed, it's working well so far,' Harriet told her. 'Remember Karen Norton from the village? She was in your tutor group at school, if I remember. She got married a year or so back and she and her husband moved in to the flat behind the kitchen. She does the cooking and housekeeping and he does the maintenance and gardening, or at least, he supervises the contractors and does the kitchen garden. His name's Markus but . . . ' she paused with a grin, then hurried on. 'He's a plumber by trade but pretty handy all round, which is useful. Plus he has, um, other talents.'

'Other talents? Is there something odd about the husband?' Edith's grey eyes narrowed as she caught the smile that passed between the driver and front-seat passenger. 'What about him? I always got on well with Karen, we were in the same gang, but we've lost touch. It'll be fun to catch up again.'

'He's a very nice young man,' Harriet told her firmly. 'You'll like him; he's very popular in the village. Anyway, as I started to say earlier, if Karen and her husband — he's Polish, by the way — if they can call me Harriet and he's only known me a couple of months, I really think you must make an effort. And you might as well say Sam, while you're about it, especially as he's likely to be around a lot more in future.'

'Oh all right, *Harriet*,' Edith sounded shy. 'What's this about you, Sam? Why are you likely to be around? Do you live in the village these days too?'

'As of next week I shall,' Sam explained. 'Harriet's neighbour lost her husband in the spring and she's moving nearer to her daughter in Hastings so she offered me first refusal on her house. It's ideal, semi-detached from Harriet's place. Contracts were exchanged almost a month ago and I'm taking another look round the cottage this afternoon before I go home.'

'Oh,' Edith looked suddenly subdued. 'Of course, I'd forgotten.' She blinked. 'Harriet told me, I think. I was so sorry to hear about . . . '

'Thank you,' Sam nodded, frowning blankly out of the car window. Even now, after some years, a sudden mention, however oblique, of his late, beloved wife could catch him unawares.

'Nearly there.' At the top of the hill Harriet swung into a narrow road, paused in a passing place nestling close to the hedgerow, which was starred with dog roses and bryony, to allow a tractor to rattle by, then headed off west towards Locksley. Just at the beginning of the village she turned left, through brick-pillared posts, the gates long gone, into the winding, pot-holed driveway of the old cream-stuccoed farmhouse that was Edith's family home, pulling up with a flourish at the front door. 'Here we are,' she said, scrambling out of the Mini to let Edith out through the driver's door.

'Here, hand me your laptop so you can scramble out. And that bag as well. That the lot?' She went to the boot and unloaded Edith's case. 'Can't stop, I'm afraid. Sam wants to catch my neighbour before she has to go out. Don't worry too much about your grandparents, Edith. I believe Walter is due out of hospital tomorrow, and there's been a rota of people in the village dropping in daily to see if your grandmother needs anything. Besides, Karen and her husband are extremely efficient and they're very kind too. Give everyone my love.'

She gave Edith a quick hug and climbed back into the ancient but gleaming Mini, leaning out for a parting word as she did a three-point turn. 'If I don't see you before, I'll certainly see you tomorrow night. We'll both be there — Sam's coming too.' As she drove back down the gravel drive to the gateway, Harriet frowned, wondering whether she should have dropped a hint. There was something else that was worrying her: the ongoing village mystery — the missing man last seen in the local pub — but no, there was no need to add that to Edith's problems. There was surely no connection, was there?

Edith waved goodbye, looking puzzled by Harriet's last remark, but she shook her head and hauled her bags up the steps and into the entrance hall. Dumping them there she hurried through the silent house to the kitchen where she paused at the door and stared at the curvaceous, auburn-haired young woman who was taking a tray of assorted mini quiches out of the vintage Aga.

'Karen?' Edith held out her hands to the other girl who, when she recognized the newcomer, straightened up in surprise, then plonked her baking tray down on the old scrubbed kitchen table and rushed forward. 'How fantastic! I met Harriet Quigley at the airport and she gave me a lift. She told me you were here but I didn't really take it in properly. You look amazing! It's great to see you again — it's been years. I love the vintage look, very Debbie Reynolds. That's new, isn't it?'

The other girl really did look stunning, Edith decided, a 1950s pin-up; her hair was in a bouncy style with a fringe and a perky yellow ribbon, and she wore a pair of what looked like genuine vintage pedal-pushers. Bright red lipstick and a crisp white blouse with a Peter Pan collar completed the picture.

'Edith?' Karen Mirowski returned the hug with affection. 'Goodness yes, it must be at least five years. I've been into vintage nearly that long.' She looked at Edith. 'You haven't changed much,' she said, then she took a step back, casting an appraising glance at her. 'No, I take that back,' she said. 'You actually look tired out. I imagine it was a long flight. I'm so glad to see you, you're really needed here, I can tell you. But why didn't you let your grandparents know you were coming home?'

Edith shrugged and smiled. 'No time. I got the message about Grandpa and hopped on a flight as soon as I could. Besides, my current job had, er, come to a natural close. It was time to come home anyway. Grandpa was cool about me working abroad for a couple of years but I know he wants me to get involved in the place now and I can't let him down.'

'Well, I'm glad; you're certainly needed here,' Karen told her frankly. 'They'll be pleased, your grandparents. You'll find them a bit shaken up at the moment.'

'Yes,' Edith looked anxious. 'Harriet's been telling me about Grandpa's accident. I'd better go and see Gran and break it to her gently that I'm home for good.'

Karen glanced at her watch. 'I'd leave it for an hour or so,' she suggested. 'You know Mr Attlin's not due out of hospital till tomorrow? And your grandmother usually spends the afternoon resting these days but she was late today and she's only just gone upstairs to the sitting room. Leave your bags down here. Markus, my husband, can take them up when he gets back. He's working on a plumbing job in Hursley all day today but he'll be back soon. He's got to get ready for a gig in Southampton.'

'Mmm, all right, thanks.' Edith sounded distracted as she stared at the array of food she had glimpsed through the open door of the larder, as well as the tray of quiches cooling on the table. 'What on earth is all this food for, Karen? There's enough to feed an army here. They haven't taken in lodgers, have they?'

'Just the one,' Karen rolled her eyes. 'That's this artist that your grandmother has invited to stay for the summer. He's — ' She broke off as the phone rang, then reached for a pencil and paper and began to make a list, pointing to the kettle. Edith shook her head, ran the tap for a glass of cold water, then turned away, frustrated. A lodger? What on earth were her grandparents thinking of? She waved to Karen, who was still busy on the phone, and went out of the back door into the courtyard formed by the angle of the mediaeval hall and the house that had been tacked on in the early 1500s.

Out in the sunshine Edith felt again the tremor of excitement that always assailed her when she came home. It had always been home, even when her life during term time was spent in London, where her mother had a high-powered job as a company lawyer. Holidays always meant the far from stately farm of the Attlin family, the old house at Locksley, near Winchester.

When she was a young child her father, an army officer, was blown up by a mortar attack while on a routine deployment with the UN peace-keeping forces in the war in Bosnia. For the four years it took Richard Attlin to die in a hospital outside London, Edith lived in Hampshire with her grandparents while her mother worked to keep them afloat, visiting her husband and daughter as often as she could. After Richard's death Edith went back to school in London but when she was fourteen her mother married again. Her new husband was a doctor, an old friend from her home town in the Scottish borders, and she moved back there with him, while Edith chose to move permanently to Locksley where she became one of Harriet Quigley's students at a school just outside Winchester.

Even with the worry about her grandparents, both at present and for the future, Edith felt herself relax. I'm home, she thought, sighing with relief. It had all come together, she realized: a longing for home that had crept up on her and the fact that the children she had been teaching were about to go to boarding school, together with the knowledge that her real job awaited her back at the farm in Hampshire. If only her grandfather was really going to be all right.

Savouring the peace and the sunshine Edith turned the corner and came out to the front of the house, to find a stranger, a tall, very thin young man, contending with Lulu, the stout family dog that looked much like a Labrador but with a curly tail. She was leaping up at him in a ridiculous parody of puppyhood and plastering his chinos with mud.

Oh God, it must be Karen's husband, she thought, running along the brick path. I hope it doesn't put him off working here. Harriet says he's a treasure and it's so hard to get reliable helpers for Gran and Grandpa. 'Down, Lulu, down. Bad dog!'

The dog arched in mid-jump at the sound of a remembered voice and twisted round, barely touching base before throwing herself at Edith who, wise in the fat almost-Labrador's ways, braced herself to receive the onslaught. After a damp but enthusiastic reunion Edith rose and looked up at the stranger.

'Ohhhh!' It was a long drawn-out gasp as her hand went to her mouth. 'But . . . but who *are* you?' She stared at him in astonishment. Not Karen's husband after all, definitely not, but who on earth could he be? Dark brown hair, a humorous quirk to the mouth, achingly familiar, but goodness, he was thin. Far *too* thin, surely?

'What's the matter?' he asked, looking anxious when she just stood there gazing at him.

'But . . . you look just like . . . ' She pulled herself together and frowned, then shook her head. 'I'm sorry, it's just . . . oh well, never mind. Can I help you? Were you looking for someone? I'm so sorry about the dog.'

'I'm fine,' he said, patting the old dog as she flopped down beside him, resting her nose on his shoe. 'I like dogs but I must admit I wouldn't have worn my best trousers if I'd known what she was like. I wanted to make a good impression on my first day, that was all.' When Edith still looked puzzled he grinned. 'I'm the new lodger,' he explained. 'I was just exploring. Who are you?'

'You mean you're the artist Karen was talking about?' She stared at him, a frown knitting her brow. 'I — oh, I'm sorry.' She shook her head. 'I don't mean to be rude, but it's a bit of a surprise. We've never taken in lodgers before and I can't think what Gran's up to. It's not as though she hasn't got a lot on her plate.'

'I suppose it must seem odd to you,' his smile was disarming, 'but you needn't worry. I insisted on paying for my bed and board even though your grandparents protested.' His smile broadened and he held out his hand. 'You must be Edith. I'm your very distant cousin, Rory Attlin.'

'Really?' She hesitated, still puzzled, then shook hands with an apologetic smile. 'I've never heard of any distant cousins. But,' she glanced at him again then looked away, 'that could explain why you look so much like . . . ' The old dog interrupted her at that moment, nuzzling a wet nose into her hand. 'Oh well, it's Gran's business after all. I'm sorry if I sounded rude, I'm a bit jet-lagged.' She gave him a friendly grin.

He smiled. 'Thanks, no problem. Just one thing: they did mention in the pub that there used to be witches here. Any truth in that? Just so I know.'

'They only say that to cadge drinks out of the unwary.' She laughed out loud at his expression. 'Caught you, did they? The truth is the Attlin women have always been practical and bossy, and yes, they probably did know a lot about herbs and folklore, but I expect you'll be safe enough.'

'Hmm.' He looked thoughtful, a sparkle in his hazel eyes. 'Have those particular genes been carried down to the present day?'

She laughed again and shook her head. 'I couldn't possibly comment. You'll have to wait and see. And watch your step.'

'Look.' He dug his hands into his pockets and smiled down at her. 'I've clearly arrived at a difficult time, but can we call a truce? I'll try and keep out of your way and not be a nuisance, but I don't want to leave. This place is magic.' He swept a comprehensive glance round the garden and looked down at her slightly shyly as if reluctant to admit to such enthusiasm.

She wasn't proof against such obvious appreciation of her home. His presence might be an unwanted complication at a time of such uncertainty and anxiety, and his appearance was something of a disturbing mystery, but the hand caressing the stone angel beside the original entrance to the hall was the hand of a lover. His expression as he gazed up at the mosaic of dressed flint that glittered above the porch, as the sun caught it, was one of startled pleasure.

'Call me Edith, everyone does. Look, I'm really sorry if I was a bit short,' she told him again. 'I shouldn't have, it's just that you look so . . . ' She frowned. 'There's a portrait, you see . . . well, I'll show you later, then you'll understand. But as I was saying, there's no point me making a fuss. If Gran thinks you should be here, then here's where you have to be.'

'She's been very helpful. We fixed things up earlier in the week and I moved in this morning. Your grandmother's friend in the village told her about me and that I was looking for somewhere to live. She vouched for me because her sister used to live next door to us.' Rory filled her in on some details. 'I'm starting a new job at the university next term and this gives me a good base for getting to know my way about and doing some leisurely house-hunting.'

Edith shivered, suddenly cold. 'Earlier in the week? You were here? When was that? Was it before or after Grandpa's accident?'

He stared at her abrupt question. 'I heard about that. It was the same day, I think, Wednesday. At least, I think it was that night he was injured, wasn't it? Why? Does it make a difference? I promise not to get underfoot.'

'It's not that . . . oh, never mind.' She still felt chilled and suddenly very tired as well as paranoid. Somebody walking over her grave, perhaps? 'I was just wondering, that's all.' She led him through the original stone-flagged entrance into Locksley Farm Place. 'Let's go and have a cup of tea,' she suggested. 'I'm parched.'

Rory lagged behind, staring up at the entrance. 'You'd never know this was here, would you,' he said, nodding towards the mediaeval building. 'Tucked round here you don't see it at all when you come up the drive, it's amazing.'

He caught up with Edith and as they crossed the great hall Rory paused to look around. The room was dominated by an enormous refectory table that stood across one end, gleaming with centuries of elbow grease. Silver pots filled with roses stood at either end and there was a larger flower arrangement in the middle.

'I see the village Flower Club ladies have been here.' Edith looked puzzled as she nodded towards the artfully elegant display. 'I wonder why. Maybe it's just a compliment to Gran as she used to be their chairman.'

Rory was clearly only half listening. 'This table is incredible,' he murmured, stroking it with an appreciative hand.

'It is, isn't it,' she agreed, giving him an approving look as her suspicions faded into the background. 'It's the genuine article too. My umpteenth great-grandmother is supposed to have pinched it from her convent during the Dissolution of the Monasteries. Though, to be more accurate, she sent for it when the convent was closed down as she had

27

already run away with my umpteenth great-grandfather. I doubt she paid anything for it; the legend says she was a tough cookie.'

'A runaway nun?' He looked intrigued.

She was gratified to note his interest so she continued. 'It's said that they were distant cousins and forbidden to marry because her family were poor. His father actually bought off her parents with the price of her dowry to the convent so he must have taken the affair seriously. There's no way of knowing why she went along with it and took her final vows. Maybe they forced her, or perhaps she was just biding her time.'

She took out a tissue and wiped up a scatter of drops of water from the flowers. 'Anyway, two years later, at the time Henry VIII started getting heavy with the monasteries, she and her cousin, Richard Attlin, turned up at the Angel House bearing a marriage certificate that might very well have been legal. Apparently, everyone turned a blind eye and it was never queried. The forbidding father had died, which was why Richard took off to fetch her and as the convent was broken up soon afterwards, I don't suppose anyone thought it was worth checking.'

'The Angel House?' Rory enquired. 'I thought it was called Locksley Farm Place?'

'Quite correct, so it is. The Angel House is

just the local name for it. The old name of the village was Locksley Angelorum and now it's officially just Locksley, which, by the way, is nothing to do with Robin of Locksley; we're a long way south of Nottingham.' She perched on the edge of the great table and watched Rory make a leisurely circuit round the room.

'This place is incredible. When I was fixing things up I didn't actually come in here,' he told her as he gazed in awe at ancient beams that spanned the soaring height of the hall, then paused, as everyone always did, to peer up the chimney of the huge stone hearth. 'Hey, I can see the sky a long way up.' He cast a sardonic glance at the smoke-blackened stonework and grinned at her. 'I see it smokes; it must be fun here in the winter.'

'Oh, I don't know,' she shrugged. 'We don't even try to heat it these days, of course — it's too expensive — but it only smokes if the wind is in the east.' She grinned and waved a hand to the far end of the room. 'Though I must admit the fireplace at the other end tends to smoke if the wind is in the north, south, east and west.'

As she spoke there was a clanging at the front door. Neither of them had noticed the sound of wheels approaching on the gravel drive but when Edith ran through the house to open up, she was confronted by an ambulance with its open rear end facing her. The driver and his mate were helping an elderly white-haired man into a wheelchair.

'Grandpa?' Edith rushed to give him a brief hug and to help settle him. 'What on earth are you doing out of the hospital? Harriet and Karen said you weren't due home till tomorrow. You really ought to do as you're told.'

'I'm sorry, love,' put in the patient transport ambulance driver, looking sympathetic. 'He insisted on discharging himself and apparently there was no way they could prevent him. He wouldn't let anyone ring up for you to fetch him and he wangled a lift with us. The best they could manage was to insist on the wheelchair in and out of the ambulance, and they nearly had to tie him in before we could set off towards the lifts.'

'Oh, I know.' Edith shot him a smile of fellow feeling. 'He's an awful, pig-headed old devil and it's much easier to give in when he's got a bee in his bonnet.'

'Well, of all the unfilial things to say . . . ' Edith ignored her grandfather's remonstrance and cajoled the driver and his colleague into carrying him, plus the wheelchair, up the stairs to his bedroom on the first floor. Rory had stayed in the background during this exchange and took no part in getting the old man upstairs, which surprised her slightly.

While Rory saw the ambulance crew off the premises Edith helped Walter Attlin into an armchair in his room. She gave him a brief run-down on her sudden arrival back in England and her fortuitous meeting with Harriet at the airport, while she carried on scolding.

'Why have you done this, Grandpa? You're not usually so headstrong and you know a broken collarbone and shock aren't something to be ignored.' She looked up as Rory hovered in the open doorway, carrying the old man's overnight bag. He gave her a slight, diffident smile as he dropped the bag on a side table and turned to leave the room. Then the old man answered her.

'Didn't Harriet tell you about my 'accident'?'

Edith could almost hear the inverted commas round the word and as she stared at him he pulled himself upright in his chair. 'I'm not leaving Penny in danger. If someone could do this to me, God knows what they might try with her, she's so frail.'

'Harriet said you believed someone drove at you deliberately,' Edith said flatly and Rory halted in the doorway and turned a surprised glance at them. 'Are you sure, Grandpa?' Edith shook her head slightly, to clear her

31

thoughts. 'But that would mean it was attempted . . . murder, wouldn't it?'

As the word dropped ominously into the silence Rory drew a startled breath. Edith looked up at him with fear in her grey eyes while Walter Attlin gave him a measuring glance, appeared satisfied with what he saw and nodded briefly to himself.

'Exactly,' he said. 'However, that's not the only reason I came home. You haven't been told yet, I gather, that your grandmother hasn't cancelled the Rotary dinner?'

'What?' It was a shriek of protest, hastily subdued as Edith recalled that her grandmother was asleep on her sofa in the converted bedroom next door. As Rory turned to her, looking puzzled, she explained. 'It's a charity do,' she said. 'We don't have to do more, in theory, than provide the venue. The Rotary Club does the rest; they bring most of the food, drink, music, decorations and so forth. The wives move in on the day and take over the arrangements and all we have to do is put in an appearance and look gracious. That's the theory. In practice, of course, it's a whole lot of hassle.' She frowned and looked suspiciously at her grandfather, who was looking studiously innocent.

'Tell me I'm wrong,' she demanded. 'Tell me it isn't tomorrow night.' He looked mulish and said nothing. 'So that's what Harriet meant when she said she and Sam Hathaway would definitely see me tomorrow night, if not before. And that's why Karen's been cooking up a storm downstairs. That would be Gran's doing; she always insists that we contribute towards the dinner.'

She whirled round and confronted the unsuspecting Rory, sudden angry tears of frustration welling up. 'You don't see, do you? You think I'm just being selfish because I'll have to work my butt off, and so will you, by the way. But it's not that. It's them, Gran and Grandpa. They'll kill themselves and all for a . . . ' she caught herself up as her grandfather looked at her, 'all for a wretched party.' She turned away, struggling to drag a tissue out of her pocket and the old man's disapproving look turned to affection as she mopped up her tears.

'It's in the Bible, darling,' he said. 'Remember? *And the greatest of these is charity.* I know it's hard for you, Edith,' he stroked her head as she knelt beside him. 'But you have to let old people kill themselves in their own way. Your grandmother is determined to have this party because it's one of our long-standing traditions. Besides, it will take her mind off this 'accident' of mine.'

He looked over the bent blonde head and

smiled at Rory. 'My dear boy, I'm forgetting my manners. It's delightful to see you again. Are you settling in comfortably? I'm afraid Edith is certainly correct on one score: you will have to work to help get this dinner under way and I'll be relying on you to stop Edith and my wife from wearing themselves into the ground. I shan't be good for much.' He smiled ruefully as Rory shook hands. 'I'm afraid this will give you a very odd idea of us, but as it's all in the family, perhaps you should consider yourself thoroughly adopted.'

Rory looked touched and flattered as he smiled. 'I'd like to be adopted, thank you, sir. But as for keeping Edith and Mrs Attlin in check, I'm not sure I'm strong enough to argue with them.'

Edith began to smile but paused at the old man's response. 'I'd almost forgotten. Don't overdo things, will you. If only from a purely selfish point of view we don't want anyone else crocking up.'

Ignoring Rory's protest, 'But that's not what I meant at all — ' Mr Attlin looked over his shoulder at Edith.

'Any chance of a cup of tea? It's like being in prison round here so I know better than to ask for a slug of whisky, even for medicinal purposes.'

Edith had been looking at Rory through

narrowed eyes, wondering about her grand-father's remark and Rory's sudden flush of embarrassment, but the old man's cunning ploy distracted her and she headed down-stairs. A backward glance showed Rory sitting down, talking earnestly to her grandfather, who was nodding agreement. To her astonish-ment she saw him clap a hand to the younger man's shoulder.

The kitchen was empty and just as Edith was waiting for the kettle to boil the phone rang. It was Karen.

'Edith? Oh good, I'm glad it's you. I had to nip over to Sainsbury's but I've got a flat tyre so I'll be a while yet. There's a list of jobs on the dresser; any chance you could make a start on them? My husband will probably be back before me, but there's still a lot you could do to help, if you wouldn't mind.'

Back upstairs, Edith found her grandfather settled in bed looking weary, with Rory finishing his unpacking and plumping pillows. They both looked up at her entrance.

'Your grandmother not awake yet?' The old man relaxed and sipped his tea. 'That's good, I'd rather she had a real rest; she's not been sleeping too well at night.'

Rory picked up his own mug of tea and followed Edith from the room. 'I think he'll drop off now,' he murmured. 'He's a lot more tired than he's letting on.' He closed the door gently behind him.

Touched by his perception she nodded, leading the way downstairs. 'I know, he has to be strong for Gran, and she has to keep going for him.' She shivered at the thought that her grandfather might have been killed the other night, instead of escaping with only shock and a broken collarbone. *If* he'd been attacked . . . *if* he hadn't imagined the whole thing . . . And Rory, however charming and pleasant he might seem, had been in the area at the time. She shivered. Did Rory, whose face was so achingly familiar, did he have a hidden motive in moving to Locksley Farm Place?

At the foot of the oak staircase Edith stopped so suddenly that Rory, just behind her, cannoned into her, only just managing to right them both.

Elvis Presley was fiddling with the switch on an electric floor polisher. When he heard them scuffling he looked up, pushed his quiff out of his eyes and gave them a shy smile.

2

Harriet Quigley looked thoughtful as she shoved her porridge into the microwave and laid the kitchen table for her breakfast. Yesterday evening had been interesting, to say the least, she mused.

Sam had been delighted with his final visit before the neighbouring cottage became his and, as he wanted to do some decorating, the plan was that he would stay with Harriet for a few days before finally moving in at the end of the following week. Living cheek by jowl would be fine by both of them. Admittedly they had spent their sixty-odd years squabbling but they weren't just first cousins; Sam was also her best friend. It would be good to have him close by. She had plenty of friends in the village and beyond, but Sam was different, Sam was special. Besides, he was beginning to emerge from the bleak wilderness that he had inhabited since the death, nearly five years ago now, of his wife Avril, who had been one of Harriet's closest friends. Village life would be good for him, always something going on . . .

'Living in this village will take his mind off

his miseries,' Harriet told the slim tabby cat as she left her mug, bowl and spoon to drain by the sink and went out to inspect the garden. Having moved to the cottage less than a year ago, she was constantly coming across new and interesting plants in the garden. Now, she bent to smell her latest discovery, an old-fashioned Crimson Glory rioting along the fence.

'You are absolutely the most beautiful thing I've ever seen,' she told the rose, then checked herself with a guilty laugh as she realized she was whispering so that the other roses shouldn't feel jealous. Turning to the Old English roses she had put in last autumn, she was glad to see they were still doing well, with *Gertrude Jekyll* galloping up the trellis. However, *Brother Cadfael* and her favourite, the *Ingenious Mr Fairchild* — who in the world thought up these names? — were showing signs of greenfly, along with the odd black spot. Spraying them, she grinned as she recalled Edith's greeting the night before when Harriet strolled in through the front door.

'Harriet? Did you know we had Elvis Presley living here?'

'Don't you mean Elveece?' Harriet tossed her keys onto a side table in the oak-panelled hall and surveyed the scene. 'I love the way he pronounces it and he doesn't mind in the least that we all copy him. Karen's the only person who ever calls him Markus. Yes, of course I knew, I told you about Karen's lovely husband, didn't I?'

'I wish you'd been a bit more specific,' Edith laughed ruefully. 'I nearly had a heart attack when he turned round and smiled at me, and Rory looked as though he'd seen a ghost. It wasn't just the physical resemblance; he was dressed all in white. It was a white boiler suit; he'd just come in from a job where he'd been decorating but for a minute I thought it was a full-on Elvis suit. You could have told me he was an Elvis impersonator in his spare time, the likeness is unnerving. We saw him in the sparkly Elvis rig-out later on, when he was going out again.'

Harriet shook her head, laughing. 'And spoil the surprise? Where is he now, anyway?'

Karen bustled in from the back hall. 'He's got a gig at a club in Southampton,' she explained as she beckoned to Edith. 'I sometimes sing with him, hence the fifties gear, but not tonight. Listen, Edith, Mrs Attlin said not to bother with supper for them tonight, she'd come down and get something, but I'm not having that. I've done them some soup and sandwiches, if you could take a tray up to them, and there's more for you and

Rory in the kitchen when you want it.' She looked at the visitor. 'There's plenty for you too, Harriet, if you like.'

'I've eaten already, thanks,' Harriet explained. 'I dropped Sam off at his flat in Winchester and had a bite to eat with him. I've come to see if there's anything I can do to help before tomorrow's shindig.'

With a nod of approval Karen waved towards Edith. 'Edith's got the list of things to do. I've got a load of ironing to get out of the way so I'll see you later.'

'Did you get anything more out of your grandfather?' Harriet asked as she and Edith set up hanging rails in a partitioned-off corner of the marquee that was set up at the entrance to the Great Hall. 'There, that should do well for a cloakroom — nice and handy for the outside loos in the yard. And the indoor loo isn't too far away either.' She nodded towards the lavatory that had been tucked under the staircase in the early days of Queen Victoria's reign by a rare Attlin who had money to spare. The blue-flowered porcelain ought to impress tomorrow night's diners, Harriet decided.

Edith sighed. 'Nope, he had his say — pretty much what you told me — and now he refuses to utter another word. I think you're right, he's clamming up so Gran doesn't get upset. You know what he's like; it happened, he survived, why make a fuss?' She shivered. 'But it's worrying me sick. He doesn't imagine things, and he's certainly not going senile. So what happened?'

★   ★   ★

With Sam in mind Harriet peered nosily over the fence at next door's garden. I wonder if he'll keep up her vegetable plot, she thought. He's not a great gardener; Avril was the one who loved doing the designing and planting, but he likes his food so perhaps he'll make an effort if it means home-grown, organic vegetables.

She sighed happily. It would be like their childhood, she thought, living next-door to each other, semi-detached in this case. However, daydreaming about the past and future brought her back to the present time. The previous evening was still on her mind.

Edith, in spite of her anxiety over her grandfather's accident, was already beginning to look more relaxed. Harriet had been quite shocked at how strung-up and brittle the girl seemed when they met at the airport the previous afternoon. A few weeks at home should put her right. Her grandparents were as hale and hearty as it was reasonable to expect at their age, in spite of Cousin Walter's accident. And money, it seemed, was not an issue for Edith at the moment.

'You know, Grandpa wanted me to have a year or two away before I have to buckle down and start working here, and I was earning fantastic money,' Edith had confided. 'I've got enough saved to tide me over for a while and besides,' she hunched her shoulders as Harriet looked sympathetic, 'you know the score, Harriet. I'm no farmer so the idea is that I take on the job of trying to make the place pay, while the new manager Grandpa's got starting at Michaelmas — Alan Nichols — runs the actual farm business.'

Yes, Harriet was more relieved about that than she let on. The death of his only son had been a shattering blow for Walter Attlin and he had buried his head in the sand for years. Only his wife's entreaties, along with Harriet's persuasions, had eventually made him agree to set up a trust that would give Edith a major share in the place at the age of twenty-five. With her birthday in January, Edith had reached that landmark, so it had only been a matter of time before she came home to take on the task. Harriet sighed, it was a daunting prospect for anyone so young, she thought, but Edith was tougher than she looked and at least the elder Attlins would have company, and if it came to it — protection, with their granddaughter and now Rory both living at Locksley Farm. She frowned for a moment. Rory . . . He seemed a nice enough lad and she had noted with some amusement the way he and Edith seemed to have fallen into much the same kind of relationship that Harriet herself had with Sam, working together but with a lot of friendly bickering. There had been that rather odd moment, though, just before Harriet took her leave.

'I'm knackered,' Rory had told her and Edith abruptly at about half past nine. 'I'm sorry, but I really need to get myself to bed if I'm to survive tomorrow.'

Harriet and Edith were about to drop in to say goodnight to Mr and Mrs Attlin and both women turned to look at him curiously as they paused outside the door of the old people's first-floor sitting room, formerly the best spare bedroom.

'Of course.' Edith sounded contrite. 'I'm sorry, Rory, I tend to get carried away. I did warn you about the bossy Attlin women, didn't I? Go and grab a decent night's sleep, you're beginning to look a bit green round the gills. Shoo.' She gave him a friendly push. 'You look as if you'd keel over in a breath of wind. Go to bed.'

He brushed aside her apology and her concern. 'I'm perfectly all right,' he snapped. 'Stop fussing. I had a fever, that's all, and it still sabotages me sometimes. I'll see you tomorrow.'

Harriet nodded while Edith stared after him as Rory turned on his heel and set off towards his room next to the narrow staircase at the end of the corridor. The two women were just about to open the door in front of them when they heard him exclaim aloud. Turning, they saw him stare, open-mouthed, at a spot on the panelled wall then, after a frozen moment, he shook his head and headed into his bedroom.

Now, Harriet pondered this episode. It hadn't looked like a spasm of pain, or sudden faintness, so did he see something? she wondered. It was a pretty ancient house, after all. She laughed and shrugged, picking up the slender, half-grown tabby cat who was weaving sinuously between her legs. 'All right, Dylan, I'll get you some breakfast instead of imagining ghosts, and you can help me sort out something to wear to the dinner tonight.'

★ ★ ★

Rory was exploring the garden at the rear of Locksley Farm Place. Somewhere around a quarter to six that morning he had struggled, sweating and terrified, out of a nightmare that was all the more terrifying for being formless. Bodies, definitely; he knew that somewhere behind the mist lay the bodies. Unable to get back to sleep he had tried reading for a while, and then checked his emails, remembering his surprise that Locksley, which seemed to him at the back of beyond, had broadband. It was a relief. It meant he could do most of his remaining paperwork from the house and not have to struggle up and down to London more than he needed. Even the thought of it made him tired, but then, everything made him tired at the moment. And not just tired; he had never felt so close to breaking down as these last few months, with tears threatening to well up at the most unexpected and inconvenient moments. He brushed a hand across his eyes as, right on cue, his eyelids began to prick with unshed tears. Oh, for God's sake. He shook his head and straightened up. Not here, not now or soon, please God. Not anywhere or any when.

He avoided the marquee set up at the entrance to the great hall, and brushed moss and twigs off an old stone seat to rest for a bit. Locksley Farm Place would do very well, he thought. It was a good place to recuperate and to stay while he looked for a place of his own; and where better to keep the promise he had made, the promise he intended to keep, no matter what? For a moment a memory ran up against the brick wall of his will; no point in dwelling on the past, not just now at any rate.

His eyes narrowed as he frowned, thinking about the old man and his assertion that someone had deliberately tried to run him down. Rory agreed with Edith that Mr Attlin was neither senile nor hysterical. The body might be ageing but the intellect was as sharp as any Rory had encountered.

Just as Edith had done, the old man had drawn a sharp breath when he first encountered his proposed lodger, while Mrs Attlin had lost colour and looked badly shaken. There had been no time yet for anyone to explain what it was about him that affected them so badly, even at a second meeting, but from Rory's point of view it was all to the good. The old chap clearly trusted him, and the old lady was warming to him, though she kept shooting glances at him when she thought she was unobserved, and now Edith too seemed disposed to take him on trust.

'Morning,' came a greeting. 'You're out and about early today.'

'Hi, Edith.' He nodded to her and brushed

more moss off the seat. She sat down and gazed with satisfaction at the house. Above the ancient studded door to the mediaeval hall the angel design, inlaid in dressed flint, glittered as it was lanced by sunlight. 'Tell me about the house, will you?'

'Do you like it? It's just an old farmhouse with a couple of quirks, really.' She waved a hand towards the old building. From the front it looked like a solid farmhouse, possibly Georgian in style, faced in cream render.

The view from the rear had surprised him during his earlier perambulations. It was clear that the major part of the house was actually Tudor, but that nobody had bothered to render the old red brick, and the stone mullions were left intact; only the front, the part that showed, had been modernized. At a right angle stood the ancient hall, built in mellow, greying stone with the original porch close to the far end, with what appeared to be some battlements added randomly on the top.

It wasn't as big as he'd thought on his preliminary visit; it was the extensions added, seemingly with no design in mind, that made the house seem to sprawl.

'Here, I spotted you from my bedroom window wandering about so I brought you this little old book. I thought you might find it interesting; it tells you a bit about the house.'

'Great, thanks. *Highways and Byways of Hampshire* by the Rev'd Sebastian Spilshaw. Let's have a look.

"The property known as Locksley Farm Place has been indiscriminately altered by succeeding owners so that now very little remains of the original apart from the small but interesting Great Hall with its handsome cruck-built timber roof. One aspect of interest to the antiquarian is that it is said to be one of the oldest continuously inhabited residences in England. The Attlin family claims descent from the original Roman who built a villa, long since vanished, although a curiously shaped stone, said to resemble an angel, remains in what is whimsically referred to as the Burial Field.' Hmm, when was he writing this? Oh, I see, 1873.'

Rory flicked through the gilt-edged pages then referred back to the section on Locksley Farm Place. 'What else does he say about the house?

"The family claim that in Saxon times a house was built on the current site is unlikely to have any foundation in reality, as no evidence of this building is available. What is not open to question is that an application

48

was made to the king, Edward I, in the late thirteenth century, requesting a licence to 'crenellate' a building on this spot. Such a licence was duly granted but the fortifications were on a modest scale and were never needed under siege.'

'I think it's amazing,' Rory announced, looking up at the house, before going back to the book. 'He's a bit dismissive of the rest of the house, isn't he? 'The mediaeval Great Hall (so called, although it is, in fact, of merely domestic proportions) now lies to the rear of a Tudor residence, originally of brick and stone, built in 1506. However, this modest edifice was criminally altered, in 1804. At that time Simon Attlin Esq. knocked down internal walls and enlarged the rooms, thus destroying all traces of the antique panelling. He also had the exterior of the Tudor building rendered and the windows replaced so that, in appearance, it now resembles any other undistinguished late Georgian farmhouse and is of no interest at all to the antiquarian.'

'Patronizing, isn't he? I rather like that weird little tower stuck on the corner, but the Reverend Sebastian is appalled: 'Unfortunately, the present owner's father made an extended visit to the Scottish Highlands some twenty years ago and succumbed to Balmoral *fever, in the erroneous belief that the addition of a would-be antique turret might enhance his house's appearance.'* '

Rory flicked through the pages and looked up with a grin. 'He's got a real downer on the family, hasn't he? Listen to this: *'Despite early pretensions to nobility — witness the application to crenellate (which, in hindsight, must be deemed over-ambitious) — the Attlin family soon sank into yeoman obscurity, where they remain to this day, although, as previously mentioned, they have not been above claiming descent, on occasion, from a Roman soldier who dwelt in the area during the latter years of the occupation of Britain. The notion that the said soldier received a blessing on his land and house by the good offices of an angel is laughable.'* What did the Attlins ever do to upset him? And what's all this about an angel's blessing?'

'Oh, one of the daughters turned down his proposal,' Edith said. 'Mind you, old Simon Attlin does seem to have been a bit of a vandal, getting rid of the panelling and so forth.' She glanced at her watch. 'Time to get a move on,' she announced. 'It's gone half eight so we'd better go and get some breakfast. I'll tell you the angel story later. The Rotarians and Inner Wheel people will be here by ten or eleven but I think we've

50

done all we can. Elveece,' she grinned at his snort of laughter, 'oh, all right, but I agree with Harriet. I love the way he says it. Elvis then, he said he'll finish polishing the floor in the Great Hall but then he's off to Romsey on another job.'

As they crossed the yard, Rory surveyed the outbuildings, which included a barn as well as the stables, none of them used for anything but storing junk.

'Seems a pity not to put this lot to use,' he ventured. 'Do you have any plans?'

'That's my job for the foreseeable future,' she shrugged. 'We need to make the place earn its keep; the house and the outbuildings too, not just the farm. When I was little there were animals in here but when my father died Grandpa lost heart and got a very good manager in. The whole character of the place altered when the fields at the back were turned over completely to arable and the livestock moved over to the new man's house down the hill.' She led the way back to the house, with a rueful smile over her shoulder. 'That's where the real working farm is and I won't be involved in that day to day; what's here is just an old house that needs to earn its keep. Any suggestions as to how that can be achieved will be extremely welcome.'

In the kitchen they found Karen looking

grey-faced. 'Sick,' she said, through gritted teeth. 'Got a migraine coming on.'

'Go back to bed this minute,' insisted Edith. 'Here, have you taken anything for it? Don't worry about us, I'll do the grandparents' breakfast and see to things here. Go!' She shooed the hesitating Karen out of the kitchen and turned to see Rory filling the kettle.

'I can cook,' he said. 'Heart attack on a plate do you?'

She laughed and nodded and arranged a tray of toast and tea for her grandparents. When she came back Rory was flipping a slice of fried bread onto a plate. 'I worked in a lorry drivers' café one summer,' he told her. 'It was a real greasy spoon. Here you are, tuck in.'

As they ate in companionable silence Edith glanced across at Rory's plate.

'Have we run out of bacon?' she asked. 'Have some of mine.'

'No.' He sounded slightly annoyed as he waved her away. 'I've temporarily gone off bacon, that's all.'

His tone was forbidding so she shrugged and subsided. While they ate they were watched by the assorted animals. The dog, Lulu, was cramped uncomfortably into a cat bed, fondly gazing at the fierce black kitten,

Percy, who was lording it in the dog's own bed. After eating, three other cats had disappeared, with an air of purposeful activity about them as they operated the cat flap, each tail an erect question mark as they embarked on a day's hunting. The shy marmalade cat had plucked up the courage to sit under the table beside Rory's feet and the old lady of the menagerie, Milly, was curled up on the sunny windowsill languidly washing her tail and pretending to be above such mundane matters as breakfast.

'It's a good thing you like cats,' commented Edith as she watched Rory seduce the ginger cat with a morsel of fried bread while the kitten pranced over to see what was on offer. 'You'll fit right in. Percy seems an awful brat, but Lulu adores him; I've seen her washing him. Gran had only just acquired him when I was home for Christmas and Lulu spent the whole time running round after him, protecting him from the other cats.'

'We always had cats at home,' Rory said shortly, then looked away from her and changed the subject by holding out a hand to the kitten, who promptly bit his finger.

'When I was home last,' she said, looking curiously at his closed expression; so many subjects were clearly taboo, 'Gran had a visitor, a Mrs Something, I forget what. I came down to make some tea and when I got back there was total chaos. Mrs Something was on her feet and dripping blood from her hand, with her chair knocked over behind her and Gran was standing by the table. She looked white with fury and she was clutching Percy tightly. It was funny afterwards but at the time Gran was in a state. She turned to me and said, 'Edith, please take Mrs Whatsit to the bathroom. I don't think she cares for cats and Percy certainly doesn't seem to care for her.'

'I got the poor woman out of the room and cleaned her up, but she was incoherent with rage. Apparently she hated cats but thought she ought to be polite as Gran seemed so keen, so she held out her hand to him. Of course, he's half vampire and half piranha so he just gave her an evil grin and took a chunk out of her finger. She left, insisting she was going straight to the doctor's to have a tetanus jab. Gran's never forgiven her for that so she certainly won't be at the party tonight.'

'How formal is this thing tonight?' Rory asked. 'I don't think anyone's said. I mean, is it black tie or what? And shouldn't there be another marquee for dancing or something? The Great Hall isn't anywhere near big enough.'

'Oops.' She clapped a hand to her mouth.

'Good job you asked. Yes, it's a real posh-frock do, dinner jacket, the works. I'd better borrow something of Gran's. She's a hoarder and never gets rid of clothes, so there's a big stash of vintage dresses dating back to the late forties. And no,' she added, 'it's not a dance, just a dinner because the hall isn't big enough to squeeze in a dance floor as well as dining tables. What about you tonight? I expect we could borrow something if you like.'

'I'll be fine,' he assured her. 'Mr Attlin says I can have the barn out the back as a temporary studio and storeroom and I've got a trunk there. I'll get my dinner jacket and take it up to my room to hang up. Do you need me for anything particular this morning?'

'Um, not really.' She shook her head, then glanced up at him. 'Tell you what, when Elvis has finished polishing the floor and the Rotary people are doing their stuff, why don't I show you the picture gallery? You'll understand then why it is that everyone gasps when they see you. Meet you at 11.30 on the first floor landing?'

★   ★   ★

'Wow!' Rory stood, almost speechless, in the doorway to the small gallery on the top floor

55

of the house. 'Oh. My. God!' he finally managed. 'I assumed it would just be attics up here, full of junk. Interesting junk perhaps, but still junk. This is incredible — why have I never heard of it? It's pure Tudor and so are some of those paintings.'

Edith had forgotten he was an artist and his enthusiasm disarmed her. 'Are you an art historian too?' she asked with interest. 'What kind of painting do you do, anyway? I don't think I've heard.'

'I'm getting something out of my system at the moment,' he said and the jagged echoes of some bitter hurt pierced her, though his face was composed and determinedly uncommunicative. He pulled himself together. 'I'll be teaching a bit of art history,' he explained. 'Along with the practical stuff. And I mostly work in acrylics and mixed media, oils now and then, but like I said, I'm having a stab at something different just now.'

The picture gallery was at the top of the Tudor house, with light coming in from the back of the building via small mullioned windows. Edith had always been led to believe that the collection ranged in quality from the frankly mediocre to some pleasantly undistinguished family portraits, some going back to early Victorian times, though a couple were known to be older. She was surprised,

56

therefore, to see that Rory was almost purring with pleasure as he loped round the rectangular, oak-panelled room.

'They're supposed to have used the gallery for exercise, but I'm not sure it's true. That sounds far too grand, this was never that kind of house — it's too small. Still, you can come up here whenever you like, but we don't really have a lot of time at the moment,' she warned, relieved to see that interest in the gallery had relaxed that extreme control over his emotions. What could possibly have hurt him so badly? Edith had known grief as a child, with her father's long-drawn-out suffering and eventual death, but that was an old sorrow. Whatever was eating Rory was raw and immediate and he withdrew politely but firmly from any comforting overtures.

'Look.' She drew him away from a dull, dark painting in a corner, that he was examining closely. 'This is Dame Margery, the one who was a nun.' She led him to a small portrait painted on a wooden panel and was about to speak when he gave a shocked gasp.

'But I *saw* her,' he said slowly. 'I swear to God I saw this woman last night, on the landing upstairs, when I was going to bed.'

'You — you couldn't have,' she exclaimed. 'She's ... ' Edith stared at him in astonishment. 'Was that what it was? When you kind-of squawked and looked gobstruck? Harriet and I both saw you jump out of your skin.'

Rory was staring at the head-and-shoulders portrait of a sixteenth-century woman. Not a young woman, he suspected; she wore a dark-green gown with a neat white ruff at the neck and her fair hair was just visible beneath a Tudor headdress with a jewel, perhaps some kind of reliquary, on a chain round her neck and an emerald ring visible on her slender hand. Her grey eyes held a thoughtful look as she stared out of the portrait towards them, while the firm lips quirked in just the suspicion of a smile.

Edith was surprised at the intensity of his gaze, then, as he let out a pent-up breath, he looked down at her — and jumped. 'What?' she demanded. 'What's the matter?'

He shook his head, looking bemused. 'I just don't know,' he told her. 'I could have sworn that this woman walked along the landing towards me last night and when I looked again, she'd disappeared. I thought I was going mad and I certainly don't believe in ghosts. But now? You look a lot like her, did you know that? Maybe I just got mixed up. God knows I was tired enough and I'm still taking some heavy-duty medication; they

58

warned me it could have some weird side effects.'

Medication? He certainly looked exhausted, Edith thought, taking note of the dark circles under his eyes, and there was that excessive thinness too. She bit back the questions on the tip of her tongue — his expression was forbidding so she smiled and shrugged. 'I wouldn't be quite so adamant about ghosts not existing,' she said mildly. 'Not when you've lived in this house a while longer. But never mind that, come over here and see this portrait by the window.

'There,' she said, pointing dramatically to a modern portrait, dating from the late 1970s. She watched with interest as Rory stared, mesmerized, at the painting of a young man with dark curly hair, startling blue eyes and the faintest promise of a dimple. Apart from the eyes, his own were hazel, it was the face Rory saw in the mirror every day when he shaved.

'But who on earth?' He turned to her, astonished, but seeing her eyes misted with tears, he understood. 'Your father, of course. No wonder everyone jumps out of their skin when they meet me. What an amazing likeness.'

He hesitated then reached out an arm in a brief, consoling squeeze. 'I heard about him in the village. You must have been very young. It's hard, I know ... ' He turned away, in embarrassment, perhaps, or to hide his own emotion as Edith, comforted, nodded her thanks, not wanting to trust her voice.

Rory stared at the picture of Richard Attlin for a few more minutes then set off on another ramble round the gallery, pausing now and then to examine a picture closely or to stand back and appraise another, with a thoughtful pursing of his lips. Much of the time, though, he spent staring round at the vaulted beams of the roof, the panelled walls and the wide, polished boards of the floor.

'I just can't believe it.' He waved a hand round at the gallery. 'How can something like this be completely unknown? It's incredible inside, like a small version of that National Trust place in Cheshire, the black and white building. Is the house listed?'

'No,' she shrugged. 'Not sure how it escaped but it did. The only reason we can think of is that nobody knows it's here, apart from friends and family and as you spotted, it's not visible from the road. Why? Do you really think it's important?'

'Important?' He stared at her in disbelief. 'Of course it's important — it's a national treasure! You need to get an expert up here as soon as you can. I bet there are all kinds of grants available for a house like this, even nowadays when funds are hard to find. It's hidden from outside too, isn't it? I wonder if they strengthened the building when they put the eighteenth-century front on the house. There's not the slightest trace of a wobble in the walls or the floor, which you'd expect, I'd have thought, after all these centuries.'

He wandered round again, admiring the mellow timbers and stroking the panelling while Edith watched and wondered about him, this hitherto unknown cousin.

'Haven't you had your portrait done yet?' he enquired as he completed his second circuit and when she shook her head, he offered, 'I'll do one of you if you like?'

Startled and doubtful, she stammered her thanks.

'Don't worry,' he told her, eyes gleaming with amused malice as he evidently read her mind. 'I promise you I'm quite good. As long as I use crayons I can colour in very nicely now, without going over the lines.'

'Oh, for goodness' sake,' she was stung to retort. 'Why are you so touchy? I didn't mean that, I — '

'Oh yes you did,' he snapped then climbed down off his high horse. 'Oh, I'm sorry, Edith. You're right, I am touchy and I do need to get over myself. I'll tell you about it some time or other, but honestly, I'm perfectly competent and I really will do a portrait of you soon. I'd like to anyway, maybe get some echoes of Dame Margery in it somehow, a stylized background of some sort, perhaps, vaguely Tudor. It'd be an interesting project.'

Mollified, she led him to a pair of portraits near the painting of her father. 'We really ought to go back and help, but I wanted you to see these two before we leave it for now. This was painted not long after they got married. Grandpa was stationed abroad for a few years at the end of the war and he met Gran when he came home on leave. Her entire family were killed by a Doodlebug bomb and the only reason she didn't die too was that she was at a Girl Guides meeting. They don't talk about it but I think she must have had a bit of a breakdown afterwards though she was getting better and living with an aunt when they met.'

'I can believe that,' he said with sympathy. 'You can see it in her eyes; she's got a haunted look, and she's very thin too.' He looked again. 'I'd never have pictured her with chestnut hair, though. I suppose I'd have assumed she was a blonde like you and Dame Margery.' He looked at the blue-eyed, fair-haired young husband in the painting.

'The colouring is different, but the features — and the rest — he's actually very like your father — and me, isn't he? The family likeness is really strong.' he murmured.

'You're a lot taller,' Edith gave him an appraising look. 'And not stockily built like them, but apart from that . . . ' She stared up at the two figures and tried to smile. 'If Grandpa had been killed last week — '

'What do you reckon actually happened?' His voice was kind as she knuckled away a tear.

'I don't know.' She shook her head in exasperation. 'It can't possibly be true, he must have been mistaken. It just isn't possible that anyone would drive at him deliberately, intending to run him down.'

She looked soberly at Rory. 'But he's so certain and the alternative, that he's cracking up mentally, is even more unthinkable. I wish I knew what to believe.'

'Let's go and see what's going on downstairs.' Rory tucked her hand into his arm and turned her gently towards the door. 'You know, when we've got more time, there are some things I'd like to do in this gallery; some research I want to carry out. I think there's something rather interesting in here that nobody seems to have noticed. More than interesting actually, but I need peace and quiet and most of all *time*, to get a proper look at it.'

She raised her eyes to his face at that.

'No, I'm not telling you. I said I need time and I'm not jumping the gun. Meanwhile, don't you go dropping any hints to anyone, not even your grandparents. I think you urgently need to get someone in to see the gallery and anyway, if I'm right about the other thing, this could be something spectacular!'

★ ★ ★

At 7.30 that evening Harriet Quigley looked round the guests knocking back champagne, or something more or less resembling champagne, in the hall at Locksley Farm Place. Aware that the organizers liked to put on the Ritz for the annual dinner, she had dressed her best in her favourite midnight-blue silk jersey with her mother's ancestral brooch in the shape of a gold acanthus leaf pinned beside the low, square neckline.

On the edge of the party she could see Karen, looking adorable in polka dots and a rustling taffeta petticoat. She was policing the Inner Wheel ladies and supervising the men in charge of the bar while keeping an unobtrusive eye on her elderly employers.

Harriet smiled and relaxed a little. With three of us at it, she told herself, they're in good hands. Like Edith, who was also watchful, she too had been worrying about Walter Attlin's accident, but looking at the well-behaved people around her she frowned. It had to have been vandals or hooligans, she thought, surely not one of these people. Nobody he knew could have tried to kill an old man, surely. The idea had her twisting round to check on him: no, he looked fine. A little frailer than usual, perhaps, but he was in his late eighties, for heaven's sake. And absolutely sane, she decided after another glance at the good-looking old man flirting happily with the village's chief flower arranger.

'Stop worrying about it, Harriet.' It was her cousin Sam, murmuring as he appeared behind her. 'You said the police have it on record and as far as I can see, that's as far as they can go. Walter seems to be recovering well so you might as well just leave it. There's nothing more you can do.'

'But it's not just that, Sam, there's this other business too; that young man who's missing, the village mystery.' She was about to enlarge on it when their hostess came over to them.

'Harriet, my dear.' Mrs Attlin, slightly built

like her granddaughter, was elegant in dove-grey lace. 'And this, of course, is your clerical cousin. How do you do, Canon Hathaway? I remember you coming here as a small boy.'

Acting on impulse, Sam bent to kiss her hand and was charmed when she blushed like a young girl, though he was aware of Harriet's sardonic grin somewhere to his left. He smiled impishly back, and Harriet felt a rush of affection. To cover her unaccustomed emotion, she turned to her hostess. 'How are you getting on with your guest, Penelope? I thought he seemed a very nice young man.'

'Oh he is,' the old lady was enthusiastic. 'He's a darling. It was a shock, of course, when we first saw him. The resemblance is so very strong.' She looked cautiously round and appeared relieved to see her husband deep in contented conversation with Edith and Rory, the latter scrubbed up nicely in formal dress. Edith looked ethereal in 1950s cream chiffon trimmed with knots of rose-pink ribbon and Harriet grinned as she wondered if Edith would be going in for vintage, like Karen. 'Walter is being very good about it, but I know it opened up old wounds for him, so I'm trying to keep his spirits up.' She smiled as she watched Edith eagerly talking to the two men. 'Edith, of course, is frantic to find out all about Rory but he says he doesn't want to talk about it at the moment so of course we're respecting his wishes. He's had quite a traumatic time of it lately.'

She drifted away to greet more guests and to talk to some of the Rotarians in charge of the event.

'Uh-oh.' Harriet interrupted Sam as he started to speak. 'I smell trouble. Look, heading straight towards us: tall, dark and dangerous, that girl with Gordon Dean. You must know him, or know of him; chairman of this, that and the other, face like a ripe tomato. He's a big business tycoon type, always in the financial papers and on the news having made yet another billion. He lives just down the road, the nearest thing there is to a next-door neighbour to the farm here. The girl is his daughter, Lara, one of my less agreeable former pupils, and she's trouble with a capital T. Just watch all the wives take a firm grip on the reins as they catch a glimpse of her.'

'Harriet, good to see you, my dear.' Harriet submitted to a hearty kiss and slight squeeze from the burly tycoon who was much of an age with her and Sam. 'And I know this is Canon Hathaway. We've met a couple of times and now I hear you're planning to join us in the village.'

Sam, not yet wise to the Locksley grapevine, looked as if he was about to engage in conversation, but Harriet, who knew Gordon Dean would bore on at interminable length about his business, his house and his orchids, aimed an unobtrusive kick at Sam's leg and introduced him to Lara Dean. As Rory and Edith came across the hall, Harriet introduced Rory as well.

'So this is Rory?' Observing her former student, Harriet thought Lara's husky voice — like the sleek black bob, the to-die-for scarlet silk jacket and slim skirt, the pert bosom and the chiselled cheekbones — was expensive and way out of Rory's league. There was a slight trace of an American accent and she was evidently pleased to encounter Rory. 'I've heard all about you from various people in London when I was there the other day, and of course the village is buzzing about you. It must be such a relief to be home at last after such a ghastly ordeal. I want you to come to our lunch party tomorrow, and tell me all about it. No, I really won't take no for an answer.'

She drew him closer to her side, linking arms while he blinked at her, looking bemused. 'Er, thank you, Lara,' he managed finally. 'I'd love to have lunch but I'm not sure about my plans for tomorrow. Maybe some other time? I'm afraid, though, that I've been warned not to discuss what happened, for security reasons. Besides, it's all over and I want to put it behind me.'

She pouted and ran a lacquered finger down his sleeve, pantomiming disappointment and Harriet, who had been watching with some amusement, hastened to his rescue. She was forestalled by a chilly intervention by Edith, who had been talking to Sam and to Gordon Dean.

'Good evening, Lara.' Her audience almost shivered at the frost in her voice. 'You look stunning. When did you come home? I'm so glad you could make it this time; I think you've missed the last few Rotary dinners, haven't you? What was it, on your honeymoon, or something, each time?'

'How sweet you look, Edith,' came the cooing response. 'I suppose that's one of your grandmother's dresses? I've been home a few days, relaxing and catching up with old friends. I must circulate now, though. I know I've been monopolizing Rory but I just had to tell him how pleased we all are to see him safe. We'll have to take the greatest care of him, of course.' She swung round and astonished Rory by brushing his cheek with her lips and, as Harriet observed with detached interest, she managed to brush against his jacket with her elegant and ample (enhanced, surely?) cleavage. Rory, Harriet thought, looked intrigued but wary and cast a hasty sidelong glance at Edith, obviously reluctant to be the meat in that particular sandwich.

Harriet smiled at him as they were summoned to dinner and she tucked him safely in between Edith and herself, with Sam on her other side.

'Are you settling in?' she asked. 'It can be quite daunting moving to such a small village. Everyone knows everything about everybody else, even if they get it all wrong, which, of course, they always do. Sam will find out for himself soon; he's completing on my neighbour's house in a matter of days and once he's here, the village will pounce and he'll find himself on this committee, and that working party, till he's hiding from the front door bell.'

Sam grinned across her. 'I'll need to get some work done first,' he told them, 'so it's very generous of Harriet to offer to put me up while I sort out a bit of decorating. The departing owner's taste is too pink and cottagey style for my liking, but it's only cosmetic, so I'll get in and just slap a coat of emulsion on. Thank goodness she didn't go the whole hog and treat the beams with that stuff that looks like black treacle; that's a devil to get rid of. I'll want to replace the horrible modern lattice windows too; they're completely wrong for an unpretentious cottage, but that can wait till I'm in. At least the ceilings are fairly high so I won't be knocking myself unconscious on a regular basis.' He nodded briefly. 'I love Winchester but it'll be good to get right out into the country, peace and quiet and nothing much happening.'

Harriet gave an exclamation and started to speak, then shook her head and frowned as Sam looked at her in surprise. 'Not now,' was all she would say. 'But we do need to talk later on.'

While they ate, Rory asked Harriet about the village and its inhabitants and she sketched in a little family history and local gossip. 'You know there's a pretty widespread rumour circulating that there's oil to be found under the land. Speculation is rife that this is the reason this anonymous buyer wants it, so they say.'

'Oil? You're kidding.' He stared at her, his mouth open. 'This isn't Texas, or the Middle East.'

'I know.' She looked sympathetic. 'But there's a history of oil all along the south coast, you know, and inland as well. It dates right back to the Romans who were involved in shale extraction. I don't suppose you've heard of Wych Farm? At Kimmeridge in Dorset, not that far away. It's been producing I don't know how many barrels of crude oil for some years. It's not that fantastic a suggestion, though I've no idea if there's any truth in it here. There was an exploratory bore hole at Chilworth, near Southampton, not so many years ago and that's only a few miles down the road.'

'But they wouldn't want to sell, would they?' he asked. 'I suppose the money would make a huge difference to them, though. I get the impression they're not exactly rolling in money.'

'No, of course they're not. Who is these days? Farmers always grumble, it's their default position, but there's no denying that farming's been in the doldrums for decades and on top of that, Walter rather lost heart when Richard, Edith's father, died.' She heaved a sigh. 'Walter's grandfather was the one who nearly bankrupted the farm in the 1929 crash and they've struggled to keep afloat ever since. About ten years ago Walter handed over the day-to-day running of the larger farm to a manager who lives over the hill, the other end of the village. Mercifully Hampshire wasn't affected by the foot-and-mouth outbreak ten years ago or more, and the Locksley herd of Aberdeen Angus is becoming internationally renowned but it's not a get-rich-quick enterprise.'

Harriet glanced across at her elderly relatives and sighed. 'I suppose you could say they're land rich and cash poor, so they've sold off the odd acre or so for building when times have been really tough, then things muddle along for a time. Unfortunately, there's always something else with a place as ancient as this.

'There's another small farm just down the road, a couple of hundred acres and a dead ringer for Cold Comfort Farm. The tenant died three or four weeks ago — a nasty old so-and-so he was, I have to say — and the offer to buy turned up practically the next day. I can see, I suppose, why somebody might conceivably want the big paddock, which does have road access, though it's much too close to this house for them even to consider it, but the anonymous buyer insists on having the adjoining Burial Field too. Have you seen it yet?' Rory shook his head. 'Oh you must, the field's covered in scrub at the moment, lying fallow for a year or so, and the copse is overgrown, but it's the heart of the family, even so. Don't you see? If this rumour is true, it alters everything.'

She liked his ready intelligence.

'You mean it becomes a matter for everyone who lives here and not just a private affair? I don't know anything about oil production, I must admit, but the impression I do have is of the countryside being laid to waste. Surely that wouldn't be allowed to happen here, would it?'

'I don't know. It seems unlikely but palms can always be greased if there's enough money involved. I gather Walter has been talking to my cousin Sam, though Sam's the soul of discretion and won't tell me.' She looked slightly put out, then shrugged. 'But it doesn't take a genius to guess that this astonishing offer featured in their discussions. As for the idea of oil under the land, I can't imagine Walter going in for drilling, not for a moment, but if someone else were to believe there could be oil here, you're talking enough money for a thousand pretty substantial bribes.' Her face reflected her anxiety and frustration. 'One thing is obvious. Whoever this mystery purchaser is, he's trying to pull a fast one on them. A parcel of land with oil under it is worth a hell of a lot more money than he's offering. They don't *want* to sell but they're old and very tired and this business the other night, Walter's broken collar-bone . . . '

He didn't try to dismiss her fears.

'You mean that Mr Attlin could be right? That someone *did* try to kill him? With him out of the way, how long would Mrs Attlin resist the pressure?'

Harriet and Rory stared at each other, their faces grim.

'I can't really discuss it,' she said, almost in a whisper, as she suddenly recalled that however sympathetic he might be, Rory was a complete stranger. 'It's not really any of my business.'

She shivered as another thought slid insidiously into her brain. Land with oil underneath it might well be worth killing for. Glancing at Rory she caught his eye and saw quite clearly that the same idea had occurred to him. Sobered, she looked down at her plate. Perhaps murder would be worth the risk — if you had no scruples and if the reserves of oil were great enough to make it worth your while. And if the only apparent obstacle happened to be one frail old man.

3

Harriet left Sam to find the whisky and glasses for a nightcap while she slipped out to water her runner beans. The cat greeted her as he ran along the top of the fence and when she picked him up she could smell smoke. 'You've been in somebody's bonfire again, Dylan,' she scolded him, burying her nose in his soft fur. 'Lovely smell of wood smoke, but mind you take care. We don't want a barbecued moggie.'

In the sitting room she found Sam poring over an ancient booklet he'd discovered on the coffee table.

'You've read this, of course?' He looked up at her with a chuckle. 'Is this true? According to this, family legend says that the founder of the Attlin family was supposed to be one Lucius Sextus Vitalis, (though how his name is known is glossed over), newly retired from the army some time around the early fourth century AD and finding himself, so the legend says, *'heart-sore and weary'*, not far from the city of Venta Belgarum — which is Winchester, of course. I suppose, like all the retired soldiers in the Roman army, he would have been given a land grant and built his villa here — all right for some. It says here that Lucius is supposed to have had a dream when the buildings were finished, that an angel appeared and blessed the house. *'There came unto him a vision of a great angel. And the angel said unto him, 'Lucius Sextus Vitalis, thou shalt live here and prosper and all thy children shall dwell here forever.''*

She looked over his shoulder. 'That little booklet was in amongst my father's things,' she commented. 'I do vaguely remember the story but it must be twenty-odd years since I read it. Mother had kept all Dad's stuff in boxes and I've only just got round to checking them. I unpacked some of the books the other day; they're just stacked on my desk until I get a chance to go through them properly. That particular one was top of the pile, though, so I fished it out to show you. It was written by a Victorian spinster, one of those poor relations people used to have.'

She grinned and went on, 'Unlike now, when we're all poor relations. Anyway, Miss Evelyn Attlin supposedly cobbled it together from ancient fragments of parchment and called it *The Atheling Chronicle* but I suspect that what she didn't know about the past, she simply invented. According to her, as I recall,

Lucius married the daughter of a local chieftain of the Belgii — it's never just a cook or bottle-washer, is it — but we don't know her name. In fact there are no further names mentioned in the chronicle until the Athelings come into the picture.'

She twitched the little book out of his hand and flicked through the pages. 'Yes, here it is. It's believed the angel story was inspired by the stone in the field. It's probably a menhir, a standing stone, but it might, if you squint sideways at it, resemble an angel. Only to the eye of faith, as far as I can tell, though. Here, read the bit about Alfred the Great — you'll like him.'

'Good grief.' Sam looked up from the yellowing booklet. 'How does he get in on the act?' He scanned the next couple of pages. 'I see, I wondered where the name came from. So Attlin was once Atheling? That sounds Anglo-Saxon. Oh, it's here, *'King's Heir. The title was borne equally by all the King's sons.'* ' He glanced up at her, and she rejoiced to see the interest in his face; Sam was definitely coming back from the desert of life without Avril. 'So it means younger ones were eligible as well, and it wasn't automatic that the eldest son would inherit. The local Atheling is said to have been a sprig of King Alfred's.

'Alfred the Great, King of Wessex, lived from AD 849 to approximately 900 and drove the Danes from his territories. He built a navy, restored law and order to his people, encouraged literacy and personally translated works from the Latin into English.' ' Sam stopped reading and grinned. 'It seems to me that Miss Evelyn is having a little difficulty here,' he laughed. 'She's trying not to admit that the Edmund Atheling that the present Attlin family are supposed to be descended from doesn't seem to have been legitimate but she's couched it in such genteel language it's hard to make out.'

'Ah well,' Harriet said philosophically. 'What's a little irregularity among friends? Didn't hurt William the Conqueror, did it? Here, put it away, it's too late for ancient history, especially written in Miss Evelyn's purple prose. I'll get us a drink.'

'I enjoyed this evening,' Sam remarked as they sipped their Laphroaig. 'I was particularly impressed by the cabaret.'

Harriet grinned. 'Yes, our Elveece is terrific, isn't he? He doesn't just look the part, he can really sing too.' She sobered suddenly. 'I was a bit surprised, though, when I was talking to him tonight, to find he had been here the same day in January that our local murder mystery took place . . . ' She

79

caught herself up. 'I mean when that young man went missing. I could have sworn Karen said they hadn't been in this neck of the woods for years till just before Easter when they heard about the job vacancy at the farm. But Elveece told me tonight that he dropped in for a drink that night, after he'd been doing a plumbing job in Hursley.' She looked thoughtful. 'He said that was the first time he'd been over here but he liked the look of the place so when Karen spotted the job here with the Attlins, he was all for it.'

'What local murder? What young man?' Sam stared at her, bemused, his whisky glass halfway to his lips. 'Who's missing? Sorry, Harriet, I haven't the slightest idea what you're talking about. And what's all this about Elvis?'

She pulled herself together. 'Of course you haven't a clue, I'm sorry. And it's not really a murder, in spite of the village scandal-mongering, just a worrying mystery. It all started when you and I went to Sicily over the New Year, remember? We'd had a pretty fraught run-up to Christmas so you came up with a last-minute bargain trip. And don't forget, as soon as we got home, you went straight off to that course you were teaching. I suppose all the commotion had died down by the time I next saw you.

'It's just that a young man called Colin Price was last seen in The Angel in Locksley just on six months ago, on the fifth of January this year. He had two pints of beer, according to the landlord, and asked about the village; just chatting, at first, until he seemed to take more of an interest and asked specifically about the old people up at Locksley Farm. And then, for some reason, he started quizzing the barman about the new vicar: what people thought of him, how long he'd been here, that kind of thing.'

She finished her whisky. 'Anyway, he hasn't been seen from that day to this, and the police are worried that he's not taken any money out of the bank since, or used his credit cards, or gone back to his flat, which was rented, for any of his belongings.' She frowned as she took Sam's glass and rinsed it in the kitchen sink, along with her own. 'I'd almost forgotten about him.' She put her head round the sitting room door, looking apologetic. 'Then there was a reminder in the local newsletter last week and on top of that there's this business with Walter's accident. God knows why I should link the two, but somehow I do.'

Sam's eyes narrowed. 'Oh, for God's sake, Harriet.' He gave an exaggerated sigh. 'You're not thinking about playing Miss Marple again, are you? Surely once was enough.' He received only a cold stare in response as she sat down again, so he shook his head, but humoured her. 'All right then, leave aside the old people for the time being and tell me about the vicar. It's John Forrester, isn't it? Why would your mystery man be interested in him? I know of him, of course, but by name only. I've never actually met him other than to pass the time of day.'

'Not a lot to tell,' she shrugged, secretly pleased to be able to use him as a sounding board. 'He was potentially a high flyer, deputy principal at a theological college and marked for stardom. Late thirties, probably, but he moved to a country parish last autumn to see if his wife's health would improve. Didn't work, though, she died a few months ago, poor soul.' She stared down at her hands. 'I suppose the vicar will get back on track soon enough, after a decent interval.' She cast a speculative glance at Sam. 'You might have come across young Mr Price yourself,' she said. 'It turns out that he was on a contract as a temporary researcher at the Stanton Resingham archive.' She frowned at his blank stare. 'You do know about it, Sam. I know you often drop in to the county reference library — it's the mass of papers that's stored there.'

'Oh yes, I remember, I've got a pass for it too, but I don't recall anyone of that name. Mind you, it must be months at least since I've had occasion to go in there. Some old boy left a legacy plus a load of cash to set up a special foundation, didn't he? With his own collection of local documents to start them off.' He looked thoughtful. 'I've only got a pass to get in on admin grounds; research isn't my province. Had this young man worked there long, then?'

'Only since the early autumn,' she told him. 'He was temping but he seems to have chopped and changed jobs a fair bit, though his references were all right, according to local report. However, he was apparently competent and he still had several months left to run on his contract. His job was pretty much routine, data inputting, I think. It doesn't seem likely to have anything to do with his disappearance.'

'Medium height, medium build, mousy hair?' Sam shrugged and rose to his feet. 'Now you come to mention it I do vaguely remember someone pointing him out to me in the cathedral refectory, but no more than that. And now it's way past midnight,' he reminded her. 'I think I'll be off to bed.' At the door he remembered something. 'Hang on, what were you saying about young Elvis?

83

I know you've got an over-active imagination, Harriet, but you surely can't link him to some rolling stone of a chap who did a bunk when his life probably got too complicated by debts or women, or both?'

'I'm sure you're right,' she agreed meekly. 'Everyone who'd been in The Angel that night was questioned, Elvis included — he told me tonight. But then, he was the one who found Walter the other night. Complete coincidence, I'm sure.'

At his questioning glance she explained. 'Elveece was coming home Wednesday after a gig in Andover and he saw tail lights heading off down the farm track. Luckily he had the sense to go and check it out and found Walter only minutes after he'd fallen and hurt himself. If he hadn't been on the scene so promptly, God knows what would have happened.'

Sam shook his head at her. 'Conjecture, Harriet, based on gossip and a fevered imagination.' He went off upstairs, leaving her frowning.

The trouble was, she fretted, recalling recent conversations with local friends, that however illogical and without a shred of evidence, the entire village believed that Colin Price had come to a sticky end. The press of local opinion was compelling, even though common sense told her that it was nonsense,

No, you're right, Sam, she said to herself as she turned off the lights and shut the cat in the kitchen. It's just another oddity, that's all. Too many oddities: Colin Price disappearing after asking about Walter and Penelope Attlin and the vicar; Elvis being at the pub at the same time that Price was last seen although I could have sworn Karen told me they hadn't been here till April; and now Walter's accident — if that's what it was.

With a shiver, Harriet recalled her conversation with Rory. *Oil.* Black gold deep in them thar hills. If it was true . . . if someone believed or actually *knew* there was oil there . . . Three coincidences . . .

★   ★   ★

Edith ran into her grandmother at about eleven the next morning.

'Oh, Edith, I'm glad you're up, darling.' Mrs Attlin was looking remarkably bright-eyed and bushy-tailed considering she had still been wide awake at about one in the morning. 'I've just had a phone call from Gordon Dean. He wanted to know if you might be at his drinks party today. It's a noon start.'

A groan from Edith brought a reproving glance. 'I'm sorry, Edith, I forgot to tell you about it. I'd written to decline for Grandpa and myself — I knew it would be too much for us, even before this business with his collarbone. However, Gordon called this morning to extend the invitation to you and Rory, as you weren't here, either of you, when he originally asked us.' She shot Edith a firm glance. 'I told him I thought you and Rory would be delighted. No, I know you don't really want to go, but if you're going to be at home for a while, you might as well make an effort and I'm sure Rory won't mind accompanying you.' She dealt her trump card. 'Grandpa would like it if you went; you know how he feels about our responsibility to maintain links with the neighbours.'

That was unanswerable so Edith nodded with an ill grace and went off to find Rory who looked equally unenthusiastic.

'Lara asked me last night,' he said. 'I told her I didn't think I'd be able to make it but if your grandfather wants us to be there, there's not much we can do about it.' He sighed heavily. 'Oh well, there's still some time till we have to get tarted up, why don't you show me around and tell me some more of the family history. I don't know any of it; nobody seems to have told my father anything. I know that, because I asked him about it when I was a kid.'

His lips tightened and she saw the shutters come down, so she led him outside, through the garden towards the old stone wall that marked the boundary between the house and the farmland. 'We're heading to this Burial Field of yours, aren't we?' he asked. 'Tell me about it.'

'It's the most ridiculously romantic story, embroidered over the centuries by ordinary people wanting to brighten up their drab lives. The actual truth, if anyone ever really knew it, was lost centuries ago. Nobody has ever done any research; the Attlins have been soldiers or farmers with no academic interests and there's never been any money to finance an archaeological dig. Mind you,' she looked thoughtful, 'I could always try getting in touch with *Time Team*, I suppose. It might be intriguing enough for them to come and poke around.'

She looked up at him, with an eager light in her eyes. 'You know what? I might just do that. Can't do any harm, they can only say no.

'Now, where was I? You'll have heard that the family is supposed to have been founded by a Roman?' He nodded and took the old book out of his pocket.

'Yup, I've got the Rev Sebastian right here, ready to rap you on the knuckles if you come up with any of your fanciful Attlin fairy tales.'

She sniffed. 'Silly old fool, he was sour about everyone in the district. No house was good enough, no land extensive enough, no family ever noble enough for his taste, and once the Attlin daughter rejected his proposal he took great delight in dismissing her forebears as lowly farmers at every opportunity. Not that they gave a toss, they *were* lowly farmers after all, and proud of it.'

She filled him in on the family legend, ending with, 'Miss Evelyn Attlin says Lucius Sextus Vitalis had some pretty important connections. But then,' she looked mischievous, 'nobody is ever descended from the rabble, it's always the nobility, never some poor sod of a foot soldier who simply ran away and deserted.'

She paused, looking at him with a slightly abashed grin. 'I know, I know, it sounds unbelievable but it's what we've always been told, so now naturally it's gospel truth. Where was I? Lucius was evidently a practical man and decided this was a good place to build, so the angel's blessing was the icing on the cake. There was a good spring; running water.' She pointed to a stream sparkling in the sunshine lower down the field. 'Good access but easily defensible too, and on a slight hill. No wonder he apparently *'looked on his work and found it fair.'* '

They had been skirting the low-lying scrub in a field away to the west of the house and she led him now towards a copse atop a rise at the far edge of the meadow. 'It's said that he had the stone carved, later on, to make it look more like an angel and built the atrium of his house around it. Money doesn't seem to have been a problem as he got going on building the house straight away. Look, this is it; this was where the central courtyard of the villa is said to have been.'

'Why did they build the new house so far from the original villa?' Rory squinted against the light as he looked back towards the farmhouse.

'Grandpa says the stream probably got silted up and turned marshy, which, in turn, would bring mosquitoes and malaria. They used to call it intermittent fever, or ague, he said. Building the new house higher upstream would solve the problem.'

'I didn't realize malaria was endemic in England,' Rory said absently, as he examined what he could see of the stone with a critical eye. It stood about four feet high, the base all but vanished under layers of earth and generations of shoots and saplings of the alders that surrounded it. 'I suppose it does look a bit like an angel,' he conceded at last. 'If you allow for two thousand years of wind and weather. And squint a bit.'

She looked at her watch. 'We've got a bit longer before we need get ready. Look, come and sit down over here for a minute.' She waved a hand towards the stone boundary wall. 'Grandpa was told that this would have been the middle of the villa complex but at some point they built that stone wall right across, probably at the time of the Enclosures, which is why the shape of the fields changed completely. That would be why the copse is in the angle of the walls and not out on its own. Anyway, Lucius finished building his house and then looked round for a wife but he took his time about it; very picky type from the sound of it. It's said that he had a fall out hunting and was nursed by *'a maiden of high repute and high beauty'*. She came from a great family, the legend says, and he *'did fall heart long and steadfastly in love with her to her great joy.'* Ain't love grand?'

She glanced at her watch. 'You might as well have the full works,' she nodded, giving him a brief run-down of the origin of the Attlin name. 'So, by-blow or not, Edmund Atheling married Edith, the last of Lucius the Roman's descendants.'

They were sitting on the sun-warmed stone of the old wall, listening to the splash of the stream that had featured in the Roman legend. Edith was making garlands, weaving heads of pinky-red clover in with starry daisies and varying the colour with speedwell and sprigs of wild thyme while Rory chewed contemplatively on a blade of grass.

'It's an amazing story,' he said lazily. 'I'm quite prepared to believe every word of it. Would I dare doubt Miss Evelyn Attlin? It's the kind of place anything could happen.' He frowned for a moment, remembering that something certainly had happened only recently but before Edith noticed his hesitation he asked casually, 'Are there any ghosts around, do you know?'

'In a place this old?' She smiled then looked curiously at him. 'You really did think you saw Dame Margery the other night, didn't you? Oh all right,' as he shook his head. 'I know you think you ought to be rational about it or blame your medication but the ghost of Lucius Sextus Vitalis has been seen in this very spot.' She waved a hand expansively to encompass the copse and the entire field. 'He is reported to wear his army uniform and looks very noble and impressive and it's said that only the family ever see him.'

It was her turn to fall silent for a moment, a thoughtful expression on her face as she stared at the ancient stone, then she scrambled to her feet. 'Time to go.'

She set off but Rory lingered by the angel stone. 'Hang on, Edith, there's something a bit odd here. It looks as if the soil's been disturbed, just here behind where the plinth must be.'

'What? Show me.' She stared as he fought his way out of the trees and pointed to the mass of soil he had spotted by the roots of an alder sapling, inches away from the ancient stone itself, but not easily visible from the field. Another tree seemed to have been jammed carelessly into a hole. There were signs that someone had definitely been at work on the bank and as Rory backed out of the mass of vegetation, he frowned as he brushed soil off his jeans.

'Could it be something to do with this oil business?' he queried. 'Drilling for oil? It seems a bit amateurish if it is.'

A small plane buzzed self-importantly overhead and Rory looked up, his puzzled frown deepening. He turned his attention back to the disturbed earth.

'Highly unlikely, I'd have thought. Much more likely old Misselbrook's been out here digging out the badgers, just the sort of thing he'd do. And he'd be sure to keep it quiet as it's not allowed these days. I suppose it *might* be amateur archaeologists, treasure-hunters,' Edith frowned. 'Fat lot of good it'll do them; only the odd shard of burnt and blackened pottery has turned up over the hundreds of years the field's been ploughed but *Time Team* has a lot to answer for. Could have been someone trying to see if there's an inscription on the stone, which there isn't. We do get them now and then, lurking about the place with their metal detectors and it's a real problem when this field is planted. Not so bad now, as it's not ploughed, but it's a flipping cheek all the same.'

The church clock struck the quarter and they looked at each other aghast.

'Not a word about this,' Edith warned as they cantered across the field towards the house. 'I shouldn't think it's anything to worry about but I don't want the grandparents upset and Grandpa gets really cross about trespassers. Besides, if it *was* old Misselbrook, Grandpa's upset enough because the old devil's just died — they'd known each other all their lives.

'We'll talk later, but for now we need to get cleaned up for this drinks party. It'll be awful,' she warned him. 'Lara Dean will latch on to you and I'll get stuck with a boring old fart, some crony of Gordon's.'

Rory followed obediently in her wake but at the field gate he turned and stared back at the distant copse. It might be badgers, he supposed, but it had looked a little too tidy for an old man bent on illegal badger killing. Treasure-seekers seemed a more likely bet, but what could they be looking for? And — the thought struck him unpleasantly out of the blue — had someone been digging there on the night a car was driven at Walter Attlin? Because — perhaps — could he have seen something he shouldn't?'

4

'Champagne, eh?' Sam took an appreciative sip from his glass and grinned at his cousin. 'And it's Veuve Cliquot too, I caught sight of the label. Very nice, bit over the top for a village drinks party, I'd have thought, but very welcome all the same.'

'I ought to feel guilty.' Harriet looked over the rim of her glass at their host. 'Enjoying Gordon's drink when I dislike almost everything about him.' She sighed and made a face. 'He tries too hard, that's the trouble, but you can trust him to serve up the best. About the only thing you *can* trust him with.'

She glanced round the room and turned back to Sam. 'How do you feel now you've had a chat with some of them? These people will be your neighbours, friends even, once you move in next door and although you don't have to embrace them whole-heartedly you'll still see a fair amount of them. You'll need to rub along.'

'They seem a nice enough bunch,' he said, smiling and nodding in answer to a friendly wave from someone. 'I've been listening to some of their concerns about this rumour that's going round, about possible oil drilling. They're very worried but nobody seems to be asking questions of the right people.'

Harriet hid a smile. Sam would fit right in, she thought, glancing across at him with deep affection, and before he knows it he'll be on the parish council and he'll be the one who asks the questions. Oh well, perhaps it will help with the bad times, when he's missing Avril even more than usual.

'They're also fretting about Walter Attlin's so-called accident.' Sam was still absorbed in village gossip. 'The police seem to be taking no further interest and apparently some bright spark of a constable suggested he could have been knocked over by a cow.'

'Oh, for goodness' sake.' Harriet was half amused, half irritated. 'Even if Walter were dotty enough to mistake a cow for a car, there's no livestock anywhere near the house. They're all over by the other farmhouse under the cowman's eagle eye. I was talking the other day to Alan, the chap who's taking over as Walter's manager come Michaelmas. He said they're planning to plough a couple of fields now old Misselbrook's popped his clogs. Alan's a local man and knew the old misery by repute, so he's delighted the old fellow won't be around to be a thorn in his side. Got all sorts of plans apparently,' she grinned. 'In fact I suspect he's had his eye on the place for a while, speculating about what might be done there. He's itching to get his hands on several of those fields, along with some near the house, including the Burial Field, and sow them as wild flower meadows. Very trendy these days and good for wildlife as well as looking lovely, and a vast improvement on the current scrub; there are even some little oak trees nearly a yard high.'

She looked sober as she returned to their anxieties. 'Going back to what you said, nobody quite likes to ask questions when Walter is so set against discussing it. He won't talk about the accident and he refuses to talk about this oil rumour, and people are fond of him and don't want to upset him. I'm surprised Gordon Dean isn't poking his nose into it on general principle. Mind you, I'd ask him about it myself, but I'm another who doesn't want to upset Walter, so I'd better not pry.'

A new arrival made her eyes gleam appreciatively. 'Oh ho, the vicar's here. Just watch the women cluster round. Not,' she added, 'that he's the only good-looking young(ish) man at this party, the place is positively swarming with them. See that brown-haired one by the bar? He's Gordon Dean's assistant, Brendan Whittaker, been here a few months, but I don't think I've seen the tall dark man who's talking to the doctor before.'

'Speaking of good-looking,' Sam murmured, 'here come Edith and Rory. He's a surprise, isn't he? The likeness is very strong, apart from his height.'

'Of course,' Harriet remembered. 'You knew Edith's father, didn't you? Yes, Rory is very clearly an Attlin. It must be quite painful for the old people but they won't let on.'

Lara Dean sauntered forward to greet the newcomers, nodding coolly to Edith, but offering a cheek to Rory and to the Reverend John Forrester. 'Have you met our new vicar, Rory? Dad tells me he's a great asset to the village and very popular with the ladies.'

Edith was amused to see that the vicar took Lara's advances in his stride, but she was less impressed by the way Rory was reacting. To be fair, he had little choice in the matter as his hostess had seized his arm and was parading him round the room to introduce him to her guests. Like Harriet, Edith had noted the surprising number of young men so she ignored Rory's rolled eyes and waded in.

'Hi, Brendan, how's it going?' She fluttered her eyelashes at the other men in the group; her grandmother had told her to be sociable, after all. 'Am I interrupting? I haven't seen

Brendan since Christmas.' Within minutes she had been offered a seat, handed a glass of champagne and a plate of nibbles had been set on a table beside her.

'I know you won't eat this, Brendan.' She nodded towards the prunes wrapped in bacon. 'I spotted some veggie snacks over there.' She held out the plate towards the tall dark American who had been talking to his host and was now giving her an appraising once-over.

'Not for me, thanks,' he grinned. 'Not bacon, with a name like Goldstein.' He took a sip of champagne. 'That's Mike Goldstein,' he told her. 'I'm here on vacation. Maybe you could show me round?'

Mike's dark eyes gleamed in admiration as Edith perched on the end of a sofa beside him. Working at home might turn out to be more fun than she'd anticipated, she mused, if Mike happened to be here for a while. And besides him, there was Rory . . . yes, well. She glanced round the room. There he was, still being paraded round by Lara, and looking tired and bored so that, in spite of her sense that there was some mystery about him, she felt a pang of sympathy, especially when he caught her watching him, and rolled his eyes.

She responded eagerly to Mike Goldstein's advances, throwing a crumb of conversation at Brendan too, acutely aware that the vicar was now a bystander, an appreciative grin on his attractively rumpled face.

After a while he came over to her and somehow cut her out from her admirers. 'Talk to me now, it's my turn,' he told her. 'I'm sorry I missed the dinner last night but I was already booked for a dull evening I couldn't get out of. I gather it went well?'

Edith had briefly been introduced to him once over the Christmas holidays when she had spent a few days at home before heading north for Hogmanay with her mother and stepfather, but otherwise she had barely spoken to him. Now she had time to take his measure, she saw that the vicar of Locksley was a very attractive proposition indeed.

'Tell me about your family's connection with the church,' he demanded. 'I'm trying to mug up so I don't sound a fool when tourists interrogate me. I've read the little booklet about it, but the Attlins have been here forever. Besides, my own special interest is the late Roman period, so the mediaeval history is a bit of a blur.'

She melted at once, never proof against appreciation of the place dearest to her heart and they were soon deep in conversation about the Attlin chronicle and the Roman story.

'The angel motif is unusual, isn't it?' he commented, shifting slightly to let Harriet into their discussion.

'Our particular angel is unique,' she reproved, then laughed at herself. 'Mind you, you might be surprised to hear that supernatural beings as a rule aren't actually that rare in Hampshire. Tell him, Edith.'

'Harriet's right,' Edith told him, as he looked incredulous. 'I don't know of any other angels as such, but there was a giant and at least a couple of dragons. The Bistern Dragon on Burley Beacon was quite undemanding, only asking for a bucket of milk every day, so it was very unsporting of the villagers to hire a dragon-slayer.'

'You're kidding.' He looked from one to the other, clearly thinking it was a wind-up.

'No, it's quite true,' Harriet assured him. 'Well, as true as any of these stories ever are. Hampshire's very rich in weird monsters. There's the Wherwell Cockatrice that was hatched by a toad from a duck's egg and lived in a cellar. That one was a real villain because it ate humans, but the locals were more enterprising. They gave it a polished shield and let it wear itself out fighting its own image, then they finished it off.'

'So the Locksley angel is quite a cut above the dragons and giants, isn't it?' The vicar,

Harriet thought, was either really interested in local lore, or perhaps it was just Edith who had caught his eye. Not sure I approve of that idea at all, she mused, recent widower and so forth, though he's certainly a charmer, an excellent preacher too.

Edith was in full flood. 'Oh yes, there aren't many stories of private, personal angels, they mostly prefer to appear to saints. None of those in our family,' she grinned. Harriet hung around, throwing a word in here and there, although she was aware that John was finding her presence irritating. Well, tough, she frowned. He must know the whole village watches his every move and I don't want Edith getting caught up in something that could rebound on her. She drifted back to her surroundings and listened as John persisted in angel talk. It was reasonable, she supposed; not every village had its own tame angel, but he seemed to really be pressing Edith about the connection between the Romans and the folk legend.

'I gather even the name of the village is connected with angels,' he said, as Edith finished telling the story of how the Roman villa had been built.

'Mmm, only a few pedants, like my grandfather, insist on using the village's full name. The post office certainly doesn't bother with it. My Latin's pretty ropey but Grandpa says it was something like *Locus Angelorum*, the place of the angels, now corrupted to Locksley. The church is St Michael and All Angels, as of course you know.'

Harriet was aware of Sam watching her so it was no surprise when he excused himself politely and made his way across the room.

'Why are you looking ruffled?' he began, when their host surged up to them with an invitation to admire his orchid collection in the large conservatory.

'Tell you later,' she whispered, so Sam tagged on for the tour. The orchids were impressive and Sam scored some Brownie points with Gordon Dean by admitting that he'd visited the Orchid Farm in Fiji on a stopover on one of his visits to his son, Christopher, in Australia. His pleasant features revealed no sign of his complete lack of interest and Harriet watched appreciatively until her attention was claimed by the tall young American who had been looking out of the conservatory window.

'Admiring Gordon's garden?' she asked with a smile.

'Admiring all the shades of green,' he said. 'I know it's the classic cliché, but I'm from Texas and we just don't have this.'

Mike Goldstein was a bit of a stereotype

himself, Harriet thought, surreptitiously admiring him. Tall, dark and handsome, with a warm, drawling voice that was very attractive. 'I gather you're ancestor hunting. Are you a colleague of Gordon's?' she asked, a sudden thought darting into her mind.

'Oh, no. I'm on a year's contract, based in London. I knew Lara in New York and when I found myself with some unexpected leave, I gave her a call. She and her father very kindly invited me to base myself here while I do my research.' At her questioning glance, he went on, 'My mother is very keen for me to find out about her family.'

'Your family's from Hampshire?'

'My father's folks escaped during one of the Russian pogroms, but my mom's ancestors didn't just originate in Hampshire, but actually in the Winchester district too.' He explained, 'I spotted a grave in the churchyard here when I blew in last week, a Melinda Zebedee who died in 1801, and that makes me wonder. My great-great-grandma's middle name was Melinda, you see, so I have hopes. My mom was very excited when I called her about it last week. Great-great-grammy's maiden name was Zebedee too, which is pretty unusual, I guess, but they say it's quite common round these parts.'

'I wouldn't say it was exactly common,'

Harriet began, only to be interrupted by Edith who had wandered into the conservatory.

'Last week?' She sounded almost fierce, Harriet thought, as she addressed the question to Mike. 'I didn't know you were here last week. What day did you arrive?'

He seemed unaware of any undercurrents as he answered. 'I guess it was Monday evening when I blew in,' he said mildly. As Harriet watched with interest she realized that Edith was still very tense, though she was trying to hide it. So what was all this about last week?

Harriet left the group, now augmented by Rory and Brendan, and wandered over to admire the view. Mike was right; the green landscape and the brilliant flower beds were wonderful, if a tad too immaculate for Harriet, whose own tastes ran to blowsy, uncorseted cottage gardens.

Now, why would Edith be worried about last week? She went back to considering her former pupil's evident anxiety. Of course, it was Wednesday evening that Walter had his accident, Harriet remembered. So Edith is — what? Suspicious of Mike? Well, why not? Harriet had her own suspicions, even though Sam was dismissive. Any stranger in the village had to be looked at, however unlikely it might seem. And not just strangers, she thought, then scolded herself. Sam's right, I'm trying to play Miss Marple again. It was probably joyriding kids who ran into Walter, and they're either shaking in their shoes in case they get caught, or else they were too high to remember a thing about it. It occurred to her that this might also be the opinion of the local police, the case not closed but not high on their list of priorities either.

Edith, meanwhile, had ranged herself alongside Sam who offered shelter from the proprietorial arm Brendan Whittaker was trying to sneak around her waist. A couple of drinks in the local pub at Christmas when she was bored seemed to have had more of an impression on Brendan than Edith liked. Her conscience was more or less clear and he'd certainly not taken it seriously at the time, so why the present display of affection?

She was rescued by Lara, of all people, who took her back into the big drawing room. 'I hope you're looking after poor Rory properly,' she cooed, settling herself in an elegant pose on a sofa and looking up at Edith.

'Rory? Of course we are,' Edith stared.

'I do hope that's so,' was the surprising comeback. 'But you can sometimes be a bit bossy, you know. I remember from school.

And he does need a lot of TLC.'

'What?' Edith was frankly astonished. 'I know he's been ill with some fever or other, but he insists he's fine now. Why on earth should I pamper a grown man? I've two elderly, real invalids to worry about.' The (admittedly justified) crack about her bossiness rankled and she managed a laugh, but at the smug expression on the other woman's face, the laugh tailed away.

'You really don't know, do you? I'm amazed.' There was no doubt Lara was enjoying herself. 'You didn't know about him being held on a drug-smuggling charge in the Far East, then? He was in prison for about nine months until he was released a month or so ago. That's why he's so thin. I believe he had a very bad time. It was a trumped-up charge, of course, but one of the guys he was with was executed. Fancy him not talking to you, of all people.'

Edith was shocked, overcome with remorse at her bullying of Rory. No wonder he hadn't carried tables and chairs for the dinner. Too shocked to care about Lara's smirking triumph — they had always loathed each other, since Lara had picked on Edith at school until the younger girl learned to retaliate — she didn't at first notice that last crack, then: 'What do you mean, 'me of all people'?' she rallied belligerently.

'Well, darling, I mean considering you're related. It's pretty amazing how much like your father he is, could be him all over again.'

'What?' Edith was dumbfounded. 'You never met my father, you didn't move to the village till after he died. How could you possibly know what he looked like?'

'I didn't,' Lara smiled sweetly. 'But when I was dressing for the dinner last night I was watching something Dad had recorded and he'd accidentally caught the last ten minutes of a documentary about local heroes in Hampshire. There was a beautifully clear shot of your father, with a mention of who he was and how he died in an attack just at the end of the Bosnian War. I had no idea how good-looking he was, and then, of course, I came across Rory an hour later. It was quite a shock.'

Edith had herself in hand now. 'I know there *was* a programme,' she admitted, 'but it was years ago. And besides, nobody else has mentioned seeing any such thing.'

'Why would they?' Lara shrugged. 'Nobody round here would say anything about it in case it upset your grandparents. Besides, the programme Dad recorded was on very late on one of the cable channels, I checked with him. I imagine the thing about your father was a repeat that followed on even later.' She rose to her feet and smiled even more sweetly as she glanced across to where Rory was talking to Sam Hathaway.

'It's a good job you two aren't an item, isn't it? For that kind of resemblance you'd have to be *very* closely related, I should think.'

★ ★ ★

'Well? Don't think I didn't spot you, Harriet, when you had young Edith pinned to the wall for interrogation at the party.' Sam was looking sternly at her as they relaxed later that afternoon over a cup of tea in her garden.

Harriet banged her cup back in the saucer, too annoyed to care if it cracked. Sam had always been an expert at winkling things out of her. 'Stop exaggerating. I did *not* interrogate her. She grabbed me because she's worried sick and she thought I might be able to help.'

Sam, who was playing truant from church, scarcely noticed his cousin's pettish behaviour. He was trying to decide whether to go back to his flat now or stay at Harriet's for another night. His place was just a place to lay his head, he mused, not a home, though nothing had been a home since Avril died. Maybe, perhaps, living next door to Harriet, his oldest and dearest friend, might go some way towards filling the aching gap. And perhaps something might turn up, something he could do to help the people here, or was that just arrogance? He made a face into his cup and shrugged; the Lord will provide, I suppose.

'Edith's been thinking along the same lines as I have,' Harriet was saying. 'In other words, she's making mental notes about strangers who were around the village last Wednesday and who could — and you needn't pounce on me, I said *could* — have been involved in her grandfather's accident.' Sam growled his disapproval and she ignored him. 'Yes, well there are several new faces around at the moment. There's Brendan Whittaker, and there's young Rory, plus Mike, the dishy Texan. And Elveece found him, of course. I just don't know what to think about any of it.' She slid a sidelong glance at his unresponsive features as she added, 'There's the vicar too.'

'What?' Sam sat up, ready for a fight. 'That's utter nonsense, Harriet. I don't know the man but he's got a perfectly good reputation. You need to watch your tongue, and warn Edith to do the same or you'll both find yourselves in trouble.'

'I'm aware of that,' she said, irritably. 'It's only you and I'm just thinking aloud but I can't help wondering if Walter's experience might be connected with the missing man. Rory wasn't here then, poor lad. I told you about what happened to him, didn't I? And even though this American friend of the Deans was in the UK, the local grapevine would have picked up on it at once if he'd been loitering round the village in January. But that still leaves Brendan and John Forrester and Elveece who were all here in January.'

'Hang on.' Sam had remembered something. 'Forrester's wife died around Christmas. You're surely not suggesting that a grieving widower had time to go bumping off your missing man, are you? Because it's indefensible, if that's what you're saying.'

'Calm down, Sam.' She got up and went into the kitchen for more tea and a couple of slices of lemon drizzle cake. 'I'm not suggesting anything, just wondering. I'll tell you one thing about the vicar that I don't like, though,' she added vigorously. 'He was definitely flirting with Edith at the party today and I don't want her mixed up with him. I know he's good-looking and I'm sorry about his wife, but the poor creature's only been dead six months so it's a bit soon for him to be taking up with another woman.'

'What did she die of?' Sam ignored Harriet's hint about Edith who, he clearly recalled, had been flirting happily away with all the young men in the room, including the vicar. He lounged back in the sunshine, munching on his piece of cake and thought about what he had heard. 'I gather she had some kind of breakdown, as far as I can recall, so I imagine it was mental health problems, poor soul, and that's why he took this living. He hoped the pace of life and the countryside would have a beneficial effect on her.'

'She was stoned,' said Harriet baldly. 'We weren't here then, we were on that New Year break in Italy, but I asked around. I wanted to make sure I didn't say anything tactless and upset him. Seems she was a fair bit older than he was and prone to hysterical jealousy, though the word is that nobody's ever heard anything against him, other women, I mean, but she was always turning up at meetings and embarrassing him. Her drug problem, which everyone suspected anyway, showed up at the inquest. I went to that, the whole village turned out in support, and it was felt John came out of it very well. Everyone was sorry for him and the general consensus, though never openly expressed, of course, was that he was well out of it.' She didn't look at her cousin. 'His wife left him an awful lot of money, they say.'

Predictably, Sam exploded in righteous indignation. 'I'm not staying to listen to this kind of gossip, Harriet,' he said, rising and heading for the house. 'I'd better go and get started on clearing out the flat. I know most of our — ' he pulled himself up short on the word and looked away, while Harriet blinked in sympathy. 'My stuff is in store but there are hundreds of books still to pack and I've left it late to start. I'll ring you tomorrow and hope you can drag your mind away from scandal and trivia.'

Harriet saw him off, hugging him affectionately. 'You're a pompous old prig, you know, but I forgive you. And regardless of your strictures, I'm going to do some poking around and see if I can find any clues to the local mystery.'

He sighed and returned the hug. 'I may be pompous,' he told her. 'But you're a nosy old biddy, Old Hat, and you need to stay out of trouble. Promise me you won't do anything stupid like wandering about at night trying to catch villains?'

Her blue eyes gleamed with mischief and Sam wished he hadn't spoken. 'I'll think about it,' was all she said, but Sam was seized with foreboding.

5

'Edith? It's Harriet. Sam's just rung me to ask if you and Rory would like to join him for dinner at the new French bistro in town tonight.' Harriet caught herself up with a faint giggle and went on, 'Well, I'll be there too, of course. Sam was cross with me earlier on but I'm obviously forgiven.' She sobered quickly. 'I hope you two can make it. Although he won't mention it, today is his wife's birthday and he finds it very tough going. Neither of us ever says anything, but Avril is always in our thoughts at this time and I know he'd welcome a bit of distraction.'

'Oh, poor Sam.' Harriet could hear the ready sympathy in Edith's voice. 'I liked Mrs Hathaway. She was always fair but you couldn't mess around in her English classes. I expect you miss her too, don't you? I'd better check whether Rory's up for it and I'll get back to you.'

★ ★ ★

Rory had disappeared immediately after the drinks party, muttering about 'work to do', so

Edith busied herself by helping Karen around the house, as well as taking a pot of tea upstairs to her grandparents.

'Tell me about Rory?' she asked, as she poured out.

The silence that greeted this innocuous question made her look up. Her grandmother looked suddenly strained and very weary, while her grandfather was scowling.

'The relationship is complicated; old sorrows, old anger, better left alone,' he growled and Mrs Attlin nodded in corroboration. 'As for discussing him, that's his business. He doesn't want it talked about so we'll respect his wishes, if you please.'

She stared at him, feeling at a loss. There was a slight edge in his voice that warned her not to press the question. She felt his disapproval but ploughed on regardless.

'What about his father? Is he still alive?'

The disapproval was marked now; she was encroaching on shaky territory but she had no idea why.

'Rory's father was killed some years ago, and his mother . . . No, I told you, Edith, I'm not prepared to discuss this with you any further.'

Puzzled and slightly hurt, Edith shrugged and left the room, leaving the old people looking at each other.

'Oh, dear,' sighed Penelope Attlin. 'Now her feelings are hurt. Do you think we should have told her everything after all?'

'Nonsense, love.' Walter shook his head. 'Rory asked us not to discuss his affairs so it's up to him to decide when — if — he tells her anything. Besides, it won't do her any harm to have a check, bossy little madam. Always was.'

The bossy little madam stomped her way downstairs and relieved her frustration by peeling the potatoes Karen handed her. After a while her temper subsided and she wandered out to the stable yard. No point pushing for the story, she told herself. If Rory asked them not to discuss it, they're not going to. I don't like to ask Rory outright, but . . . She sighed and shook herself. Lara's mocking hint had disturbed her more than she cared to admit, even to herself, but surely there couldn't be anything in it? Her father had always been her hero and the idea that he . . . no, it was preposterous.

She pushed open the stable door, knocking as she did so, and looked in — at images from hell. Huge canvases of red and orange light screamed at her from all sides of the open space. Jagged black wounds scored the searing nightmare colours. There were no shapes, no forms, no figures in this landscape of pain and fear.

Recoiling in shock she turned away involuntarily and came upon another picture that was somehow infinitely sad, a small, swirling green canvas. An oasis, perhaps? She couldn't make it out but it spoke of grief and longing.

And I sneered at his offer to paint me, she winced, as she slowly became aware that he was looking at her. His face was blank, features schooled into immobility, but his hazel eyes were watchful.

She put out a tentative hand. 'Rory — '

'I was backpacking last year,' he said, turning his head away. 'I was due to start working at the university here in the autumn so there was the summer to fill. Mum had died only a couple of months earlier so there wasn't anything to go home for. I'd broken up with my girlfriend too so a trip out East seemed as good an idea as any.

'It was fine until Mitch, the guy from college that I was with, met this local man in a bar and when he offered us a lift in his Jeep to share expenses, we jumped at it. He seemed okay and we bummed around the countryside with him for a few more days till we were going through Customs.'

He shrugged. 'It was the old story. Couple

of gullible young idiots who were horrified to find our bags stuffed with heroin, but his luck ran out when one of the Customs people recognized him from a wanted list.

'I won't bore you with the details but in a way, that helped Mitch and me. Because the local guy was a known smuggler they accepted that we'd been caught in his net, but they still threw us in jail. He, the other guy, was charged, tried and found guilty all in a rush, but because they were angling for a deal with the British government, they held off executing him, using us as the bargaining point.'

Again came the resigned shrug. 'We were told afterwards that was probably why we were arrested in the first place but whatever the truth of it, we served their purpose. It took them nine months to sort everything out and in the end they cleaned us up, kitted us out in smart new gear and took us out of the cell, so we thought we were home and dry. But they had one last surprise for us — they forced us to watch the smuggler's execution.'

He ignored her shocked gasp. 'It was all very hush-hush and we were told to keep a low profile once we got home — other Europeans in the same jail, you see. God only knows how that Lara woman found out about it. I must remember to shut her up. Anyway, my university job was held open for me so

118

after debriefing and counselling, here I am.'

It was hard to know what to say and Edith was grateful that he was looking more himself again. 'These are for an Amnesty exhibition in the New Year,' he told her as she stared again at the flaring paintings, then his glance flickered towards the small green canvas. 'I was glad Mum was dead. It would have been hell for her; she had no family left.' He went to the sink and started to clean his brushes. 'She had a cerebral haemorrhage, right out of the blue. She was only forty-nine.'

That seemed to be his last word on the subject so Edith let it go.

'Harriet's just rung to invite us out to dinner with her and Sam tonight. I said I'd ask you.' She explained the circumstances behind the invitation and was relieved at his immediate agreement.

★ ★ ★

The new French bistro almost lived up to its own hype so Harriet was able to set aside her concerns and be, frankly, greedy. A glance at the other two reassured her. Rory was looking more relaxed and Edith too seemed more herself. Sam was — well, she hid a sigh — Sam was his usual pleasant self, delighted that his two young guests were enjoying their

119

meal, but Harriet knew that on this of all days, his wife's death was very much with him. A lot of topics to avoid in conversation, she thought, it's a flipping minefield: mustn't talk about Avril; better not mention Rory and what happened to him, even though I'm guessing he's told Edith about it now. Plus there's Walter's accident, which is better avoided, and Sam will hit the roof if I bring up the topic of the local 'murder mystery'.

'I wanted to sound you out about this missing man, Harriet.' Edith looked up in surprise as Harriet choked on a sip of Merlot. 'You okay?' As Harriet nodded, avoiding Sam's affronted expression, Edith went on, 'Well, I've been talking to people about it, at the party today and to Karen, among others. It all sounds a bit odd, I have to admit, and at least four people solemnly told me they were quite convinced he's been murdered.'

She gave a sudden giggle as she caught Harriet's eye. 'The silliest idea is that he was a spy and MI5 have done away with him, for reasons unspecified but believed to originate from the fact that he asked a lot of questions and a pair of sunglasses was spotted in the top pocket of his jacket. As it was January, the dark glasses are held to be deeply suspicious. On the other hand I also heard that the sinister reason he was asking about Grandpa

120

was that he was investigating his military career. However, as Grandpa came out of the army after the Korean War, sixty years ago, that seems unlikely. Nobody can give me a good reason as to why this stranger, who's probably just done a bunk, should have been bumped off, but it's worrying when you consider Grandpa's accident as well.'

Sam clucked his tongue in annoyance. 'Oh, for heaven's sake, Edith, not you as well? I've had Harriet adding two and two and making seventeen on the same topic. And,' he shot a warning glance at his cousin, 'I suggest you both keep quiet about your wilder theories. There's a man missing and the police admit they have some concerns. It's not a matter for idle speculation.'

Edith blinked and looked anxiously at Harriet, who laughed at her. 'He's a clergyman, he has to say things like that. Don't worry, it goes with the job. If Sam and Rory don't want to discuss the village goings-on, you'd better drop round for coffee with me tomorrow, Edith. We can sum up the evidence, or lack of it, then.'

★ ★ ★

Just before midnight Edith jolted awake, a partially formed idea nagging away at the back of her mind. Sleep proved elusive so she scrambled out of bed and looked out at the moonlit farm, silver and black in the shadows. All the anxiety about her grandfather's health, along with the fairly parlous state of the farm's finances, clamoured in her head, and she was just about to draw the curtain again when a glint of light caught her eye, two fields away. She squinted and spotted the light for a brief, second time; a torch held downwards, perhaps? It looked as though it was coming from the Burial Field. But that's not possible, she gasped. You can't see that far from my window.

About to dial 999 and summon the cavalry, she hesitated as another movement distracted her. This time it was a moving shadow, man-shaped, and it was running swiftly across the garden below her. As the man crossed a patch of moonlight she gasped: it was Rory.

It was enough to galvanize her into action and she dressed quickly. Slipping on jeans and T-shirt and thrusting her feet into trainers, she rootled in a drawer for the torch that always used to be there, found it and ran quietly downstairs. He had been coming from the direction of the study and, guessing that he had left the glass door open for his return, she left the house the same way.

Halfway across the first field she almost

blundered into a pile of sawn logs and timber. Of course, Gran had told her about the oak tree. No wonder she could suddenly see out of her window, the tree had been struck by lightning earlier in the year. She caught up with Rory as he hesitated at the field gate, some yards in front of her, then turned aghast at the slight sound she made as her shoe knocked against a stone.

'For God's sake, Edith,' he hissed in outrage. 'I nearly had a heart attack. Why are you . . . ? Oh, never mind. Here, just get behind this hawthorn hedge so they can't see us. And keep quiet.'

'Who is it? How many? I can see two of them, is that all? What are they doing?' Edith peered through the branches, gently holding back some leaves as she stared indignantly at the distant figures. 'Bloody treasure-seekers, that's who they'll be. I'm calling — ' She patted her back pocket and made a face. 'My mobile's on my bedside table. Have you got yours?'

'No. Stupid, aren't we?' He craned his neck to look more closely. 'I can only see two of them as well. They haven't got metal detectors, though. Can you see? They're poking around the base of your old angel stone but they're not using — ' He broke off abruptly. 'There's something peculiar about their heads but I can't see what it is from here.'

'Oh, for goodness' sake,' Edith smothered a giggle. 'They're wearing balaclavas!'

'You're kidding.' He squinted the hundred yards or so across the field and shook his head in astonishment. 'So? Bank robbers? Commandos? What — ?'

'That's Brendan Whittaker,' she interrupted, indicating the slighter, shorter man. 'I'm sure of it. Look, he's got really sloping shoulders. I reckon he has his suit jackets built up, but I've noticed he's a lot less impressive in casual clothes. Yup, I'm sure that's Brendan. Now what is he up to? I wonder.'

Rory was still staring at the scene. 'I know this sounds mad, but surely that's the vicar? The other guy, I mean.'

The long, angular figure wielding a shovel certainly looked familiar and Edith had just turned towards her companion when, at that moment, the shovel struck a stone with a loud jarring clang, audible to the onlookers. The expletive that ripped from the tall figure was unmistakably transatlantic in tone. Not the vicar after all.

'Mike Goldstein?' They strained to listen but the words were inaudible, only the soft but urgent murmur that followed.

'What are we going to . . . ?' Edith began, then she caught a glimpse of Rory's face in the moonlight. He was grey with sudden exhaustion and the story of his imprisonment came flooding back. She felt a pang of sympathy. 'Come on.' She tugged at his arm. 'Let's get back home. We can't deal with this on our own. Look, if we keep to the hedgerow we'll be in shadow.'

He made a token protest but caved in as she half pulled him across to the house and in through the glass door. At his bedroom door, Rory paused for breath then stood still, staring rigidly at the wall. Edith stared. She could see nothing but ancient oak panelling but suddenly it struck her. This was where Rory had supposedly seen — or, in spite of all his camouflage about medication, she suspected that he *had* seen — the Locksley ghost.

★ ★ ★

Harriet fussed around the kitchen, her wits unusually astray as she tried to make sense of everything. Sometimes she thought that Sam, who was back in Belfast for a night, winding up his project, had the right of it and she was making something out of nothing. There was still that nagging doubt, though, and she was

125

glad she had dropped him at Southampton airport early that morning so there was no need to worry that he'd turn up today to apply his caustic common sense and laugh at her tentative theories. Edith, on the other hand, although generally speaking as sensible and practical as Harriet herself, would definitely be ready to discuss, discard and revisit all those theories.

What's more, Harriet smiled reminiscently, Edith could keep a secret. Even the threat of detention had not made her tell who had sprayed paint on an unpopular teacher's car. Harriet grinned as she remembered Edith, her hands spattered with incriminating paint, acting like an Angela Brazil schoolgirl and defiantly refusing to sneak. The situation was eventually resolved by a tearful confession from the culprit who admitted the crime, whereupon Edith stopped being a martyr and explained that the paint was only on her because she had found the discarded aerosol and put it in the bin.

The front doorbell rang and she greeted her former pupil with affection. 'I've had a baking session,' she said, leading the way to the garden. 'I had a sudden, uncharacteristic urge to make a coffee and walnut sponge, so you're my first victim. Tea or coffee?'

'Harriet.' Edith put down her coffee mug

and spoke abruptly, abandoning the gentle chat about local affairs. 'What do you know about John Forrester?'

'The vicar?' Harriet temporized. Here it was again; the vicar's name kept cropping up, even if it was only in her own imaginings. Not only the vicar though; the village's tame tycoon, Gordon Dean, was in there too, along with his minion, Brendan, and now his good-looking American visitor, Mike Goldstein.

'Harriet?' Edith was staring at her, curiosity written all over her face. 'Are you okay?'

'What? Yes, of course. Sorry, I was lost in thought. Where were we . . . oh yes, John Forrester. What do you want to know?'

'You're stalling,' accused Edith. 'I asked first. But, oh, all right. I was talking to him yesterday, at the party.'

'I know,' Harriet agreed. 'I saw. He was looking very interested in your conversation. About the Roman origins of the farm, wasn't it?'

'That's just it.' Edith frowned and picked at a loose thread on the pocket of her jeans. 'He *was* asking about the Romans. He claimed the late Roman period was his particular interest and in fact he was full of it when I was talking to him and I thought nothing of it, but I've been going over what we said, and it seems to me now that he wasn't really all that clued up. He has a superficial knowledge, I admit, but he's an educated man and he's clearly mugged up on local history to get along with his parishioners, which is a perfectly sensible thing to do.

'It's not that, however, that makes me wonder. I've met lots of enthusiasts, you know, archaeologists and so forth, and when I first went to university I innocently let slip that we had our own villa at the bottom of the garden, so to speak. I soon learned to keep quiet, though, otherwise I'd be besieged by history buffs trying to pin me to the wall and scour my brain for details. Still happens occasionally, though I keep it quiet; they're always angling to come and poke around the place but they never have any funding. Besides, Grandpa's never been keen on strangers poking about on his land. But the point is, Harriet,' Edith looked across at her hostess, 'I can recognize a true enthusiast a mile off, is what I'm saying. I checked with Grandpa and the vicar hasn't simply asked if he could come and take a look round. Grandpa would have been delighted, but John also made one or two slips about the Roman withdrawal from Britain that didn't sit well with his supposed interest.'

'So what are you saying?' Harriet was

intrigued, and aware of a deepening of the elusive anxiety she had felt at the previous day's party. 'Couldn't it just be that he was trying to impress an attractive young woman?'

'Maybe.' Edith shrugged and took the second slice of cake that Harriet was offering. 'I didn't get that sense, not then, anyway.' She munched thoughtfully, and went on, 'Once or twice, though, he really did come across as a genuine enthusiast, but it wasn't about the Romans. It was when he was talking about King Alfred and especially about Alfred's son, Edmund Atheling. You remember Edmund? The ancestor who's supposed to have married the heiress, Edith, the one who was descended from the original Roman founding father.' She wiped crumbs from her mouth. 'He wanted to know if there are any family documents or legends about Edmund and he was particularly interested in Edmund's mother.'

'And are there any?' Harriet was just about keeping up with all the history. 'I got the booklet out for Sam to read but I only skimmed through it. I haven't read it properly for donkey's years. Who was his mother, anyway?'

'According to Miss Evelyn Attlin, she was Aelfryth, daughter of a local lordling. Nobody

129

seems to have been scandalized by her affair with Alfred and there's no record of a subsequent marriage, just a brief mention that she lived out the rest of her life with her son and daughter-in-law, doing good works.'

They looked at each other and shrugged. 'I suppose I can understand the vicar's interest in King Alfred,' Harriet said. 'He's an interesting character and pivotal to English history. Not known as a womanizer either, so a reputed son, born the wrong side of the blanket, would certainly throw new light on him.' She cast a curious glance at her visitor. 'Do you like him?' she enquired casually. 'John Forrester, I mean. I find him a little too pleased with himself,' she added, as a prompt.

'I don't know.' Edith's response was accompanied by a look of indecision. 'He's certainly very self-confident but it's not long since he lost his wife, so it feels a bit uncomfortable. What you said,' she looked suddenly anxious as she turned to Harriet, 'about him trying to impress me, I mean. I think that's what he was doing as well, but I also had the feeling that the thing about Edmund Atheling was more important to him, if you see what I mean.' She fiddled with her coffee spoon and raised anxious grey eyes to her former headmistress. 'But why would he bother? To pretend, I mean. Who cares if he likes Saxons better than Romans? Nobody round here, that's for sure.'

Harriet looked thoughtful and poured more coffee in answer to Edith's nod. 'They were all at it,' Edith confessed. 'Trying to impress me, I mean. It was a bit embarrassing, really, but Brendan was definitely coming on to me, and so was Mike, the Texan guy. It wasn't just John.'

'John?' Harriet gave her a wry look.

'That's the other thing,' Edith said. 'I was just leaving this morning, to come round to yours, when the phone rang. The landline, not my mobile. It was John Forrester, asking me out to dinner tonight.'

She glanced up as Harriet stifled an exclamation. 'What? Oh, don't worry, Harriet. I'm not stupid, I know what the village gossips are like. I'll be on my best behaviour for dinner with the vicar and make sure we eat somewhere publicly. Anyway,' she looked put out, 'Rory got a call from Lara; he's off to dinner with her tonight too.'

'She'll eat him alive and spit out the pips.' Harriet was diverted. 'I always reckoned she was a *femme fatale*, the minute she walked into my school all that time ago. There wasn't a male creature in the school, staff or student, who didn't fall over his own feet in confusion whenever she cast a glance at him, and she's learned quite a few more tricks since then. Poor Rory.' There was a lurking twinkle in her eyes at the thought, then she reflected for a few minutes. 'So, apart from your undoubted physical attributes, Edith, why do you suppose all these men are on your case?'

'I don't know.' Edith looked puzzled. 'But that's not all I wanted to discuss with you. Something happened last night.'

She filled Harriet in on the previous night's surprising goings-on in the Burial Field and was slightly shocked by her ex-headmistress's reaction.

Oddly enough, Harriet showed no surprise, but was insistent as she said, 'Yes, well, that settles it, Edith. You simply *have* to call the police; this has got to be connected with the attack on your grandfather.'

'I know, I did call them, this morning.' Edith hunched her shoulders. 'I called the contact number we got after Grandpa's accident and got a frazzled-sounding woman who took my name and said she'd pass on the message, but they were short-handed and it might be a few days before anyone gets around to us.' She made a face. 'I got the distinct impression that what she really meant was that we'd be lucky if anyone turned up at all. But I thought someone ought to know. I haven't dared tell Grandpa; he directly said I wasn't to interfere because he doesn't want Gran upset, and anyway, they're both pretty frail. I suspect the woman I spoke to just put it down to kids mucking about, but at least I've reported it.'

'I'm glad to see you've got a smidgen of common sense, Edith,' Harriet spoke sternly and she was frowning. 'Walter has been a soldier and a farmer for most of his eighty-something years and neither profession is known for its weakling qualities. Penelope is tough too, for all her delicate appearance.' She thought about it for a moment then met Edith's eyes. 'Oh, all right. I've no authority to butt in, but you must promise not to do anything stupid if you spot them another night. No *Famous Five* stuff, please, and if you do go off on some idiotic tangent, for God's sake leave a note or text me.'

There was a mulish expression on Edith's face but Harriet sighed and, driven by a feeling of urgency, gave it one last try before she changed the subject.

'Look, I had a phone call just now . . . ' She caught herself up — that had been in confidence, though she would tell Sam when she had a chance. 'I meant to say, if anything else does happen, you simply have to make a fuss when you report it. I'll do it for you, if you like. I'm not afraid of your grandfather and I'm good at yelling at people.' As her visitor fidgeted, still looking indecisive, Harriet changed the subject briskly. 'Come and look at my latest treasures while I make some more coffee.'

Distracted, as her hostess intended, by the change of topic, Edith made straight for the large doll's house that stood in Harriet's small dining room. Her ex-head's collection of miniatures had been legendary at school and once a year, as a fundraiser, the house and contents were put on display. Edith had never lost her delight in the tiny pieces, many of them little masterpieces and of museum quality, costing so much that Harriet sometimes had to catch her breath when she thought of her bank balance.

'Look on the table,' she told Edith now. 'There's a silver toast rack and a muffin dish, as well as the most minute salt and pepper. I always like to keep the new things out, so I can gloat. There's a magnifying glass there, you can check out the details.'

★   ★   ★

When the phone rang again, half an hour later, Harriet was on her own. Edith had set out for home, slightly comforted by talking it over with one of the few people whom she held in genuine respect and affection. Harriet could be exasperating sometimes, with her complacent air of being always in the right, but — as Edith was only too well aware — Harriet very often *was* in the right. It was infuriating but reassuring, and it made her ex-headmistress a safe sounding board for ideas that came out more than half insane.

Harriet flapped for a moment until she spotted the phone on the sofa. 'Sam? Where are you? Belfast? Is there something wrong?' She listened intently as her cousin told her to be quiet and hear him out. 'Goodness,' she said slowly, when he insisted she listen. 'That's interesting.' She frowned for a moment then, 'Look, I know you've only got a minute, but this is important. Edith's just been round and told me a crazy tale.'

She relayed the story of the midnight digging in the Burial Field and when he exclaimed, she said, 'No, she's not been dreaming. I had a call from Rory Attlin just before she got here, telling me the same story. He's worried that she might get herself involved in some foolhardy attempt to find out what's going on. Edith says she got in touch with the police, but they were too busy to react. You can't blame them, I suppose; they said Walter's accident sounded like joyriding kids and there was no evidence, and now this latest episode sounds like treasure hunters.

'Rory rang me because he's starting to be really anxious. He doesn't know the area and he's worried about the old people as well as Edith, plus he knows he's not fit enough to cope with any boys' own adventures she might drag him into.'

She broke off as a tall figure appeared at her front gate. 'Talk of the devil, Sam, here's Rory, just about to ring the bell. Is it okay if I tell him what you've just told me? He's got his head screwed on and I gather from what the Attlins have said that he can keep his mouth shut.'

She opened the door to her unexpected visitor. 'Rory, come in. I've just been talking to Sam and he's come up with something that makes our wilder imaginings seem tame!'

6

'I just had a narrow escape,' Rory told her as she handed him a mug of coffee and a slice of cake. 'Edith scorched past me on her bike but luckily I spotted her first and dodged behind a tree. I don't want to get into a fight about going into Winchester to the police station and making a fuss so they'll come out and take a look at things here, or at least, not till I've had a chance to discuss it with someone rational. She's so frightened of worrying her grandparents that she can't think straight.'

'She'll calm down,' Harriet reassured him. 'Part of it is guilt because she wasn't here when Walter was injured. Absolute nonsense, of course, and he's told her so more than once, but it's hard to be rational where the people you love are concerned.' She cursed herself when a brief spasm of misery crossed Rory's face. Poor lad, he was singularly short of people to love, by all accounts. She rushed into the latest development.

'Sam rang to tell me about a conversation he's just had on the plane to Belfast. It's yet another bit of information that somehow seems to be related to all the peculiar goings-on round here lately.' She shook her head, frowning. 'Seems to me there are far too many things that don't add up. Oh well, this is what Sam had to say.

'He was sitting next to an old colleague on the plane, someone he'd not seen for ages, and they fell into shop talk, as you do. Then the other man asked if he'd been involved in the inquiry into missing documents at the Stanton Resingham archive. Sam said no, he'd not heard anything about that, so his friend, who sounds a bit of a gossip, told him it had all been kept very hush-hush, on a need-to-know basis, very cops and robbers. It seems a rare manuscript turned up at auction abroad late last year and sold for a pretty impressive sum. The trouble was, some very similar pages turned up a few months later at the archive and there was a bit of a panic because some academic recognized them as being from the same manuscript. Unfortunately the vendor had insisted on anonymity and had disappeared by then, along with the cash.'

Rory looked bewildered. 'Okay,' he said slowly. 'I'm not sure where this is taking us, but go on.'

'The subsequent inquiries,' said Harriet, 'revealed that about half the documents in the archive had so far been examined over the previous year, so it was decided to go through them again — fine-tooth comb stuff — and see if they could work out what, if anything, was missing. Not an easy job, as you can imagine. The whole archive was just a mass of documents collected by this old antiquarian, and his notion of collating was impressionistic to say the least, but he'd left a lot of money in cash to finance the whole thing so they'd got it under way.

'Anyway,' she stopped suddenly, with a slightly shamefaced grin. 'Oops, sorry, Rory, I'm slipping back into Miss Q mode. Stop me if I start lecturing or giving you order marks for running in the corridors or smoking behind the bike sheds. Where was I? Ah yes. They soon realized from various references that there were other things missing; some whole manuscripts, in some cases, in others just the odd page. The galling thing was that they could tell that the missing items must have been wonderful, not just from their historical perspective, but in some cases as objects of astonishing beauty. There was apparently a note referring to a mediaeval breviary, with scribbled descriptions of the illuminations, a work of art from the sound of it — and not a trace of the actual item to be found.'

'God, that's a tragedy.' Rory was horrified

and Harriet remembered belatedly that he was an artist himself. 'Did Sam say if they'd got any clues?'

'Apparently they had a pretty good security system including individual key codes, which are swiped in. You know how it works: when the card is swiped, the time, date and ID are recorded, and when the codes were checked there were no discrepancies. The only person whose card came up was the researcher who was employed to work in the archive. He'd been vetted and passed as honest and well qualified, references panned out okay, no reason to doubt his credentials.'

She paused. 'The only trouble is, his name was Colin Price, and he's been missing since the beginning of January this year.' Rory glanced at her and was struck by the gravity of her expression. 'The last known sighting of him was on the fifth of January when he had a couple of pints at The Angel in Locksley. While he was there he was very interested in the village and particularly asked about the church, the vicar and the history of the Attlin family up at Locksley Farm Place.'

She looked down at her folded hands and then at Rory, her blue eyes shadowed and anxious. 'He hasn't been seen since.'

'Bloody hell!' Rory stared at her. 'I heard

about that, Edith's convinced his disappearance has got something to do with her grandfather's accident *and* with this midnight poking-about by the angel stone.' He finished his coffee and nodded abstractedly as Harriet offered a refill. 'I thought she was imagining things but then, I don't really know her very well.'

'She's not one for flying off on a tangent,' Harriet told him, looking thoughtful. 'Most of the time she's logical and practical, but this is about her family and Edith is very close to her grandparents. You've heard about her father? Yes, well that was a very difficult time for her, obviously. A tragedy like that could warp anyone but Edith's mother bravely bore the brunt of it herself in London, while the Attlins kept Edith safe down here. She's turned out remarkably well-balanced, on the whole.' She grinned suddenly. 'I can't imagine what she'd say if she heard me say that; she imagines she was one of the scourges of my time at her school. She wasn't, though, but I was probably more aware of her because of the distant relationship, even though she's only just been brave enough to drop the 'Miss Quigley'.

'Anyway, anything that touches her family sends her into a panic and, of course, the old people are just that — old. Edith can't bear to think of anything happening to hurt them.'

Rory digested this in silence then asked, 'Why would this Colin Price have been asking about the vicar, do you think? I can understand an interest in the farm — loads of history there and he was a researcher, after all. He could have been hoping to get a lead on whether there might be stuff in the archive, things that might be saleable; but why the vicar?'

'No idea.' Harriet shook her head. 'I've racked my brains and Sam was no help. It's public knowledge that John Forrester was looking like a high-flyer, maybe even a fast-track to a bishopric, who knows? But his wife, who was a bit older, I think, seems to have had a lot of problems and had a breakdown, so last autumn he was appointed here to cover the four parishes. I suppose the thinking was that she could recuperate more easily; we're quite high up here and out in the country, so there's more air and less hustle and bustle.' She made a face. 'At least, that would be the official thinking, I suppose. In fact, of course, there's as much stress in the country as in the town, if not more. Just fewer people and less noise.' She cut another slice of cake and put it, unasked, on Rory's plate. 'The trouble is, not everyone is happy with the way a village works, everyone knowing your business. I'm not sure Gillian Forrester was too keen on that aspect of her new life.'

'How did she die, then?' Rory was curious. 'The vicar's wife, I mean. It can't have been long ago, from what you're saying, but he was hardly playing the heartbroken widower at that party yesterday.'

'It was New Year's Eve,' said Harriet. 'Sam and I were in Italy on a short break after a particularly stressful time. I heard about it when we came home. Apparently the move to the country wasn't proving the success he'd hoped for, and Mrs Forrester reeled around most of the time in a daze. Nobody seemed sure if it was drink or drugs, either prescription or illegal, but the consensus was that she was out of it all the time. She wasn't popular; she'd upset most of the village in the short time she was here, by being rude about everything. The pub was too noisy and needed smartening up, and the food they served was inedible.' She broke off and grinned. 'That was true enough when she first moved here,' she said, 'though it's been in new hands since just before Christmas, and is doing very well. However, it was hardly tactful to complain loudly in the public bar one night, only days after she'd arrived in the place. She also moaned about the vicarage — too big, too draughty — and she was sarcastic about the village shop, said it was pathetic and run by amateurs. That really got up people's noses as it won a prize last year for being a well-run community effort.'

Harriet sighed. 'I tried, we all did, but the poor, silly woman alienated everyone who would have tried to make friends with her and there's only so much you can do, or offer, without becoming a pest. Perhaps if she'd made an effort, responded to the various overtures, her health might have improved. However, the night she died the vicar was at bell-ringing practice in the belfry. Our bells are famous locally and the New Year changes are particularly fine. He was invited to bless the bells, and I believe he had a go at ringing too. Apparently he got home around 12.30 a.m. after they'd toasted the bells with champagne, and found her dead on the hall floor. She'd obviously staggered out of bed — she was in her nightdress — and the supposition is that she'd been going down to the kitchen. Or maybe the bathroom, the stairs are next to it and it was thought she could have made a mistake. The inquest found she was doped up to the eyeballs and wouldn't have known which way was up.'

'That's horrible.' Rory was shocked. 'I didn't take to the vicar but that's an awful thing to happen. What about him? You said people sympathized with him, and you can see why; do they like him, though?'

Harriet considered the question. 'It's early days yet,' she said slowly. 'Our old vicar was extremely popular and died in harness so it would be tricky at first for anyone new to come here, big shoes to fill, kind of thing. John Forrester had only been in situ for a couple of months before the tragedy struck so in a sense he's not had time to establish himself in the normal way. He's devastatingly attractive, of course, even though he's not strictly handsome, and a lot of the females in the parish are rather taken with him.' She grinned, looking slightly sheepish. 'I can understand that; he's very charming and he looks fabulous in his vestments. His sermons are well thought out, not too long but not skimped. He's good at the pastoral side and the committees he's inevitably on are pleased to find he's firm and decisive, while managing to be tactful at the same time, and that's quite a rare skill.'

'You don't like him,' Rory accused her. 'Never mind how attractive and charming he is, or how well he does his job, you still don't like him.'

'I didn't say that,' she argued but shrugged as he looked sceptical. 'Oh all right, but this is strictly *entre nous*. He's everything I said,

145

and more, but I somehow feel, whatever he does and says, that he's acting a part. I can't put it more directly than that and it's not a crime. It may simply be that he finds that the way to cope with his wife's death. Or it might just be that he's an actor, as many clergy are at heart, politicians too; there's certainly a kind of glamour about him and people who are born like that can't help putting on a performance. It's so instinctive to them that they don't realize they're doing it.'

'I feel pretty confused, you know.' Rory sipped his third cup of coffee. 'All this talk of mysteries and missing people may be moonshine, but you can't get away from the fact that Mr Attlin was hit by a car. And you're adamant that he wouldn't have imagined that?' She nodded and Rory carried on. 'Plus there's the metal-detector guys last night. They were definitely there and up to something, but whether they're part of the other weird stuff happening round here, or just a coincidence, is beyond me.'

'Edith says John Forrester wasn't the only one making up to her yesterday,' Harriet said, watching him closely. 'I noticed it myself. Brendan was hovering round her, but that's nothing new. He was around at Christmas when she was home and I think she did go out for a drink with him, but nothing else happened, she says. What was odd, though, was that Gordon Dean was being very free with his compliments and that's not like him; his tastes usually run to older, more sophisticated women. And of course the Texan chap, Mike Goldstein, he was buzzing round her too.' She gave him a direct, blue-eyed glance. 'Come to think of it, what do *you* think of Edith?'

He coloured slightly, the flush bright against the sallow, fading tan. 'I like her,' he said frankly, 'but she holds back. We'll be talking and laughing and getting on fine, really friendly, maybe something a bit more, and then she'll suddenly stop and look upset. I don't know what it is, whether I've annoyed her, though I don't think it's that. She was okay before we went to that party but since then she's been really odd.'

'She hasn't mentioned anything to me,' Harriet said, frowning as she thought back to her conversation with Edith. 'I wouldn't worry too much. She's a very straightforward kind of girl so if there's something about you that's bothering her, you'll find out sooner or later. And it can't be anything too serious or she'd have had you booted out of the house by now, make no mistake.'

★   ★   ★

At 7.30 that evening Edith was peering surreptitiously out of a window in the hall, watching the drive, when Rory's footsteps behind her made her jump.

'Blimey,' he exclaimed. 'What's the matter with you? You jumped right out of your skin.'

'I wasn't expecting you to be creeping around.' She was flustered and glared at him. 'Oh, I'm sorry, Rory.' She held out an olive branch. 'It's all this cloak-and-dagger stuff getting on my nerves, treasure hunters and Grandpa's accident and Harriet suddenly turning into the local wise woman who's seen something nasty in the woodshed.'

'Maybe you ought to cancel your date with the vicar,' he suggested, looking hopeful.

Her eyes narrowed. 'Have you been talking to Harriet?' She carried on without waiting for an answer. 'I'll tell you what I told her. I'm not an idiot and I don't propose to give the local mafia anything to gossip about. It'll be a casual dinner in a public place, on a friendly basis and nothing else.' He just looked at her and she shrugged. 'Oh, all right, yes, I do want to sound him out about one or two things.' She gave him a rapid rundown of her conversation with the vicar at the previous day's party. 'I'll be tactful, but I'd like to see if he does have interests other than the late Roman period.'

Rory hesitated then clearly decided against saying anything but his concern was clearly apparent. He looked at his watch and gave her an awkward pat on the shoulder instead. 'Have a good time,' he said kindly, 'but be careful. Locksley is starting to look like a village in *Midsomer Murders*, creepy characters all over the place.'

'I'll be fine,' she snapped as he turned to go. 'I wish you and Harriet would stop treating me like a kid, so stop behaving like a big bro . . . ' Her mouth shut on a gasp and he stared back at her curiously, but the glare he received was forbidding enough to make him take the hint.

Why on earth did I say a thing like that? Edith was aghast. Not for a moment did she believe Lara Dean's veiled slur about Rory and her own father, but the unsettling idea had nevertheless been planted in her head and she couldn't leave it alone.

The sound of tyres on the gravel drive rescued her from her distracting thoughts and she opened the front door to see Rory going off in one direction in his elderly rattletrap, while a sleek Alfa Romeo drew up with a flourish and John Forrester, as polished and sexy as his car, jumped out and came over to greet her.

Sure that Rory could still see her she

bestowed a glowing smile of welcome on the vicar and accepted a kiss on the cheek. 'What a gorgeous car,' she told him. 'I'm so envious. I'm planning on buying some kind of transport myself, but it won't be anything like this beauty.' She was about to take the passenger seat he was offering when she spotted something. 'That's nasty,' she said, with sympathy, 'the dent on your wing. What was it? A traffic shunt or something?'

'Nothing so glamorous.' He looked rueful. 'I miscalculated the tricky angle of the vicarage drive just now and had an argument with the gatepost. Didn't you notice the brick dust embedded in the metal? I'm a fair driver, normally, so I can only plead a distracted mind. You look lovely, by the way.'

The smile that accompanied this remark made her feel slightly uncomfortable. Was it possible John Forrester was actually interested in her for her own sake? If so, things could get a tad awkward. She shifted uneasily in the expensive leather seat, sidetracked for a moment as she wondered how a Church of England clergyman could rise to such a car. Oh well, she hunched her shoulders slightly, it's only dinner and if he is harbouring ideas about me, it's no big deal, I'll just put him straight.

'Where are we going?' she enquired,

putting her misgivings aside as they turned out of the village.

'I thought we'd try Stockbridge. Plenty of good pubs there so I've booked a table,' he told her. 'I hope that's okay with you?'

'Perfect,' she approved. And it was: great food, not too far from home and right on the wide main street so that even the most determined village gossip couldn't make an assignation out of it.

He was a good driver so she relaxed and studied him under her lashes. Devastatingly good-looking in a craggy, lived-in kind of way — everyone was right about that — with reddish-brown hair and laughter lines at the corners of the eyes that almost matched his hair. Long and lean and tanned, he was casually dressed with no sign of a dog collar and she wondered just how old he was; late thirties, she decided.

'Well?' He had caught her studying him. 'Do I pass muster? Have you been given instructions on how to handle a randy vicar?'

She was annoyed at her involuntary blush but she grinned anyway and shook her head. In spite of Rory and Harriet's strictures the vicar turned out to be a charming companion with a dry, sardonic line in humour and they laughed over their meal like old friends. Harriet was right, in a way, she thought. He was pleased with himself but it was quite an endearing conceit salted with self-deprecation. It came as something of a surprise to her that John didn't drink.

'I used to drink too much,' he confessed. 'Then — oh, I don't know, I realized one day that a talkative drunk doesn't make an ideal clergyman, so I stopped.'

Edith was touched and wondered if there had been more to it; the shadow on his face suggested as much. She changed the subject and they swapped stories of student days, Edith filling him in on her experiences with the rich and famous in California, while he had her laughing helplessly at tales of some of the eccentrics he'd encountered in his first curacy.

'I didn't really want to enter the Church,' he mused. 'It was my grandmother's idea and to be honest, she bribed me to do it.'

Edith sat and stared at him, round-eyed, so that he burst out laughing.

'Don't look so horrified. It was one of those cases where Granny knew best. She insisted that I'd be happy in the Church and she was right, though I refused even to consider it to begin with. I read English but when she suggested I go to theological college with a view to taking orders, the incentive of having her leave me her not inconsiderable fortune weighed pretty heavily.'

His eyes danced with cynical amusement. 'Then she left the lot to the National Trust with a note to me, saying that, like cream and scum, I was the sort who would always bob up to the top, and that she knew I would prefer her to follow her conscience.'

As they lingered over their coffee John leaned back in his chair, looking at Edith with a considered expression. 'I'm intrigued by your friend, Harriet Quigley,' he said. 'She's a real character, isn't she? What's her story?'

A character? Edith had to hide a smile, picturing Harriet's outrage at the description. 'Harriet's great,' she said. 'She was head at my school, but she's also a distant cousin of my grandfather. What is it that intrigues you about her?'

'She seems to know all about everyone,' he shrugged. 'Not that anyone's accused her of being a gossip, but there's a feeling that Harriet is a power to be reckoned with. And what about Sam Hathaway? Do you know him well?'

'Harriet's definitely not a gossip.' Edith sounded indignant but settled her ruffled feathers. 'I don't know Sam very well but his wife was head of English at my school, and Harriet's best friend too. I was upset when she died about four years ago and I should

153

think Harriet was devastated.' She thought for a moment, John was still looking interested. 'I believe Sam was a parish priest before Mrs Hathaway died, that's how he became an honorary canon of the cathedral, but now he's working in the Diocesan Office. I suppose he gave up his parish when his wife died, but I don't really know. He's nice, though.' She glanced at John. 'Do you like him?'

'I've not had any dealings with him,' was the answer. 'But he's well regarded and certainly seems very pleasant.'

That seemed to be the end of the conversation and Edith took a surreptitious look at her watch. Dinner had been delicious and John was good company, but she was finding it increasingly difficult to create an opening whereby she could find out about his interest in her home.

Oh well, she decided. It's now or never, but as she opened her mouth to speak, John leaned forward.

'I'd like to tell you about my wife.' He spoke abruptly, looking down at his coffee cup, then back at her. 'Do you mind? Or would it bother you?'

She was nonplussed; it began to seem as though he might be making a play for her, but there could only be one answer to such a question. 'Of course, tell me whatever you want. I'm so sorry about your wife's death. I didn't meet her when I was home at Christmas but it was such a brief visit, only a few days, and then I went up to my mother's in Scotland. I think your wife wasn't well at the time.'

He looked away from her, then began. 'Gillian was a few years older.' He shrugged and said, 'Well, to be honest, there was nearly ten years between our ages but it never made any difference. A high-flying career in the City had done two things for her: it made her very wealthy but eventually it burned her out, so she was looking for a complete change of lifestyle when we met. She was extremely beautiful and I fell for her like a ton of bricks; it was only a month or so after my grandmother died, just over five years ago, and I suppose I had some idea of replacing the family I'd lost. My parents were killed when I was twelve and Granny brought me up so we were very close, even long after I was ordained.

'Anyway, it was pushing it, at her age, to think about babies, and she always said she didn't want them, but all of a sudden it somehow became the most important thing in the world to her. She had various tests and it was when it became clear she couldn't have children that she began to change. By then I'd found that Granny was right and that being in orders suited me down to the ground, so I was happy in my job. I tried to persuade Gill that I loved her for herself, that we could make a life without children, but she wouldn't believe me.'

His face twisted and Edith broke in, anxious to deflect anything too heavy, 'Don't tell me any more,' she said. 'I can see it's painful.'

'No, I'd like to tell you. I haven't talked about her to anyone else in the village; it hasn't seemed the right thing to do, but . . . ' He frowned and picked up the cafetière to pour more coffee. 'It was after she had the test results that she started taking drugs. Nothing too serious at first and I, stupidly, thought she was getting over the disappointment and beginning to look forward to a future that could still be good, but it didn't last long, that phase. Soon she was shooting up regularly. I never managed to find out how she got her supplies — addicts can be incredibly cunning. It got worse after we moved here last autumn, but I could never catch her out.'

He sighed and brushed a hand over his face, then went on with his story. 'The saddest thing of all was that she refused to

156

accept that she was a drug user. She used to insist to me, to the doctor, to anyone she met, that she was violently anti-substance abuse, that she would never take drugs, it was against her religious convictions. Even with the needle marks on her arms she still wouldn't admit it, even to herself.

'In the end it killed her, of course. I expect you've heard the bare bones of the story: I was at the last bell-ringing practice before the great New Year performance and I joined the ringers for a pint in the pub before going home. You know the vicarage, I'm sure, and you'll know that the staircase is rather grand mid-Victorian and the tiles rather special. She was lying on the floor at the foot of the stairs; she'd broken her neck on those damned encaustic tiles.'

'Oh, John.' Edith was overcome with sympathy. 'What a dreadful thing to happen.'

'I don't want you to have the wrong idea about Gillian. You know what the gossip mill is in Locksley and there have been some rumours about her behaviour. But we were married for five years.' His eyes pleaded with her to believe him. 'And she was a wonderful woman — when her demon didn't have her in its grasp.' He shook his head. 'I loved her but life hasn't been easy these last few years and I want you to know that I've never looked at another woman — until now.'

She was grateful that he said no more but got up to pay the tab. It's all getting a bit heavy, she thought, and I feel awful now. I'll have to be careful what I say and not get into a situation where he and I are alone again, I don't want to hurt his feelings.

There were no awkward silences during the journey home and Edith began to breathe easy again until John pulled over in a leafy lane about half a mile from the village. A shiver of excitement seized her, and the promises she had made to Harriet and to Rory flew out of the window. There was something irresistibly naughty about the idea of being kissed by a vicar, she thought, and kissing was definitely what was on his mind.

Kissing was something he was well qualified to do, she decided, when she could draw breath. For a few moments she responded enthusiastically, then he drew back and smiled at her.

'You're the most delectable ex-governess I've ever kissed.' His voice held a smile in the dark. 'I've been wanting to do this ever since I set eyes on you at Gordon Dean's party.'

Mention of the party brought her to her senses and in spite of her resolution to find out what she could, she couldn't help stiffening. The memory of the midnight treasure-seekers intruded and with it the recollection that, charming and sexy though he might be, John Forrester was a new widower and that Harriet, whose opinion she valued, had misgivings about him.

'There's something I ought to tell you,' he began slowly, his tone portentous.

She shifted away from him, back into her seat, seized with a sudden longing for the safety of home.

'It's about Brendan Whittaker; I know he's a friend of yours.'

'Huh?' The anticlimax had her sitting up straight at once. 'He's not really a friend, just an occasional acquaintance. What about him?'

'Oh, nothing concrete. It's just that I've been getting the impression he's up to something that might be illegal. I can't give away too much, but as you'll imagine, I'm pretty hot on drugs and so forth, and one or two of the things he's said to me suggest there's something pretty dicey going on. It's very recent; I bumped into him at the pub the other day and stayed for a pint. He and that American, Goldstein, were thick as thieves and Brendan let slip a couple of things that made me wonder.'

He refused to elaborate, in spite of her urgent questioning. 'It's too vague,' he told her. 'I'll sound Brendan out again. Oh, don't worry,' he laughed at her expression, 'I'm no hero, I'll keep a low profile.'

Edith was astonished. This was the last development she had anticipated. A cold dash of cynicism suggested that John could be deflecting suspicion onto the other two men, but why should he? Harriet was the only person who had articulated any misgivings about him, and then in the privacy of her own home. Besides, even Harriet seemed more dismayed at the idea of the vicar coming on to Edith, rather than engaging in some — what? — criminal activity.

It was nearly half past nine. 'I know it's early, but I really ought to be getting back,' she told him. 'I love being at home but the downside is that the grandparents can't get to sleep until I get safely back. It's a bit like being a teenager again.'

When he drew up at the front door, she was taken aback as he reached over and pulled her to him. This time, when he kissed her, there was a pent-up passion that shook her, and try as she might she couldn't help a slight recoil. He let her go at once, with a rueful laugh,

'Sorry, Edith. Snogging in a parked car is completely naff. It's been a long time, is the only excuse I have; next time I'll be a perfect gentleman, I promise.'

Flustered, she scrambled out of the car, murmuring thanks for the evening and as he drove away, she was torn between slight indignation at his assumption that there would *be* a next time, and the lost opportunity to question him further about his keen interest in her family history.

7

There was only panic. Harriet held herself completely still, afraid to move, aware of pain and worse than pain: complete and abject terror. Whatever cradled her, some kind of metal framework she concluded, reaching out a tentative finger to touch, rocked and shivered precariously under her, frightening her so much that she could scarcely breathe. There was something else, its weight heavy on her chest and in the moments of consciousness she explored that too. Gradually, thankfully, she recognized her handbag and there, tucked in the bag's front pocket and blessedly easy to reach, sat her phone.

The darkness came and went, along with fragments of memory. Driving down the track, an impression of danger screaming down on her, then silence and the fearful rocking.

★   ★   ★

'My head hurts.' Harriet struggled to turn away from the bright light shining down on her. What was happening? Where . . . ? 'No,'

162

she whispered. 'I'm *not* going to say it . . . '
But she did, anyway. 'Where am I?' *Damn!* 'I
was in the car . . . '

A soothing voice hushed her. 'Don't worry,
Harriet, you're in hospital; we're just taking
you down to X-ray,' it said. 'You've been in an
accident but you seem to be all in one piece
and it looks as though everything is working.
We think you might have had a bit of a bump
on your head so we're just making absolutely
sure you're all right.'

There *was* a car; she definitely remembered
a car coming full-on at her, headlights
blazing.

'Somebody drove into me.' She was awake
again and aware of a uniformed policewoman
standing a few feet away. The girl's face
brightened into interest and she bent over
Harriet. 'Did you see who it was, Miss
Quigley?' she asked, pen poised over her
notebook.

Harriet tried to shake her head. 'Ugh, that
hurts,' she muttered. 'No, his lights dazzled
me but I think it was a sports car, long and
low, anyway.'

She roused herself and was glad to see a
cup of tea wavering into view. 'Concussion?'
she asked the nurse who turned out to be
holding it.

'Only a mild one. You were incredibly

lucky.' The middle-aged man helped her to sit up to drink. 'You went through the barricade and over into the quarry. You must have been very brave, managing to get hold of your phone, or you could have been there all night. The crew who brought you in said it was a miracle you survived at all. God knows what would have happened if you hadn't been driving such a light-weight, ancient vehicle. As it was, the trees caught the car and held you up there.'

'Car?' She let out a cry of protest. 'Oh no, not the Mini. My mother loved that car; she had it from new, back in 1960,' she mourned.

''Fraid so,' he sympathized. 'It's a write-off. I'm so sorry, but maybe you should look on it as having saved your life. A guardian angel Mini?'

★　★　★

'Edith?' The voice was urgent, slightly familiar, a man she knew but couldn't bring to mind straight away.

'Hmm? Yes? Who? What's the matter?' A glance at her watch showed a quarter to seven; a call at this time of the morning wasn't going to be good news.

'It's Sam Hathaway,' he said, his voice ragged with anxiety. 'I had a call from

Harriet. She's in hospital, Winchester. I don't know the details but she seems to have had an accident last night. She swears she's all right, apart from slight concussion, but she'll need a lift home.'

He interrupted Edith's cries of distress. 'She sounded okay, honestly, Edith, just shocked and tired. The thing is, my plane is delayed with some technical fault so I'm still stuck in Belfast and won't get back to Southampton airport till late this morning. Could you pick her up, do you think? You can? Great.' His relief was audible. 'She says any time after breakfast. And no matter how much fuss she makes, whatever she says, will you take her back to your place till I can get back? She shouldn't be left on her own.'

A call to the hospital confirmed Sam's message. Miss Harriet Quigley would be ready for collection any time after half past nine, so shortly after nine o'clock Edith and Rory set out on their way to Winchester in Rory's car.

'You didn't get any details, then?' Rory was taking the winding lane steadily, too many tractors in these parts to be complacent. 'No idea what kind of accident? Or where?'

'Nothing. Only that she's okay apart from mild concussion. We're to take her home with us, which I'd do anyway, even without Sam saying so. She's family after all.' The treacherous memory of Lara's hint slid unbidden into her mind and she shied away from speculating about Rory's own relationship to the family.

'How was your evening?' she asked.

'Fine,' he shrugged, looking surprised at the abrupt change of subject. 'I managed to dodge any suggestion of another date — she's so not my type.' He grinned at Edith. 'I'm not a tight-arse but I'm not made of money either and she's pretty high maintenance, financially and every other way, I should think. We went back to her place after dinner at the Hotel du Vin,' he continued. 'I managed to find out that her father *does* have interests in oil — North Sea, Middle East, mostly — but he's also got some connections with a couple of on-shore drilling outfits.'

'She surely didn't tell you that, did she?' Edith looked sceptical. 'Oops, turn left here, sorry.'

'Of course she didn't. There were some papers left on a side table and I sneaked a look while she was getting the drinks. All I got from Lara was a hint that she and Brendan have an on-off thing going, whenever they both happen to be single. Apparently her father thinks highly of him, though whether he'd be quite as acceptable as a third son-in-law is open to question.

'Anyway, I did find out that when Lara is otherwise engaged Brendan's been lumbered with looking after their Texan visitor and that they were out on the town last night.' He surprised her with a sudden laugh. 'Apparently, both of them have been enthusing about you and are planning to ask you out, which Lara clearly doesn't find amusing. She doesn't seem to like Harriet much either, says she's too inquisitive.'

He concentrated as they turned into the hospital multi-storey and as they parked he asked, 'How about you and the vicar? Did you find out anything?'

She gave him a brief outline of John's story, about his wife's sorry end and about his theories regarding Brendan.

'Hmm,' was all he said as he held the door open for her.

'You're as bad as Harriet,' she scolded him. 'Why can't you two just believe he's a decent kind of guy, who has lost his wife and is trying to distract himself by doing his job, reading up on history and so forth? And that that's all there is to it?' The trouble was, she admitted to herself, that pretty much everyone was beginning to look suspicious to her, even the vicar.

'You could be right,' he surprised her, but

there was no time for more discussion. They'd arrived at the hospital. Edith explained who she was and the nurse nodded.

'Miss Quigley just needs rest,' she said, checking her notes. 'She won't be on her own, will she? Good. There's just one thing,' her voice was lowered. 'When she first came in she kept insisting that someone pushed her car deliberately into the quarry . . .'

She looked startled at their outcry. 'Oh, yes, didn't you know? It's a miracle that she wasn't killed. Has to have been a drunk driver, of course, nobody would do such a thing on purpose, but somehow or other she ended up going through the barrier and landing in the trees.' She dismissed them kindly. 'You'll find her in the day room,' she said.

'Shh, this isn't the time to discuss it.' Rory grabbed her hand as Edith opened her mouth. 'Come on, let's go and rescue her.'

Harriet had been leaning back in her chair, her hand to her head, and wondering whether her throbbing headache would ever go away. At Edith and Rory's approach she opened her eyes and managed a smile of greeting.

'I'm fine, Edith, don't make a fuss, just — ' Her eyes widened as she saw John Forrester hurrying into the day room accompanied by the staff nurse on duty. 'Oh, for God's sake,' she muttered and caught Rory's eye. 'Follow my lead,' she hissed, to his bewilderment, reaching for his hand and shutting her eyes.

'I came as soon as I heard,' John told them, bending over to look at Harriet. 'How is she? Hasn't she come round yet? Has she said what happened?'

The staff nurse fluttered round him, and Edith eyed her with distaste. Is that how I was last night? she wondered, and frowned at the idea. The frown deepened as she spotted the undeniable interest in his eyes as he smiled down at the nurse. Never looked at another woman indeed, she fumed.

'She can't remember much,' Rory said firmly, glaring at Edith as she turned to him in surprise. 'Except that it must have been a drunk going too fast.' There was an approving pressure on his hand and he glanced down at Harriet. 'Of course, she's getting on, and at her age, memory loss is quite terrifying,' he added, deciding to embroider the story. 'And it's very upsetting for her not to recall anything about her accident.'

'Whenever she's ready.' The nurse nodded coolly to Edith and turned to the vicar. 'Can I ask you to come and talk to one of our other patients?' she suggested. 'He's very agitated and I'm sure he'll calm down if you have a word.'

John nodded goodbye and followed in her train, leaving Edith puzzled, Rory amused, and Harriet torn between laughter and annoyance.

'How dare you suggest I'm going senile,' she snapped, opening her eyes and tapping Rory lightly on the hand. 'That wretched man will patronize me now for the rest of my days.'

'I'm sorry, Harriet.' Rory was contrite. 'It was the best I could think of at short notice when you did your dying swan act. But what's this about someone driving at you deliberately? The nurse said that's what you claimed when they brought you in here.'

'Quite true.' Harriet gathered up her handbag. 'I'll tell you about it later, not here, though.' She thought quickly then, 'Edith, do me a favour, will you? Rory will drive me home, I'm sure, but I'd be really grateful if you would run after the vicar and ask him to give you a lift to my cottage when he's done here. I'll need some clothes.' She made a face. 'Sam's been on to me and the nurse was adamant that I'm to go to the farm till he's able to look after me. Yes, thanks, Edith,' she grinned as her former pupil spoke eagerly. 'I've rather taken it for granted, I'm afraid, that I can cadge a bed from you for tonight and I've written a list of things I'll probably need. Here you are, and please, not a word about what I just said, to the vicar or anyone else. Keep to the story that it must have been a drunk driver. I don't want anything else to get out.'

She and Rory watched as Edith disappeared after the vicar.

'So?' He looked at her. '*Were* you deliberately pushed into the quarry?'

'Yes,' she sighed, looking weary. 'I'll tell you about it when I've gathered my wits, but just now I really want to get out of here.' She glanced at him with a speculative eye. 'Can I persuade you to take me back to my place?' she asked and made a face as he shook his head. 'I thought not. The farm's the best bet really; my closest friend in the village has just set off on a family trip to Cornwall and Sam is in the throes of packing up his flat. I suppose I can't really stay with him among the tea chests but I'll try to persuade him to move in with me. He's due to do that next week. No,' she rubbed her eyes, 'I'm getting confused, it's tomorrow the sale is due to be completed, so he can do some decorating in his new place. Meanwhile he's got to report back to the office today on his Belfast trip, so a night or two at the farm will have to do.'

'So, Harriet.' Rory packed his cargo tenderly into the front passenger seat. 'What is it that you want to talk to me about that you don't want Edith to hear?'

He concentrated on navigating the hospital car park and headed for the hills. Harriet was frowning, so he asked again. 'Well? I have no idea what the hell's going on in Locksley but it doesn't look good.'

Harriet shook her head. I don't want to involve these two kids in whatever's happening, she thought. Then she glanced at Rory. Nonsense, woman, she sighed. He's a grown man, they're both adults, come to that, and they're involved anyway.

'I think we covered everything yesterday morning,' she told him. 'Cousin Walter's accident; the missing man, Colin Price, and his job at the archive; the news that valuable, if not priceless, items from the archive have turned up in European auctions. And now there's someone messing about in a field where it's been rumoured for centuries that a Roman ruin exists. Just because you recognized them it doesn't follow that they aren't simply treasure hunters out on the off-chance, doesn't have to be something more sinister. God only knows.' She leaned back and closed her eyes for a moment. 'Sam has some more news,' she said flatly, as she subsided into silence.

After a few minutes she perked up and smiled at her driver. 'You're a restful kind of man, Rory,' she told him. 'Thank you for not nagging me for an explanation. I just needed to gather my thoughts.'

He felt absurdly flattered at her commendation; praise from Harriet Quigley was something to respect. 'I'm still convalescent myself,' he explained briefly. 'I know it's hard to think straight sometimes. So, what did your cousin Sam have to say?'

'He rang just after breakfast to check up on me. Apparently he's been making some calls while he's stuck at the airport, doing some digging around. He's come up with a report that's just come in; the clergy can be astonishingly indiscreet sometimes, thank goodness. Anyway, the European police have produced an identikit picture of a man believed to have been the vendor of the missal that was sold recently.'

She paused dramatically. 'Guess.'

'Colin Price, I presume?' Rory sounded excited.

'None other.' She shrugged. 'It's good news and bad, I'm afraid. Interesting in that it ties Price in with the disappearances from the archive but bad news in that nobody has the slightest idea how to find him. Leaving aside the theories flying round the village, that he's been done away with, this part of the world is awash, literally, with inlets and harbours, boats, marinas, yacht clubs, all making it easy to get out of the country in a hurry. And that's not even considering the commercial traffic, ferries, airports, etc, which he could have used.'

Rory turned into the farm drive and drew up at the front door. Karen, jazzy today in a 1960s psychedelic-print shift dress, came running out.

'Harriet, you poor thing. Come on in; coffee's ready, decaf in the circumstances or you can have tea or hot chocolate if you'd rather. Then you can either go to bed straight away or go and relax with Mrs Attlin. She's upstairs and looking forward to seeing you.'

'Rory?' Harriet smiled her thanks to Karen and turned to her chauffeur. 'I hope you don't mind, but I promised Sam you'd pick him up from Southampton airport at midday. He has to check in at the office but before that he says he'll buy you lunch and give you a quick unofficial tour of the Stanton Resingham archive if you'd like?' She shot him a conspiratorial glance. 'No need to mention it to Edith till you get home.'

★   ★   ★

It was soothing, Harriet decided, to sit in a pretty, old fashioned bedroom-cum-sitting room and be served with lunch — even though it was only soup and a cheese sandwich — and later, afternoon tea, in company with a pair of delightful elderly relatives. Not something you'd want to do every day, but once in a while it was like stepping back in time. She smiled her thanks as Karen bustled in bearing more tea and Penelope Attlin leaned forward to pour out.

'I was just thinking,' Harriet observed, 'that I feel as though I'm in a period drama.' As Penelope glanced at her in surprise, Harriet explained. 'You know, tea that I haven't had to make myself in a mug, and served in beautiful old china. Karen is a perfect treasure!'

'She is,' agreed Walter, slathering butter on a crumpet. 'She says much the same, Harriet. She told me she likes to pretend she's the senior parlour maid in a period piece on television, *Downton Abbey*, perhaps, though that's way out of our league.' He looked thoughtful, a lurking twinkle in his eye. 'I can just see Karen in a maid's outfit, complete with frilly cap and apron.' Mrs Attlin gave him a wifely look and he grinned, 'Seems a harmless kind of daydream to pass the time and as you say, she's very good to us. I find it a little less convincing though, when I try to picture Elveece in the role of the perfect butler.'

175

'I'm glad to see you're recovering, Walter,' Harriet changed the subject as she looked across at the old man. 'Your colour is much better and I notice you're moving about more comfortably. Have you had any further thoughts about what happened the other night?'

'No.' Walter Attlin spoke sharply, then clearly felt the need to apologize. 'I beg your pardon, Harriet, I know you mean well, but I don't want to talk about it. No harm done in the end.'

His wife rolled her eyes at Harriet and turned the conversation to the Test Match, so cricket occupied them until Rory turned up, accompanied by Sam Hathaway. Sam shook hands with the Attlins while his eyes checked out his cousin. Satisfied with what he saw, he nodded to her and came across the room.

'Silly idiot,' was his fond greeting, as he bent to give her a hug. 'I hope you weren't playing detectives?' This last was in a lower tone and he grinned at her indignant expression. 'Okay, okay, keep your hair on. Rory told me what you said. It seems incredible but a lot of peculiar things seem to be happening around here lately. And you didn't manage to get a look at the car or the number plate?'

She answered in a similarly low voice. 'No,

I didn't, but I'll tell you one thing, I think it was someone from the village.'

'What?' Mindful of the other people in the room, Sam's exclamation had to be muted, but he frowned at her. 'How do you make that out?' he demanded. 'And come to that, what were you doing near a quarry on some farm track anyway?'

'Oh, of course, I forgot you wouldn't know about it yet. It's a short cut,' she explained. 'Hold on a minute, we can't stay here whispering.'

She rose and spoke softly to her hostess who turned her head at the movement. 'I'm going to lie down for half an hour, Penny, do excuse me. Sam will make sure I don't fall over on the way.'

Safely in her room, she dismissed Sam's attempt to make her lie down. 'Nonsense, it was just an excuse, I'll be fine sitting here in the quiet; I just didn't want to disturb Walter and Penny. Now, what was I saying? Oh yes, the short cut. It cuts off a long meandering corner if you avoid the road to the village and nip across. It's Walter's land but he's never minded and most people in the village use it to save time.'

She turned eagerly to him. 'But that's my point, Sam. Nobody else would use it, because it doesn't go anywhere, apart from the village. And I know it wasn't somebody who spotted me on the main road and for some reason decided to follow me, because I'd only just started up again when whoever it was came up over the brow of the hill. I had to stop to take a phone call from one of the people at the meeting I'd just been to in King's Somborne. That took ages, so I reckon I was parked up there for a good ten minutes.'

Sam's blue eyes were narrowed in anxiety as he sat, waiting for the end of the story. 'I feel sick when I think about it,' she confessed shakily and was glad of Sam's warm hand clasping her own. 'I'd just started up the engine and set off, still only doing about ten or fifteen miles an hour — it's a bit rough up there — when this car appeared. It seemed to slow down for a minute, then the lights blazed at me and he came straight at me and hit the side of the Mini as he swerved away at the last minute. I'm quite sure it was deliberate.' She paused and whispered, 'You see what I'm saying? He wasn't following me; he was heading for the village via the short cut and when he recognized me, he decided to kill me.'

8

'Well?' Edith nodded her thanks as Rory handed her a cappuccino. Winchester was always a popular call for tourists, particularly on a sunny morning in summer, and two or three coachloads had already crowded into the cathedral refectory. The groups of visitors were refreshing the body after traipsing round the city; shortly they would be disappearing into the cool, dark peace of the cathedral to refresh the soul.

'What do you want to know?' he hedged.

'We didn't get a chance to talk yesterday,' she said. 'What with Harriet staying and Gran inviting Sam to stay for supper. He took you round the archive, didn't he? Did you find out anything?'

Rory shook his head. 'Nothing new,' he confessed. 'It was an interesting experience, though, and just a brief glimpse of some of the documents made me itch to get stuck in and delve deeper. I might volunteer to help with the research when I'm settled — they're short-handed. Mostly though, Sam was worrying about Harriet and wondering what she's got herself into that someone would go for her like this.'

He paused, then continued, 'I don't know if you've had a chance to talk to her, but you ought to know what's been going on.' He ran through the background and then filled her in on Sam's most recent brief history of the missing researcher and the vicar's tenuous connection with him.

'The police asked Forrester about Colin Price but they seem to have been pretty gentle with him, from what Sam told me.' He responded to her questioning look with a shrug. 'They had no reason to press him anyway, but the thing is, the night Price was last seen in the village was the night before Mrs Forrester's funeral. The police asked the vicar if Price had told him anything that might suggest he was about to abscond with his ill-gotten gains, but the vicar said he had no recollection of seeing Price at that time, let alone talking to him. Who could wonder at it? The poor bloke must have been in a complete state the whole time.'

'You've changed your tune,' she said. 'I thought you didn't like him.'

'I don't, but that's no reason not to feel sorry for him. Anyway, Sam doesn't like him either, but that doesn't stop him giving Forrester an alibi for when someone was knocking down your grandfather.'

She looked up, startled. 'What do you mean?'

'On the night in question, Sam was at a diocesan discussion, attended by a dozen-or-so local clergy, including John Forrester. The meeting didn't go smoothly and things got heated — nothing to do with Forrester or Sam — so what with having to calm everyone down, Sam said it was late finishing. And then one of the others suggested they go back to his place for a nightcap. About eight or nine people accepted, including John Forrester, though Sam says he never actually got to speak to Forrester that night, partly because he barely knows him and mostly because he, Sam, was drawn into a debate with a couple of friends. Anyway, by the time the vicar left Winchester, even driving his flashy car, he'd hardly have been in a position to run down your grandfather out in the fields.'

She nodded slowly and he glanced at her in surprise. 'I thought you'd be pleased.'

'I suppose so, it's just . . . ' She hesitated and sipped her coffee. 'Ugh, it's gone cold.' She pushed her cup aside, shaking her head when he offered her another. 'It's just that yesterday, when John ran me home via Harriet's place, I fed the cat and then left John in her sitting room while I went upstairs to collect the things on her list. When I came down again, he didn't hear me at first, and I found him in her study, flicking through some papers on her desk. He straightened up at once and moved away, making some comment about having picked up the papers from the floor. He said he'd gone in there by mistake while looking for the loo and that it must have been the cat that scattered them, unless Harriet was very untidy and he didn't think that for a moment.'

She tried to remember. 'He went to put Harriet's bag in the car while I locked up, so he didn't see me take a sneaky look at the paperwork on the desk. The first thing I saw was the name, Colin Price. It jumped out at me from what looked like a précis of the problems at the archive, something Harriet must have written down to try and make sense of it.'

She stood up as Rory glanced at his watch. 'I don't believe John is involved in anything shady,' she said as they made for the exit. 'But, but if he is,' her voice faltered and she hunched her shoulders anxiously. 'If he is, he knows now that Harriet has been nosing around about the Stanton Resingham archive and she can only have got that information from Sam.'

★   ★   ★

Sam Hathaway was fidgeting uneasily. For once, as he stood in the longest cathedral nave in Europe, he was unconscious of the soaring beauty of the pillars and arches. Harriet had slept well the previous night, she had assured him when he called her earlier, and said she was planning to return to her cottage the following day.

That much was a relief, but Sam found himself haunted by the thought of how miraculously she had survived the accident, haunted too by the desolation that her death would have caused him. What the hell was going on in Locksley village? One of the prettiest spots imaginable, painted so often that it was difficult, some days, to get near the church or the village duck pond for easels and hefty great bags of painting gear, while artists sat hunched on little folding stools. An old farmer run down on his own land; a respectable middle-aged woman deliberately driven into a disused quarry and only saved by a clump of trees that clung to a craggy chalk face. These things simply didn't happen in his and Harriet's world.

It was just on eleven and Rory was due to arrive any time now for his guided tour of the cathedral. Sam sighed; no chance to discuss the unlikely crime wave in his new home village, not with the companion he had picked up on his way here.

A familiar voice had hailed him as he walked down the High Street after a visit to his solicitor, to the bank and to his estate agent, to check on today's arrangements for the completion on the cottage.

'Sam? Sam Hathaway? My dear fellow, it's been too long. How are you?'

An elderly man, rotund in clerical suit and dog collar, was puffing towards him, hands outstretched in greeting.

'Oliver.' Sam halted in his tracks and shook hands. His friendship with Dr Sutherland dated back years, to the days when Sam, having exchanged electrical engineering for the church, was newly out of theological college and about to take up his first curacy in Oliver's parish. Dr Sutherland had proved to be a kind and effective mentor and Sam had held him in considerable respect and affection ever since.

Lately, however, there had been another, sadder link between the two men. Celia Sutherland had died only a week before Sam's beloved Avril, and the older man had continually sought out his former curate, finding solace in their shared widowed state.

Only I didn't find solace in it, Sam growled to himself as they turned their steps towards the cathedral. Mrs Sutherland had been in her seventies, Avril twenty years younger, all those years stolen from them. It wasn't fair. Sam felt himself tighten with the strain of not yelling the words out loud. Even now, nearly five years after her death, the loss of Avril was unbearable; would never heal. All he could hope for was that the move to the cottage next to Harriet would turn his thoughts in other directions.

'What are you up to these days, Sam?' For a moment he had forgotten Dr Sutherland but he pulled himself together and gave a brief rundown of his activities, adding, with a glance at his watch, that he must be on his way to meet someone at the cathedral.

'Good idea.' The old man gave a benign nod. 'I'll walk down with you. Just the thing, a wash and brush-up for the soul. Don't like to go too many days without dropping in, and it must be getting on for a week at least since I was last at a service there.'

Sam gave in with a good grace and slowed his long-legged stride to suit the old man's wheezes. As they turned into The Square, Oliver Sutherland paused and looked behind them, then shook his head, tugging at Sam's sleeve.

'Been hearing about you, Sam,' he said. 'Someone said you've been poking about in the matter of that missing research chappie.

That true?' He studied Sam's startled expression and laughed gustily. 'Never mind, never mind,' he puffed. 'Don't tell me anything, none of my business anyway. Just thought you ought to know your investigations haven't gone unnoticed.'

At the West Door, Sam, who was still looking thoughtful, took off his slightly battered but elegant panama hat, shooting a grin at his friend as he did so.

'I see you still insist on wearing that ruddy panama,' snorted the old man as Sam had known he would. 'I should think everyone in town knows you by it, damned silly affectation.'

'No such thing,' Sam countered robustly. Their sparring was long-established and affectionate. 'You know perfectly well it was a birthday present from Avril. She liked me in it so I'll damned well wear it whenever I want to.'

'Oh, well, she was a lovely woman, so I suppose you'll suit yourself.' The reply was an amiable grunt, then Oliver Sutherland went on, 'I'll tell you what, though, you might lend me that poncy silk handkerchief you also insist on festooning yourself with. I'm hot and sticky and my own handkerchief is wringing wet.'

Sam hesitated for a split second then shrugged and handed over the sky-blue silk handkerchief that he wore tucked in his breast pocket. Like the panama it was a relic of one of Avril's occasional attempts to smarten up her husband. He had resisted her at the time, grumbling loudly, but since her death he had tried to make it up to her by turning out on sunny days in the outfit she had prescribed: cream linen jacket, silk handkerchief and the panama from Gieves & Hawkes in the town.

He had his fair share of vanity and knew that the outfit suited his tall, lean figure and that the blue of the handkerchief brought out the matching blue of his eyes. Harriet teased him about the hat, accusing him of only wearing it so that he could doff it with a flourish when he encountered any female acquaintances, thus revealing his impressively thick silver hair.

Sam always countered the slander by pointing out that Harriet was only jealous. Her own mousy hair had turned pepper and salt in her early forties and when it became evident that she hadn't inherited the same genes as Sam, she had gone a discreet honey-blonde instead.

Now, inside the cool glory of the cathedral, Sam looked round and caught sight of Edith, scuttling along in the wake of Rory's long strides.

'You got stuck with her, I see?' His eyes twinkled as he noted Rory's glance of dismay when he spotted Dr Sutherland. 'Me too,' he nodded, then turned to introduce them all.

'So,' the old man said, after shaking hands. 'Are you poking your noses into this business too?' He wagged a finger at them both. 'I've just warned our friend here that he ought to leave it to the authorities, and — something you ought to know, young Sam,' he frowned at his friend, 'I think you're being followed. I'm sure I spotted someone keeping a close eye on you just now.'

'What?' Sam smothered his incredulous exclamation. 'For heaven's sake, Oliver, you saw no such thing!' He stared at the other man and shook his head. 'This isn't some back alley in gangland, and we're not playing cops and robbers. Now, we're going up to look at the cathedral library. What about you?'

'I'll stay on guard.' The old man sounded undaunted by Sam's scolding. 'Here, by the Wilberforce tomb.' He waved a fond hand at the exuberant Victorian gothic angels. 'I'll hoot like an owl to warn you if I see the same bloke again; tall fellow, dark hair, sunglasses. Noticed him particularly, definitely keeping an eye on you.'

'You silly old fool.' Sam clapped an

affectionate hand on his friend's shoulder. 'God help anyone who does get into your clutches; you'd talk them to death.'

Oliver Sutherland grinned cheerfully at Rory and Edith who were watching in amusement. 'Might pop into the chapel next door for a sit-down in a minute, actually. Check on things through the iron grilles,' he whispered, his face alight with mischief. 'Here, Sam, you'd better give me that wretched hat of yours. It'll only get in the way.'

Sam, who was attempting to stuff the panama into his jacket pocket, gave in and meekly passed it over to the old man who immediately began to fan himself with it. 'All right, you old fraud,' he laughed. 'You can come out to lunch with us when we're done here, but only on condition you buy me a drink to compensate for all the aggro you cause me.'

The Triforium Gallery was crowded but Edith and Rory were happy to squeeze in and look at the various treasures.

'I haven't been up here for ages,' Edith said, pointing out a silhouette of Jane Austen, 'done by herself', according to the inscription on the back. 'Don't let me forget to show you her memorial on our way out.'

Sam looked on benignly as they admired a

green bowl made of fluted glass. 'That's said to have contained the heart of King Canute,' he told them. 'The bowl was found at Shaftesbury, where he died, but he was buried here in Winchester. It's said to be the only complete piece of Late Saxon glass in England. It's a crying shame you can't finance a dig in your Burial Field, you might come up with some treasures of your own. Maybe you'll get a grant some day. Now come along, time to take a look in the library. You mustn't miss the Winchester Bible.'

As Rory followed Sam, Edith leaned over the balcony and gazed down at the pinnacles of the Wilberforce tomb. A large party of tourists was milling around and as she watched, Dr Sutherland glanced up and waved to her, pointing to the Venerable Chapel at the side. She smiled and nodded as he turned to make his way through the throng and into the chapel, then she followed the others down to the library. A last glance downward showed her the old man parked comfortably on a chair, with Sam's panama on his chest and Sam's blue silk handkerchief being used as a fan. Edith felt faintly disconcerted, dismissing as ridiculous an indefinable sense of dismay, something out of tune, something she had just seen.

The library was fascinating and Rory, in

particular, spent ages admiring the famous Winchester Bible, the masterpiece commissioned by King Stephen's brother, the Prince Bishop of Winchester.

Rory quoted from the leaflet he'd bought: 'It was written on the finest parchment, each sheet a complete hide, requiring the slaughter in all of some two hundred and fifty calves.' He looked at the other two, his eyes gleaming. 'I've a good mind to try my hand at some illuminated capitals,' he said. 'I had some fun with icons a year or so back, and this wouldn't be too dissimilar.'

Sam's phone beeped and he looked eagerly at the incoming text. 'Oh great, we've completed. The cottage is mine.' He acknowledged their congratulations then looked at his watch again. 'Seen enough? Right, let's go down and winkle old Oliver out of wherever he's dozing. I promised him lunch and he'll be ready for it by now. We'll make it a celebration.'

There was no sign of the portly clergyman on guard by the tomb so Rory stuck his head into the chapel. He gave a sudden exclamation and withdrew, beckoning Sam with a shocked expression.

'What the . . . ?' Sam shoved him aside and hurried in, with Edith on his heels. Rory glanced round briefly and followed them.

Oliver Sutherland was leaning back comfortably in a corner, feet stretched out on a kneeler. His head was tilted against the carved wood of the pew, with Sam's panama hat slipping down from where it had been precariously balanced over his face, with the brim now resting on his chest. The hand that had been holding Sam's handkerchief as a fan lay lax at his side, the handkerchief a blue splash of silk on the floor. He looked as though he was taking a peaceful nap as any elderly cleric in his mid-eighties is surely entitled to do. But he appeared to be quite, quite dead.

9

The next half-hour was a nightmare jumble of discreet panic. The last thing anyone wanted was to have a commotion in the cathedral, which was packed with visitors. Disruption, however, turned out to be unavoidable.

Sam Hathaway took control. Rory had taken up the old man's wrist and finding no trace of a pulse, looked round for guidance. As Sam, trying to summon up what he knew of resuscitation, took Rory's place at the old man's side, the only other occupant of the chapel, a middle-aged woman who had been sitting in quiet meditation in the opposite corner, now rose in concern.

'Is something wrong? Can I help? I used to be a nurse.' Her accent was Canadian and Rory saw, from her comprehensive glance, that she understood the situation. To Sam's relief, she took over, directing him to help her lay Oliver Sutherland down and begin CPR, so Sam told Rory to hurry to the booth at the cathedral entrance to alert the authorities and to call for a first-aider.

'There's an ambulance on its way,' Rory

panted, returning within minutes. 'The first-aider should be — Oh.' He was interrupted by the woman who had followed him in. She quickly assessed the situation and nodded to Sam to change places with her. He took a pace back, then spotted his panama hat on the tiled floor, partly obscuring the puddle of blue silk, his handkerchief. As he reached to pick them up he glanced at the still, serene old face and bent his head in a moment's quiet prayer.

Rory, after one look at Edith's chalk-white cheeks and dazed expression, pushed her into a pew and looked to Sam for instructions. Grieved, but not shocked, Sam was sure there was nothing to be done for his old friend, though he knew that CPR would continue until further help arrived.

'You stay here and keep people out,' he said crisply to Rory. 'Here, put the rope across and stand guard. I'd better go and report to the powers-that-be what's happening.'

Within less time than seemed possible the ambulance crew were on the spot and a defibrillator put into use but Sam wasn't surprised when they made a quiet decision to stop trying.

'I'll go with him to the hospital,' he told the anxious group in the chapel. 'Rory, can you talk to people here?' At Rory's nod, Sam followed the discreet procession to a side door.

'How peaceful he looked, the poor old gentleman,' remarked the Canadian nurse. 'And what a nice way to go for a minister, right here in the cathedral.' She patted Edith's hand. 'There, dear, don't take it too hard. Is he your grandfather?'

'No-o,' Edith roused herself. 'I don't really know him at all. I'm sorry, I don't know why I was so upset.' She mopped her tears away. 'I suppose it made me think about my own grandparents. How silly, what an unhelpful thing to do.'

Rory reappeared, having given all the information he could to the authorities. He glanced anxiously at Edith, but was reassured by the colour returning to her cheeks.

'Poor old chap,' he commented. 'I suppose it was a heart attack, it'll come out at the post mortem, I suppose. Mind you,' he added, 'he did have a couple of nasty scratches on his hand and wrist. I wonder what caused that?'

The Canadian woman shook her head in dismissal. 'I noticed them too, but it's nothing to worry about. I'd guess those are cat scratches. Does he have a cat, do you know? Failing that, it could be rose thorns or brambles if he was a gardener. Anything could have caused it; they weren't freshly done.'

He hunched his shoulders as he nodded in agreement. 'You didn't notice anything odd in here, did you?' he asked her in a low voice. 'Nobody talking to him, upsetting him or something like that?'

'He might have been agitated and had a heart attack, you mean?' She looked thoughtful for a moment. 'No, I can't say I noticed. I did see him put his hat over his face, because it reminded me of my father. He always did that if he wanted a quiet snooze.

'A party of tourists looked in at one time, with a guide, but you can't get many people in here so they mostly didn't stay. Some of them sat down for a moment and one or two knelt in quiet prayer, I think. I'm sorry, honey,' she smiled mistily. 'I wasn't really noticing much, I was thinking about Angus, my late husband. He would have loved this place so much.'

She blinked away a tear then, as Sam Hathaway reappeared, she became practical. 'Now then, if we're not needed here, why don't we go get a cup of coffee or something?' She spoke to Edith, patting her arm as she did so, and Sam nodded.

'That sounds like a good idea. You go, Edith. I decided not to go to the hospital in the end. There's a lot to be sorted out at a time like this, so I'm going round to Oliver's place to make a start on phone calls and so forth.'

'I'll stay with Sam and see if he needs a hand,' Rory announced. 'Where will you go, Edith? You ought to have something to eat, you're white as a sheet.'

She shook her head, nauseated at the thought of food, but the Canadian lady, who introduced herself as Margaret Mackenzie from St John, New Brunswick, interrupted.

'I'm staying at the hotel right by the cathedral. You can't miss it. We'll be in the main lounge. You come and find us there — we'll be fine,' and she waved the two men on their way.

'I know you don't feel like eating, but you'll feel all the better for it,' she insisted, and beamed approval as Edith absent-mindedly polished off a plate of biscuits. Refilling their cups, she enquired, 'Why were you so upset, honey? You mentioned your grandparents. Have you recently lost them? That old gentleman must have been well over eighty, and he looked so peaceful. Death is nothing to fear when it comes so gently.'

'It was just silly hysteria and not the slightest bit of help to anyone,' Edith said apologetically. She explained a little of her situation and found the older woman warmly sympathetic.

A call came in. Rory. 'We'll be a while,' he told her. 'Why don't you have lunch with Mrs Mackenzie at her hotel? Sam and I will grab a bite to eat and one of us, probably me, will get back to you as soon as possible.'

The next couple of hours passed in peaceful conversation about this and that, and Edith was feeling much calmer when Rory appeared at about three o'clock — without Sam and looking slightly amused.

'I dropped Sam off at his flat to pick up the last of his bits and pieces and then he'll make his way over to Locksley.' He accepted a cup of coffee and went on, 'He's going to camp in his new house for tonight at least, though he'll probably move in next door to keep an eye on Harriet when she gets home tomorrow.' He grinned at them. 'The thing is, I've got something of Dr Sutherland's in the car. We went round to his house first and Sam got in touch with the old boy's solicitor and his son in Toronto. There wasn't much else we could do except that when we got there Sam remembered the cat.'

Edith and Mrs Mackenzie looked up. 'He did have a cat after all, then?' the older woman remarked. 'That could explain the scratches on his wrist.'

'Well, it could,' Rory said doubtfully. 'But Sam says Hector, the cat, is far too laid back to scratch anyone and too fat and idle to lift a paw.' A reminiscent smile flickered across his face. 'He's certainly fat and he weighs a ton, but he didn't even twitch a whisker when we got him into the cat basket. Oh, didn't I say? Sam's decided to take him on. Hector can camp in Sam's spare room till he feels settled. The son in Toronto wouldn't want a cat; he lives in a high-rise block of flats anyway.'

The Canadian woman was still looking concerned and Rory added, 'I mentioned the scratches to Sam and he says Dr Sutherland was always complaining about brambles so that's most likely how he got the scratches. They colonized his garden from the patch of common land next door and he was fighting a constant battle against them.'

It was time to go. Edith rose to her feet and put out her hand to Mrs Mackenzie. 'I can't thank you enough for your kindness,' she said. 'It's been lovely to meet you, even under such sad circumstances. You must come over to Locksley soon; are you here for long?'

Margaret surprised her with a quick, sympathetic hug. 'I'd love to, honey. I'm based here in Winchester for another five days though I'm off to Salisbury for the day tomorrow, and Chichester the day after that. I like to have a theme for my vacations,' she confessed with a smile. 'Last time it was castles, the time before that was royal palaces and this year I'm visiting cathedrals.'

As they took their leave Rory had a last word with the Canadian visitor. 'If you do happen to remember anything, anything at all that strikes you as odd, I mean about the old chap, will you give me a call?'

She shot him a curious glance and surveyed him very thoughtfully, but nodded and promised, in spite of her repeated assurances that there was nothing at all out of the ordinary that she could recall.

As Rory edged the car out of the city and headed towards the hills Edith sat in the back seat talking to their unexpected feline passenger. Hector was curled up in an extra-large cat-travel basket, gazing out with placid, gooseberry-green eyes and responding amiably to her polite advances. She had to agree with Rory that a cat so large and indolent was probably not going to be scratching anyone anytime soon, so it must have been the brambles after all.

At Sam's new home, the semi-detached twin of Harriet's cottage, they used the key he had given Rory and carted Hector and his belongings upstairs to the back bedroom.

Sam's furniture from the flat had been delivered the previous day and besides his own room, the spare room had a carpet, a pair of twin beds and a chest of drawers already, though there were no curtains as yet.

'He should be all right,' Edith said hopefully as they watched the hefty grey and white tabby uncurl himself from his basket to take a languid stroll round his new quarters. A sniff of approval at his food and water bowl, a disdainful glance at the litter tray, ready for action and tucked away in a corner, and Hector stalked off to his own bed where he promptly fell asleep.

As she waited for Rory to double-lock the front door, Edith was startled to see a sleek silver Porsche parked alongside Rory's elderly Vauxhall, and Brendan Whittaker coming down Harriet's front path, next door. He looked disconcerted to see them.

'Oh, er, I was looking for Miss Quigley,' he said, looking self-consciously at the expensive-looking bouquet of lilies he was carrying. 'Gordon wanted me to see her and make sure she was comfortable.'

'She's at our house,' Edith told him, surprised. 'Didn't you know? I'll take the flowers for her if you like?' She looked round but Rory had disappeared down the side path, so she walked to the gate. 'That's a nasty scrape on your wing, what have you been up to?'

'That?' He shrugged as she indicated a mark on his car. 'Nothing to do with me — some fool parking badly. I found it like that when I got back to the car. Bloody nuisance, though; I'll have to put in a claim unless I can get it done privately.'

'Hard luck,' she sympathized. 'Did whoever did it leave their name and insurance details?'

'Of course not.' He stared at her. 'Never mind that, how about a drink sometime soon? Tonight maybe? No, of course you can't tonight, but tomorrow perhaps. I've scarcely seen you since you came home.'

'It's only been a few days.' She fobbed him off with a mumble about her grandparents and he drove off as Rory reappeared.

'I was just checking Harriet's back door,' he said. 'In case anyone's been poking about in there. It's all over the village that she's up at the farm, so why didn't lover-boy know?'

'He's not,' Edith was frowning. 'He's just someone to have a laugh with now and then. But what did he mean, I can't have a drink tonight? Why not?'

Back at the farm she soon found out.

'You're in the dog house,' Karen informed her with a cheerful grin. 'The vicar phoned earlier to remind you that you'd promised to go out with him for a drink tonight and asked what time he should pick you up.'

'No I didn't.' Edith was indignant. 'I said sometime or other, not tonight. Anyway, why does that put me in the dog house? It's not a crime.'

'It is to your grandfather,' Karen shrugged, and bent to take out some trays of tiny sausage rolls from the oven. 'He doesn't approve of the vicar making up to you. And you needn't look at me like that; I heard him tell the vicar that himself.'

'He did?' Edith was irritated but impressed all the same. Her grandfather rarely interfered in her life.

'Uh-huh.' Karen deftly put more oven trays, this time of minute vol-aux-vents, in to cook. 'Mr Attlin took the call from the vicar this morning and told him you couldn't go out tonight as we're having a small drinks party. Then he invited the vicar anyway and told him straight out that he felt it wasn't wise for a man in his position to be seen out and about with other women so soon after his wife's death and he advised caution.'

'Drinks party?' Edith was startled but the evidence was before her eyes: cocktail savouries, canapés, assorted bottles and glasses, on every available surface. 'Have they gone mad? It's only a day or so ago that we had the Rotary dinner here. What on earth do they want a drinks party for?'

'You'd better ask Rory,' was the only response she got as Karen disappeared into the large, walk-in larder.

'Don't shoot!' He held up a hand in supplication. 'Cousin Walter rang me after Sam and I left you in the cathedral. I forgot to tell you, with everything else that was happening. He told me they were having a small celebration drinks party and asked me to get on to Gordon Dean and invite his household, so I did. They're all coming and I gather your grandmother has been on the phone so most of the village will be coming too. Sam can't make it, by the way, he's got something on in Southampton tonight. I've no idea what the party's about, though.'

'Well, there's one good thing,' remarked Karen. 'We've got some olives. I asked the vicar to pick some up from the man in the market, seeing as he was on his way to Winchester, and he dropped them in an hour or so ago.'

'He's been to Winchester today?' Rory made an obvious effort to control his start of surprise as he turned to Karen. 'What time was that, then?'

'About 10.15, more or less.' She looked surprised. 'I bumped into him at the village shop and passed the time of day. He mentioned where he was off to and I just said that if he happened to be walking through the market, would he pick up some olives for the party.' She was working as she spoke and soon had a tray ready. 'Here, make yourselves useful and take some tea upstairs.'

★   ★   ★

'My dear child.' Edith's grandfather glanced across at his wife and smiled. 'The party is a makeshift attempt to dig myself out of a very deep hole. Today, as I'm sure you have forgotten, as I did, I'm ashamed to say, is our wedding anniversary. It's fifty-nine years to the day that I did the decent thing and made an honest woman of your grandmother. The party is an impromptu way of apology.'

Penelope Attlin nodded and smiled. 'He did trot out his usual excuse,' she said with a mock frown at her husband. 'You know, he says he doesn't like to rake up old grievances and anniversaries are best forgotten.'

During the laughter that followed Walter Attlin's ancient family joke, Rory glanced across at Harriet. She was looking decidedly weary and he went over to sit beside her.

'Don't say it,' she answered his concerned look. 'I know I look a wreck. I'm worn out.

Penelope and Walter are being lovely but I'm going to call it a day soon and head for bed. I'm in no state for a party and besides, the painkillers I'm on are making me very woozy.' She had dark circles under her eyes but managed a smile as Rory described Sam's new housemate. 'Bless him,' she nodded. 'Soft as butter, Sam's heart, but a cat will be good company for him. I look forward to meeting Hector and to getting home to my own little moggie tomorrow.'

'What do you think about this party tonight, Harriet?' Rory was still wondering about it.

'I think Walter is lighting fires to keep the darkness away,' she said, surprising him, and smiled faintly at his reaction. 'Or the modern equivalent,' she explained. 'I mean he's insistent that his accident hasn't put the fear of God in him and having a party is one way of showing he's not to be browbeaten. Besides,' she added, 'as he always says himself, old people have to kill themselves in their own way. They survived last Friday's dinner remarkably unscathed, so why not a small drinks do in their own home? And a fifty-ninth wedding anniversary is reason enough.'

Rory nodded and got up to corner the old man. 'Cousin Walter,' he murmured, 'did you really not see who it was, who drove into you, I mean?'

His host eyed him with resignation. 'You're just like the rest of them, aren't you?' he sighed. 'I suppose Edith's got you playing detectives with her? Oh yes,' he grunted with amusement. 'You think anything goes unnoticed round here? It's all over the village that you've been poking about in the archives with Sam Hathaway and that he's been asking lots of questions. And Edith has been going about practically wearing a deerstalker.' He glanced across the room and caught Harriet's eye. 'You too, I gather?'

He waved aside Rory's indignant denial and Harriet's sudden, anxious frown. 'If you must know, I didn't actually see who it was but I did have a kind of intuition, some sixth sense. I felt sure it was the four-by-four that belongs to Gordon Dean.'

To Rory's intense irritation Edith interrupted at that point, full of something she'd just remembered. She had clearly not overheard the exchange between the two men.

'Grandpa, when you had your accident — ' She looked haughtily at Rory and Walter who had burst out laughing. 'I'm sorry? I didn't realize it was something to laugh about. Anyway,' — she could never bear a grudge

— 'I was thinking about it earlier on. You were very cagey about it. Did you see something? Or someone?' She looked suddenly confused and a little shamefaced. 'I mean, you didn't see Lucius, did you, Grandpa? Lucius Sextus Vitalis?'

This was greeted by gasps and Rory was about to make some sarcastic remark when he glimpsed his elderly relative's expression.

'You mean . . . you really think you *did* see him?' He goggled at the old man in disbelief.

'I don't know.' Walter Attlin sounded defensive but he went on, 'I don't honestly know what I saw. I wasn't going to mention it, and if either of you breathes a whisper, I'll skin you alive. That goes for you too, Harriet. I refuse to be branded a senile old dodderer.'

He took a deep breath. 'It was at the moment I realized that the noise I could hear was actually a car. I half-turned and managed to jump out of the way, and I'd have been fine if I hadn't gone and tripped, which is how I broke my damned collarbone. I thought I saw someone in the distance, over by the angel stone.'

Edith and Harriet stared wide-eyed, while Rory tried to maintain his scepticism in the face of the old man's level voice and evident sincerity.

'It was the briefest possible glimpse, an

impression of a figure standing there; and there was a flash of something silvery.' Again he shook his head, something defiant in his attitude. 'I know it sounds insane but it made me think of armour, of a Roman breastplate.'

10

Edith had snatched a brief conversation with Harriet just after tea, but when she looked in on her an hour or two later, hoping for a further discussion, Harriet was drowsing comfortably, already tucked up in bed.

'It's bliss, sometimes,' she admitted. 'Just giving in to whatever is getting on top of you. You were right, Sam was right. I'm better off here tonight while I'm still so woozy. But tomorrow,' she looked defiant, 'tomorrow I'm going home. Sam will either be next door in his own house, or in mine — or more probably pottering between the two. I'll be fine.'

''Course you will,' Edith nodded. 'Tough as old boots, aren't you? Did you know we used to call you Boudicca at school?' As Harriet nodded, looking smug, Edith shrugged. 'I might have known we'd never have got anything past you. But listen, Harriet,' she suddenly sobered. 'What about what Grandpa said? I know the farm is supposed to be haunted but he's never mentioned seeing anything before.'

'Well,' Harriet's tone was bracing, 'for a start I don't think you need to panic about

Walter losing his marbles. Maybe he did see a ghost. Who are we to argue with him? Although,' she gave it some consideration, 'I'm more inclined to think it was the clouds parting and a shaft of moonlight briefly glancing on a tree trunk or something.' She closed her eyes for a moment before she added, 'I wouldn't dream of contradicting him, though. If it was the family's tame Roman he's not going to cause trouble for his descendants, is he? Although,' her eyes snapped open, 'I felt I'd better not rile Walter by wondering why Lucius would have felt the need to wear his army breastplate long after he'd become a civilian.'

She snuggled down and waved a languid hand at her visitor. 'You'd better go back to your guests,' she said. 'Whatever those pills are that I'm taking, they're pretty strong and I'm almost asleep as it is. Off you go; if it's anything like that lunchtime do at Gordon's, you'll spend your time fending off unwanted advances. Have they all turned up yet? The vicar and Brendan, *et al*?'

'I expect they'll be there,' Edith told her as she turned to go. 'I think they were just bored at Gordon's party, and I was a novelty. I'll fight them off, no worries.' She picked anxiously at her thumbnail. 'I don't know what to think now, though. Not after seeing them — ' She broke off in mid-sentence. Harriet was in no state to be worried, even though Edith was more and more confused about the supposed treasure-seekers and their activities.

'You might be right.' Harriet sounded drowsy. 'Be careful, love. I just don't like any of them, but I'm too doped-up to remember why at the moment.' She roused herself reluctantly to add, 'I never actually said thank you, Edith, for nipping back to feed my cat. I expect he was glad to see you.'

Edith nodded and left the room, thinking hard. Now was not the time, she frowned, to tell Harriet that she'd felt something different about the cottage when she had nipped in to check on Harriet's cat an hour ago. There was no sign of forced entry but she thought papers could have been moved and some of Harriet's bits and pieces were out of place. A cursory look round the house reinforced the sense of intrusion — a bedroom door now open when Edith knew she had shut it herself — but there was no concrete evidence and nothing seemed to be missing. Time enough to tell Harriet tomorrow morning or perhaps it would be better to tell Sam instead.

As she approached the galleried landing in the oldest part of the house, Edith jumped out of her skin as Rory loomed out of the shadows. He reached out instinctively to steady her and then somehow she was in his arms and he was kissing her. For a moment she responded, then all her uncertainties and confusion about him reasserted themselves.

'No ... ' she whispered as she pulled herself away, leaving him to stare as she headed for the top of the stairs. Before he could speak she had halted abruptly.

'Oh my God.' Her horrified whisper reached him and he looked over the balustrade to see what had shocked her.

'He looked like Sam,' she said, gripping the carved wooden banister. 'In the cathedral, I've just remembered. Dr Sutherland looked a lot like Sam from where I was looking down at him.'

'So? I wouldn't have said there was much resemblance between them.' Rory peered down into the Great Hall but could see nothing out of the ordinary. Twenty-or-so assorted neighbours were standing about, chatting and drinking, as a convivial hum rose up to them. 'What are you talking about, Edith? What the hell's the matter?'

'When we were in the cathedral,' she told him, 'you and Sam were already on the move and I looked down from the gallery. There was a crowd, a bit like this one, and Dr Sutherland spotted me and waved. I waved back to him and he pointed to the chapel, to show he was going in there.' She faltered, her difficulties with Rory forgotten. 'But when I looked down again, on the way down, I felt odd, unsettled I suppose. I've only just realized why. I couldn't see Dr Sutherland's face, just his silver hair and cream jacket. And Sam's panama hat stuck over his face, I suppose to help him snooze.' She stared at Rory. 'And Sam's blue hanky; he was using it to fan himself.'

'But why has that got you in such a state?' He was puzzled and took another look over the railing. 'It'd be more to the point if you'd seen this tall, dark man Dr Sutherland reckoned he'd seen following him and Sam. I'd forgotten about that till now.' As he gazed downwards, Brendan Whittaker sauntered across the room, nodding in passing to the American, Mike Goldstein. 'Have you checked if either of those two just happened to be visiting the cathedral today?'

Edith was still lost in thought, still looking shaken, and Rory continued, trying to work out what her problem was. 'Sam thought it was nonsense, this tall stranger, we all did; an old man being mischievous, teasing his friend. But,' he stared at her, 'what are we saying, Edith? That someone somehow harmed the old boy? It was a heart attack, the

214

doctor said so. How could it be anything else? And what's this about Sam and Dr Sutherland?'

'I don't know.' She shivered, looking so forlorn that he put a tentative arm round her shoulders, tightening his grasp when she didn't recoil. 'I just thought . . . what if someone *did* kill him? But what if it was a mistake?'

She turned to him, wide-eyed. 'Why would anyone want to harm an old man? Nobody, as far as we know. But what if . . . ' She faltered, fumbling for words. 'Suppose it was a mistake. Suppose it was Sam who was supposed to die. He's been asking an awful lot of questions; maybe he asked one too many, the wrong one.' She shivered and didn't move away when he reached for her hand. 'What can we do?' she went on. 'The police would laugh at us or more likely charge us with wasting their time. They're stretched and you saw how high on their list they put my call about the other night — nobody's been to check it out yet. You can't blame them; they believe a drunk driver pushed Harriet off the road. Harriet says it was deliberate and she believes it was someone local. An old man dies peacefully in a cathedral and another old man trips and breaks his collarbone. And what about the missing man, last seen in this village?' She shivered. 'Plus, I think someone has been in Harriet's house, poking about in her desk and among her things.'

At his exclamation of surprise she explained her earlier feeling of unease, then sighed. 'This won't do, we're supposed to be on duty. We'd better go and mingle.'

'Tomorrow morning,' he said firmly, still holding her hand, 'we're going to the cops, whether they laugh at us or not. This is all too weird and we *have* to get help.'

Downstairs, Rory was captured by members of the local art group while Edith greeted old friends, explaining that she was back for good and planning to start investigating ways of making the property pay for its keep. 'I've got loads of vague ideas,' she explained to one of her grandmother's cronies. 'I've emailed a friend from uni who knows about converting old buildings and I want to see if we can turn the stables into holiday lets. It must be possible to do something with them. Anyway, that's just one avenue to explore.'

She nodded to another old friend. 'Gran's talking about turning downstairs into a flat for them and letting me make over some rooms on the first floor. That way we'll be independent but close enough for company.

As for Karen,' she paused and waved to her old school friend who was bustling past with a tray of canapés, 'I'm just praying she and Elveece will stay on for ever and ever.'

Her attention was claimed by Brendan, who had Mike Goldstein in tow. 'How's poor old Harriet coping?' Brendan sounded solicitous and even as she murmured a polite answer, Edith had to stifle a grin at the thought of Harriet's outrage at such familiarity.

The tall American chipped in. 'I heard about Miss Quigley's accident,' he remarked in his attractive drawl. 'She's got to be a tough old bird to have survived something like that. You must have your hands full, with a party on top of everything.' He smiled down at her, a gleam in his dark eyes. 'What made you decide to have a party, tonight of all nights? Is this an example of the well-known British stiff upper lip?'

'Harriet's gone to bed,' she told him. 'She's not too good tonight, but she's very resilient. Now, can I get you another drink?'

Rory was heading for the kitchen with a tray of empty glasses when his phone rang. 'Sam? Hang on, reception's not too good here, I'll nip outside. That better? Harriet's fine, in case you're worried; she's tucked up in bed, fast asleep.'

217

'I hope to goodness she stays there,' Sam retorted. 'But it's not Harriet I wanted to talk about. I've been doing some more poking about, turning over the odd stone, and I bumped into a very old friend tonight. Nothing to do with the diocese — he's a retired engineer who was a colleague of mine before I entered the Church. He used to have some contacts with the oil business. I know I can trust him, though I swore him to secrecy anyway and I told him about all these ill-informed rumours of oil prospecting.'

'Did he come up with anything?' Rory was intrigued.

'I'm not sure. He says himself he's been out of that world for twenty years or more, and the technology's moved on rapidly, which obviously makes his know-how a bit dated. He was intrigued, though, and told me that there are several ways of sussing out if there's oil around. You can do aerial surveys to measure the magnetic fields, plus there are airborne radar and satellite images that map the earth's surface. He pointed out that besides the commercial flights from Southampton Airport there are several smaller flights, instructors, and so on, and who's to know what they're looking for as they fly overhead? He's not suggesting that anything like this has actually been done, though he's promised to put out some discreet feelers tomorrow, but you get the picture?'

Rory grunted, remembering a light aircraft that had been circling overhead a few days ago. Sam went on, 'I made some notes, hang on. Right, a seismic survey would record differences in how rocks reflect shock waves and there are also ways to measure magnetic and electrical fields; variations in any field can signal a rock layer that could be interesting. But my friend did say that a lot of this will probably be done by computer these days. This is just background info.'

Sam paused, and Rory could hear him riffling through his notes. 'I'd better hurry up,' he said and Rory could hear the laugh in his voice. 'I'm supposed to be on a pee break; they'll start worrying about my prostate. Okay, here we are. Apparently, at about Easter time, there was a gang of people in diving gear over at the Hag's Hole.' Intent on his report he missed Rory's interrogative, 'Huh?'

'The grapevine said it was a team from the university, scuba diving or something, but what my friend said is that there's another gadget called a sniffer that's used underwater to detect traces of gaseous hydrocarbons. For instance if they were bubbling up from an oil reservoir.'

Rory was about to comment when Sam cursed quietly. 'Damn, got to get back in to the meeting. Look, ask Walter Attlin about the Hag's Hole but try not to alarm him. He's got his own fish to fry and I can't betray a confidence, but one thing I can assure you is that *he's* not looking for oil. So if someone else *is*, they're doing it for their own ends.'

Even allowing for Sam's elderly acquaintance to be completely out of date regarding current oil exploration, Rory thought there was enough there for food for thought. He drifted back into the party and sought out his cousin Walter.

'Don't look at me like that,' said the old man with a smile. 'I know Edith's been watching me like a hawk, but I'm fine, and so is Penelope. How are you getting on with the neighbours?'

'Fine, they're a nice bunch. But somebody mentioned a place called the Hag's Hole and I didn't get a chance to find out more. It sounds a bit indelicate, I thought.'

This time the old man laughed out loud. 'Indelicate? Of course it is, this village is full of indelicate people! No, it's always been called that, witches and so forth, I expect, as well as the God-awful stench that hangs about the place. It's a biggish pond, a lake really, on land that belongs to me but which

I've leased to Gordon Dean for the last couple of years. It's next to his boundary and I believe he originally had some idea of cleaning it up and stocking it with trout. Hasn't happened, though, I could have told him so.'

'Wonder why it smells?' Rory was intrigued. 'Could it be methane bubbling up, maybe?' He was remembering Sam's parting shot before he hurried back to his meeting. 'According to my informant,' Sam had told him. 'The best detection device of all in the oil world used to be someone who feels it in his bones, kind of 'reads' the rocks. Someone with a nose for it. Someone,' he had added, 'in the oil business might well come from Texas.'

There was no time to consider the problem. Walter Attlin kept Rory by his side, introducing him to this neighbour, nodding to another, making sure that nobody was stuck for long with a bore. 'Staff College,' he twinkled on catching Rory's eye. 'Army training never leaves you; don't let a group get too big and never let anyone get trapped in a corner. Ah, Lara. How are you, my dear? Your father not with you? Business in London? What a pity. And this must be your American friend. I've heard about him, of course.'

They shook hands and Walter nodded to

Rory. 'Have you two been introduced?'

'Not formally,' Rory answered as Edith came up to them.

'I must remedy that,' the old man was smiling. 'Mr Goldstein, let me introduce my cousin, Dr Rory Attlin.'

'Your cousin?' Lara's interruption sounded incredulous. 'I understood he was — '

The temperature lowered until even Lara had the grace to look abashed. Edith looked startled and anxious but Walter Attlin spoke with a measured dignity. 'Certainly, my dear.' He was politeness personified, in spite of Lara's own rudeness. 'There was some kind of family quarrel a couple of generations ago and my great-uncle ran away from home. He was Rory's great-great-grandfather and sadly the two branches of the family were separated. Fortunately, Rory made contact with us when he came down to talk about his new job, and we're delighted to have the opportunity of healing an ancient rift.'

Edith had time to notice Lara's chagrin, along with the bashful but pleased expression on Rory's face, before the significance hit her. So there was no mystery, no dark family secret. As he had claimed all along, Rory was a distant cousin, nothing more, and she had been making a complete fool of herself. The rest was sheer spite on Lara's part, fuelled perhaps by speculation: the likeness really was remarkable.

The arrival of the vicar gave Edith no time to analyze her relief. He opened his eyes at her slightly distrait manner and, to her intense irritation, it was clear that he was putting it down to pleasure at seeing him. Pride made her pull herself together as she escorted John Forrester towards the drinks. 'I hear you were thinking we might go out for a drink tonight? Sorry about that but it's been pretty chaotic round here, what with Harriet moving in with us.'

'I hadn't realized she was going to do that, but it makes sense, I suppose. I did try calling her but she hasn't replied to my voicemail. I don't think she likes me very much.'

'Oh no,' Edith murmured. 'She's very shocked, of course, and not really thinking straight.'

He looked curiously at her and cleared his throat. 'I was surprised Mr and Mrs Attlin decided to go ahead with their party, in view of everything.'

'Oh, they wouldn't cancel, not when everyone was coming,' she said. 'And it won't affect Harriet, after all. She's doped to the eyeballs and won't hear a thing from downstairs.'

She wondered at all the concern for

Harriet. Brendan and Mike Goldstein had sent their sympathy and now here was the vicar at it as well, though it could simply be professional courtesy on his part. She took a sip from her glass and changed tack very firmly.

'You're looking very smart,' she commented. 'Most unvicarish.'

'How kind,' he grinned complacently, as he glanced down at his dark-grey, herringbone tweed jacket, expensive and understated, as were all his clothes. 'I like to strike a balance between fogeyish and über-trendy and when I spotted this in *Gieves & Hawkes* in Winchester at lunchtime today when I gave our American visitor a lift in, I decided it was about as daring as the village would tolerate.'

'Mike Goldstein was in Winchester today?' She tried not to weight her question too heavily, but her mind was racing. No time to think about it now, though, not with John Forrester smiling down at her. For a moment she felt her pulse race — he really was unreasonably attractive — but even as she smiled in response, she glanced up to see Rory pause just behind the vicar. A frown wrinkled his forehead but he must have felt her eyes on him because he glanced up and grinned at her. Of course, it was true after all, she scolded herself, aware that John Forrester would assume her sudden blush was for his benefit. What a fool she'd been, her only possible excuse a mixture of anxiety and jetlag. Grandpa wouldn't lie. If Rory happened to be his grandson, illegitimate or not, he would have said so. It must be so and besides, now she came to think of it, Rory would never have kissed her if the relationship had been closer. But why did Gran look so sad when anyone mentioned Rory's father? She'd never known him, so what was the mystery?

Rory was about to speak when his phone rang. 'Sorry,' he called as he headed outside again. This time it was a woman's voice, with a slight accent. She sounded familiar.

'It's Margaret Mackenzie,' she announced. 'I was at the cathedral this afternoon? I've just remembered something.'

11

The Great Hall was dark and shadowy, echoing with strange, unearthly chords. Harriet was watching some kind of ceremony, performed by a central robed figure, tall and magisterial, silhouetted against the dazzling light shining in from the front windows. The figure took a step towards her and she woke in a flutter as she realized it was an angel.

She should have slept the night through, judging by the number of painkillers she had taken, but no, here she was at — she groaned as she glanced at her watch — just after 2.30 a.m. Her head aching and feeling uneasy after the strange dream. She sat up and wondered what to do. Karen had thoughtfully left a kettle and tea things in case of need, but it didn't appeal. She staggered slightly as she went to the bathroom and on the way back she crossed over to the window.

A flash, a second flash, hastily dowsed. Torches? The moonlight made them superfluous and she could just make out a figure right over at the far edge of the Burial Field. Oh not again. There hadn't been much time to think about Edith and Rory's glimpse of the

226

two men, Brendan and Mike Goldstein, who had been up to no good in the same place. Edith had rung the police but too much had happened since, and that odd little incident had slipped Harriet's mind. But what on earth were they up to now? Treasure-hunting, presumably, but what treasure? It was widely known locally that the remains of a Roman villa were supposed to be under the field and it was Walter Attlin's cherished dream that one day there would be enough money to finance a proper dig. It was also known, however, that the field had been ploughed and planted for centuries and that nothing but fragments of pottery had ever shown up.

Harriet tried to clear her throbbing head. There was no time for that puzzle but what should she do? If I'm going out there to see what's happening, she shivered, I'm not going alone. Sam would never forgive me and anyway, I'm not that stupid, but — she hesitated — someone needs to check it out.

Not Edith, though. Harriet dismissed the idea immediately. If anything happened, if there was an accident of some kind, it would kill the old people. Sam was too far away so it would have to be Rory; she certainly couldn't handle this on her own, even though Edith would be furious when she found she had been sidelined. Harriet scrambled into jeans and a sweatshirt, thrusting her feet into canvas shoes. Grabbing her phone and her car keys, with their built-in torch, she stumbled out into the corridor and made her way to Rory's room.

'Rory, wake up.' She shook him with increasing urgency. 'Somebody's digging in the Burial Field again. Oh, for goodness' sake, Rory, wake up, will you?'

When he peered groggily at her, yawning and protesting, she gave him a brief outline of the situation. 'We've got to call the police.'

'I think you're right.' He was still yawning and rubbing his eyes as he stared out of his window. 'Blimey, I saw movement too, something glinting in the moonlight. But what do we tell the cops? Wouldn't they just think it's poachers? Is that going to be high on their list of priorities? I don't know anything about what goes on in the countryside.'

'Even if it *is* just poachers,' she said firmly, 'they've no right to be there and that's reason enough to tell the police. Look, can you see to get dressed? I don't want to put the light on, it might make them suspicious.'

'Oh, all right,' he grumbled. 'Go away for a minute, Harriet. I sleep in the nude. I'm sure you've seen it all before but I'm shy, so push off.'

He heard a stifled, surprisingly youthful giggle as she wandered over towards the window while he struggled into his clothes. A shaft of moonlight caught something sparkling on the polished mahogany of the tallboy and Harriet took a closer look.

'Rory?' There was an odd note in her voice and he raised his head. 'Where — where did you get this?' He zipped up his jeans and crossed the room to examine the tiny thing in the centre of her palm, the light glinting off the intricate twists and loops of silver wire.

'That? It's a bit of one of Edith's earrings, isn't it? I spotted in nestling in the weave of your precious vicar's jacket this evening, on one of the sleeves. I nicked it without mentioning it to him, I've no wish to talk to him anyway. I meant to hand it over to Edith but we all went to bed fairly early and I completely forgot about it.'

She looked at the delicate little object and then met his eye, looking very sober. 'But this isn't an earring, Rory. It belongs to me. It's a miniature silver toast rack from my doll's house collection.'

They stared at each other, Harriet looking bewildered and increasingly disturbed. She frowned and looked out of the window again at the distant figure, then back at the miniature. 'This is new,' she said slowly. 'It arrived by registered post the day before yesterday and I'd only set it on the side table with my other most recent treasures just before Edith came in for coffee with me.'

Rory slipped on his trainers as Harriet added, 'The only time the vicar can have got this tangled up in his jacket is when he gave Edith a lift to the village to pick up the things I asked her to fetch; in other words it had to be yesterday afternoon.'

'But that's not . . . ' Rory stood up, still frowning. 'I overheard him at the party telling Edith he only bought that jacket in Winchester at lunchtime today, I mean yesterday. He said he bought it especially for the party and was boasting about it not being too trendy to upset all the old fogeys in the village.'

'You're sure it was on his jacket? It couldn't have brushed off someone else's clothes?'

'No chance. I had to give it quite a tug to free it up from the tweed. I'm surprised he didn't notice me but he was too busy hitting on Edith. I was sure it was an earring; I assumed she lost it when she went out to dinner with him the other night.' He peered closely at the tiny silver bauble. 'A toast rack, really?'

Harriet sat down hastily. 'No, I'm all right, don't fuss. It's just the pills I'm taking, and I have to admit it's come as a shock. If that jacket was new at lunchtime yesterday that means he must have broken into my cottage sometime the same afternoon, not on his visit with Edith the day before. At any rate it can only have been just before he turned up at the party. But why?'

'Edith said he was looking at some notes you'd made,' Rory remembered. 'When he was there with her, I mean. He blamed the cat because the papers were on the floor, but when Edith took them off him, to replace them on your desk, she said the name Colin Price jumped out at her. Maybe that's what he spotted. But why would that bother him?'

Harriet had her mobile in her hand. 'We need to call the cops,' she said, her tone decisive, the momentary weakness vanished.

'No, wait, I've just remembered something else.' He caught at her arm. 'I had a call from the Canadian lady who was in the chapel. You know, she took Edith to lunch after we found Sam's friend in the chapel. She rang about half-past nine last night and I'd forgotten all about it till now. She said she noticed the party of German tourists who were milling about in the chapel but it had only just occurred to her that there was another man in there too. Mrs Mackenzie didn't think it could be important but as I'd asked her to let me know *anything* at all, she decided to call me. I asked her if she could describe him, and she said it was only a clergyman who was praying beside the old chap, Dr Sutherland.'

'What?'

'I know.' He hunched his shoulders, looking perturbed. 'I asked her about this clergyman and she said she hadn't taken much notice of him; she was busy with her own memories of her late husband and in any case, several of the tourists knelt to pray briefly. Mrs Mackenzie said she hadn't even thought about him till I asked, after all, a vicar in a cathedral is a bit like wallpaper, so much what you expect to be there that you don't even see it after a while. But when she thought about it, it seemed a bit odd. She'd seen Dr Sutherland enter the chapel and sit down but she was lost in her own thoughts so she didn't see the other man come in, or leave, come to that. She couldn't describe him but she did tell me she thought he was probably in his thirties with reddish-brown hair.'

Silence hung between them until Harriet brushed a hand across her eyes. 'I can't make head or tail of it,' she said irritably and moved over towards the window again. 'They've gone,' she gasped, and pointed as Rory joined her. 'Here, see if you can make out anything.'

'There's no sign of movement,' he agreed, after a moment. 'I'm going to take a look — and before you say anything,' he forestalled her protest, 'I'll take precautions, I'm not an idiot.'

Harriet still held her mobile phone in her hand. Sam, she breathed as Rory disappeared downstairs. I know I promised him I wouldn't do anything stupid but there's no way I'm leaving Rory by himself. Let me think . . . Inspiration struck and she sent Sam a text. *'Checking activity in BField. Rory with me. Not stupid. H.'*

Tucking her phone into the back pocket of her jeans, she was at the head of the stairs when a thought intruded. Better spend a penny, she muttered to herself. I can just imagine Rory's face if I say I need to nip behind a tree.

What with attending to the call of nature, she was some minutes behind her fellow conspirator but she could just glimpse him as he circled the Burial Field, using the old stone wall as both guideline and shelter. Harriet took a deep breath and followed suit, her mind racing madly. Why did the image of John Forrester praying beside the old clergyman make her shudder in distaste? John was a cleric himself, after all, and the old man had died of a heart attack, hadn't he? Or if he hadn't, how in the world could John have killed him undetected and, what was even more to the point, *why* in the world should John, or anyone else, have killed him? Oliver Sutherland was a cheerful old man who did nobody any harm and was popular and well respected among his former colleagues and parishioners.

Perhaps it was a heart attack. Or a stroke and maybe John had found him already dead? But no, surely in that case the natural thing to do would be to summon help, as Sam and Rory and Edith had done. I don't like the vicar, Harriet admitted to herself, in a moment of honesty, but no, he couldn't, he wouldn't — to somehow murder an old man in a cathedral, of all blasphemous things to do.

It must be a mistake, but Rory was insistent. Mrs Mackenzie was a calm, rational witness who was adamant that she had noticed a youngish man of the cloth quietly praying beside an older colleague. It was a kind and thoughtful act but if that were all, Harriet wondered with a heavy heart, why had John not raised the alarm himself? Why had he not even mentioned the circumstance?

The snatched conversation she'd had with Rory a few minutes earlier made it clear that the subject of the sad death in the cathedral had not been raised at the drinks party, probably because most of the guests were in ignorance. But even allowing for John to be showing consideration to his elderly hosts, who most probably had been acquaintances, if not friends, of the elderly Dr Sutherland, surely the normal thing for him to have done was at least to sympathize in private with Edith and Rory?

She caught up with Rory at the corner of the two fields, where the stone walls joined to make a sheltered spot for a clump of blackthorn bushes, their flowers all gone and the sloes showing hard and green. From there they had a reasonably clear view of the tangled thicket further up the rise, where the ancient stone stood. They crouched there, in the rank grass and nettles, straining to see, to hear. A sudden clang, of metal against stone, made them both freeze and Harriet could hear her heart thumping as Rory touched her arm and pointed towards the angel stone.

'Who?' She breathed the question and he pointed again. A figure, tall and angular, was silhouetted against the silvery light; it was Gordon Dean's visitor from Texas, Mike Goldstein, unmistakable in his lean length. As she and Rory held their breath, he dropped to his knees and seemed to be peering at something beside the angel stone. Or was it something below the stone? Harriet felt a frisson of excitement; could they be excavating the Roman ruins?

Even though recent Attlins had been unable to finance any serious exploration, most people in the area knew the legends and, in Harriet's opinion, her cousin Walter had been incredibly lucky that no enterprising treasure-seekers had so far disturbed the ruins. It looked as though his luck had run out now, because anyone with an innocent interest in archaeology would hardly be out here, secretly, in the middle of the night.

Rory was watching silently while Harriet speculated. Surely Mike Goldstein and his henchman — it would be Brendan Whittaker; her money was on him — surely they couldn't believe that the rewards of such a dig would be enough to justify such a hole-and-corner venture. This wasn't a fabled site like Sutton Hoo, or, nearer home, the Roman palace of Fishbourne, a few miles along the coast towards Chichester. Harriet recalled her history. Fishbourne was the home of Cogidubnus, king of the Regni, and recognized by the occupying Romans as a sub-ruler but Lucius Sextus Vitalis, the supposed founder of the Attlin family, had only been a retired soldier who married into the local gentry. Alfred's son had been the family's one essay into major-league high society and since then they had kept a low profile: dutiful soldiers, hard-working farmers, solid citizens, with no shooting stars or shining lights. The Locksley villa was small potatoes.

'We'd better get back to the house,' Rory whispered. 'Wonder where they parked their car?'

'It's down the back lane.' The voice, from about six feet behind them, made them both freeze. 'Oh, don't look so fed up.' It was Brendan Whittaker, a gun in his hand pointed straight at Harriet. 'You're well hidden. It's your bad luck that I missed the first turning or I'd never have spotted you. But now, oh dear me.' His tone was mocking. 'I thought you had more sense, Miss Quigley. No,' as Rory straightened up, 'no heroics please, Dr Attlin, or I'll have to kill you both. Now get over there to where my, er, colleague is.'

Harriet stumbled along behind, achingly conscious of Brendan's gun He whistled to the other man who had hastily donned his black balaclava — why on earth? — and who now stood, saw in hand, beside a pile of cut saplings. Without a word he gestured with his other hand to what was revealed as a hole, roughly a metre square, at the base of the ancient plinth. Neatly set aside was a turf 'lid' resting on a wooden base, together with some of the uprooted scrub that had been scattered carelessly around. There was no sign of the heap of excavated soil that Harriet would have expected, she noticed, without properly registering the thought, but there was no time to wonder.

Brendan pushed Rory to his knees and with the other man covering Harriet herself, briskly lashed his captive's wrists with baler twine that he took out of his pocket. Rory uttered a wrathful protest but to Harriet's horror, Mike Goldstein who had so far not uttered a word, swung his shovel at Rory's head. Even though he managed to twist away, the back of the blade still clanged viciously against his skull and he dropped to the ground, still and grey in the moonlight, and to Harriet's extreme distress, apparently dead.

'You *bastard!*' She lost control then, shrieking with rage and anguish. 'You barbarian, get out of my way, let me see to him.' Kicking and screaming, beside herself with fury, she scratched and howled, fighting against Brendan's restraining grasp. The other man ignored her completely and casually gave Rory a shove down into the ruins. As she landed a lucky punch on him, Brendan let out a yelp of pain and loosened his grip.

Harriet twisted away but it was no use. Rory's captor reached out and caught her, then, barely pausing, picked her up and dropped her down after Rory.

Terrified and breathless she heard Brendan's voice; he was arguing with the other man. 'There was no need for that, they're harmless. You can't . . . '

As she dropped she heard the other man's harsh grunt of laughter at Brendan's protest, then nothing else mattered as she braced herself for the fall, but somehow, miraculously, she was jolted but undamaged, apart from scratching herself on the heaps of scrub and saplings that Brendan and his crony had thrown down out of sight. This, she realized, was what had saved her from injury. Even more fortuitously, she hadn't landed on Rory.

As she took a shuddering breath there was a further horror. The light from the moon vanished as the turf 'lid' was replaced over the gaping hole about ten feet above and Harriet winced as a scatter of earth and small stones bounced off her face.

Muffled sounds from above suggested that their attackers were replacing the uprooted scrub and then there was silence. Harriet's bowels wrenched with an agonizing spasm of terror but somehow she managed to control herself, putting her emotions on hold so that she could attend to Rory. Where the hell was Rory? Fearfully, she blundered about on all fours, almost kneeling on him when she located him at last. She groped feverishly for a hand, a pulse, but although she eventually located his wrist, she could feel no pulse, not even a flutter.

★　★　★

Sam Hathaway couldn't sleep. Although the dinner on offer at the meeting had been substantial, mostly what Harriet always called 'a manly meal', a roast with plenty of potatoes and a hearty steamed pudding and custard to follow, he had eaten sparingly. It felt strange, camping in the cottage, strange but not unpleasant and the cat in the next room gave him a comforting sense of not being alone. Harriet would laugh when she heard that after a trip to the bathroom just before 2.30 a.m., he had nipped downstairs: coffee for himself; cat treats for Fat Hector, who snoozed happily in a corner until Sam coaxed him out to be stroked and admired. It felt good, he thought, listening to the tentative purring. Although Avril's severe allergies had made pets impossible, Sam was inclined to agree with his cousin that a house needed a cat to make it a home.

Harriet. He wondered how she was feeling, praying that her concussion was as slight as the doctor had assured him and shivered at the thought of life without her. Harriet had been his mainstay in the dreadful days after Avril's death and in the bleak darkness that followed, how could he manage without her? Fear made him reach out for his phone, to check on her.

Pure selfishness! He frowned in the darkness and withdrew his hand. His cousin would be tucked up in bed at the farm, doped to the eyeballs and waited on hand and foot. A panic call at this time of night was the last thing she needed. He settled down and managed at last to grab a couple more hours of restless sleep.

Harriet could safely wait till the morning.

12

At last, Harriet found a pulse. Thank God, Rory wasn't dead after all. She almost broke down then but years of self-control came to her rescue and she forced herself to relax, steadying her breathing, keeping her fingers lightly but firmly on Rory's wrist. The pulse seemed a little stronger and she swallowed once or twice, gulping with relief.

'Rory? Can you hear me?' Over the thumping of her own heart she heard a murmur, a breath taken and a thread of a whisper.

'S'posed to be a cure, you know.' The faint laugh in his voice was the most welcome sound in the world. 'Country air, family reunion, nothing strenuous.'

'Nonsense.' Her brisk reply was under-mined by a slight wobble in the voice, but she rallied as she ran her hands over him. 'Always something going on in a country village, you know; you need to man up, put hair on your chest. Now, do you think there's anything broken? I'm sure you hurt all over, but can you tell if there's any serious damage? Here, I've got my Swiss Army knife, I'll cut that stupid baler twine so you can poke about. We'll need all our strength to get out of this predicament.'

'Mmm, no, no bones broken.' His voice was beginning to sound stronger. 'There isn't a single bit of me that isn't agony and my knee hurts where I must have banged it as I landed, but it's not broken.'

There was silence as he explored the extent of his injuries. 'Got a headache, but I don't think my skull's damaged. What about you, Harriet? You've already got concussion. Did they hurt you?'

'Not really.' She sighed and gave his hand a companionable squeeze to reassure them both. 'I felt sick with fright when he walloped you with the spade but they didn't actually hurt me, just dropped me into the hole. I can't believe we didn't break our necks but when they cut back all the shrubbery, they must have chucked everything down here to hide the evidence. A lucky break for us.'

'Don't say break,' Rory groaned, and shifted uneasily. 'Ugh, I think I have got a cracked rib after all, that bastard kicked me when I fell. He was aiming at my balls, I'm sure of it. Good job I managed to hunch up just as I passed out, otherwise I'd be singing soprano for the rest of my life.'

The feeble joke made them both feel better

and Harriet fished out her key ring again. 'Here, there's a torch on it,' she grunted. 'Stupid little pencil light but better than nothing. Let's have a look at where we are.'

'Swiss Army knife? Torch? Harriet, if I had to choose who to be thrown in a gloomy hole with, you'd always be my first choice!' He rubbed his sore knee. 'I suppose you were a Girl Guide?'

'And a Brown Owl,' she added, thoughtfully shining the sliver of light around the shaft above their heads. 'Useful motto: '*Be Prepared*'. Unfortunately I forgot to pack a gun and a picnic tonight, let alone a JCB to dig us out of here.'

'God, I'm stupid.' He was feeling very gingerly in a pocket. 'I forgot all about my phone. It's got a light and we can — It's gone.' He sounded aghast and she patted his arm.

'It probably fell out of your pocket while they were giving you a good going-over,' she consoled him. 'I'm just surprised they didn't search us as a precaution. Just as well.' She held up her own mobile triumphantly. 'It's not one of those state-of-the-art gadgets like yours, just a bog-standard basic model, but it's better than nothing.' She peered at it and shook her head. 'Just as I thought, there's no signal down here.' She shrugged, settling

244

herself more comfortably as she tried to ignore the rank smell that pervaded the place; nothing mattered now she knew Rory was more or less in one piece.

'Let's take a breather before we start worrying about signals or trying to get out of here. I shouldn't think that makeshift cover would take much pushing, but it's ten or more feet up, so you'd certainly have to give me a bunk up (which you're in no state to do) and I've no head for heights anyway. But we'll keep that as a last resort. We're safe enough down here for now.' She held out her key ring. 'Here, you have this and I'll use my phone and pray the battery holds up.'

'Safe? If you say so.' He shone the light round. 'What I'd really like to know is, what the hell is going on?'

'None of it makes sense,' Harriet declared. 'I thought it looked as though John Forrester had something to do with Dr Sutherland's death, though I don't see what he could possibly gain by that. Even if it was John whom your Canadian lady saw in the cathedral, it doesn't mean he killed the old man, though it's a tad suspicious that he didn't mention anything to you or Edith at the party. I also thought he must be involved with the missing items from the archives and with Colin Price; maybe that he knew where

Price had gone.' She shook her head slowly looking bewildered. 'I just don't see how. The police interviewed everyone at the time and as far as I know, word round the village was that John never actually saw Price. Besides, according to Sam's mole in high places, nothing's been stolen since Price disappeared.

'Another thing I don't get,' Harriet paused, before continuing, 'is what any of it has to do with oil, which is where you might expect Brendan to be involved, or at least Brendan and his boss. And none of it has anything at all to do with looking up ancestors, as far as I can see.'

'I think you're right about that,' Rory added his two-pennyworth. 'I think the whole ancestor thing could be a cover and that Mike Goldstein was brought over here to act as a dowser.' He explained about Sam's discoveries. 'I know Sam's friend said he wasn't up to date on techniques, but maybe there's still a place for a kind of human sniffer dog. Though it might just be that he's connected with the oil industry anyway.'

'Hmm.' Harriet digested this snippet of information. 'It's a bit tenuous, isn't it, solely based on the fact that he's from Texas. Might be lying, after all. And what about the business with Walter Attlin? The vicar has a cast-iron alibi for that, but it could have been Brendan, or Mike Goldstein. But why would they want to do that?'

'Maybe Walter saw something. Or it might be that they *thought* he could have seen something. Sounds a high-risk strategy, though, so maybe it was blind panic.'

'And then there's me.' Harriet's voice sounded very small and she was grateful when Rory reached out to clasp her hand. 'Who was it who pushed me over the quarry? Someone on his way to the village via the short cut, no question, but who? The vicar's car had a dent on the wing, but Edith spotted that *before* I went through the fence.' She thought it over. 'He dropped Edith home by ten that night, she told me. I suppose he could have gone out again later.'

'Brendan's car had a nasty scrape too,' Rory offered. 'He told Edith he got it in a car park, didn't see who it was. But why would either of them want to get rid of you, Harriet? I mean the whole village is agog with rumours about prospecting for oil, at least three people told me so before I'd been here half a day. And if someone thought Sam was asking too many questions, why attack you and not Sam? Might as well bump off the whole village while he was at it.' He sucked in a sharp breath. This was definitely not the moment, he decided, to let Harriet know of Edith's suspicion that Sam might have been the intended victim in the cathedral.

Harriet sat silent for a moment or two. 'Right, let's stop asking questions, we've no way of knowing what the truth is,' she said firmly. 'I vote we suss out what there is down here.'

The meagre beam from her phone showed that they were in a small, square space that had a shaft let in from above and a culvert leading off at the side. Harriet crawled over to take a look and let out a squeal of fright as she came face to face with a pair of bright golden eyes, reflected in the thin line of light.

'*What* — ' She rocked back on her heels, gasping for breath, as a ginger cat prowled up to her and head-butted her with great affection. 'It's Toby, he's Penelope's cat,' she called to Rory, who had rolled over onto his hands and knees, preparing to crawl somehow to her rescue. 'But how on earth did you get in here?' She stroked the cat with shaking hands and shone the torch into the shadows.

'Rory, the brickwork is amazing. I'm sure it's Roman.' Sidetracked for a moment, she ran her hands over the arched roof of the low tunnel. 'Oh, my Lord, I wonder if it could be the hypocaust. I can't imagine what else it could be. Oh.' She was breathless with excitement. 'This means there really was a villa and we're underneath it. And,' relief suddenly hit her, 'if the cat can get in, perhaps we can get out the same way.'

She crawled back to sit beside Rory, and the ginger cat immediately scrambled onto her lap, rubbing his cheeks against her chin. She stroked him absently, while shining the torch this way and that.

A few feet to the side of the main shaft, visible through broken brickwork, was a fall of earth that looked to Harriet like the remains of a badger's sett. She peered at it, shining the light towards the brick arch that might once have been the villa's heating system.

'Damn, it's collapsed, of course it would have. I knew it was too good to be true. Look, there's no way we can force our way through that rubble and hundreds of years worth of roots.' She was bitterly disappointed. 'But how did the cat get through?'

'I think somebody's been down here, you know, it's in pretty good nick for something that hasn't been seen in sixteen hundred years,' Rory said slowly, frowning as he shone the torch over the tile and stone piers, obscured in most places by hanging roots, rubble and more earth falls.

'But it *has* been seen,' Harriet protested.

'Look, someone's been shoring up some of those pillars and if you look up at the shaft we dropped down, you can see it's been added at a later date. The brickwork is rough and the opening up from here has been hacked about to make it bigger.'

She racked her brains. 'It's a while since I taught any Roman history,' she confessed, 'but I think we must be in some kind of cistern. According to that old book about the Attlin family history, the angel stone is supposed to be where the atrium was, you know, the centre courtyard-cum-entrance hall. In a Roman villa the atrium would have had an opening called the compluvium; it wouldn't have been roofed right over and rain falling through would be collected in a shallow pool underneath, to be drained away into a water tank underneath.'

'You mean we could be in the water tank?' Rory's imagination was fired and he swung the torch up and down the shaft. 'I think you're right. Look, it's definitely made of lead, you can see where it's drooped down into folds; lead does that when it's neglected. It's incredible it wasn't stolen. Later generations knew about this place, they must have done, and for some reason came down here and made some alterations. I wonder why.'

'But it's in that old book.' Harriet was

excited, their danger forgotten. 'There's a mention of a priest's hole at the farm but nobody's ever been able to find it. Suppose it wasn't in the house at all, but that the family knew about this space and made it bigger, to use as a hiding place.'

An involuntary shudder made her hug herself for comfort. 'Dear God, imagine being a priest in hiding, stuck down here till someone came to tell you it was safe, and terrified all the time that someone would give you away.' She cast a fearful glance round at the shadows. 'Think what capture meant; torture, hanging, drawing and quartering.' A thought struck her. 'Ugh, I just hope we don't stumble over a skeleton, one of those poor devils who never made it out!'

'You're supposed to be the little ray of sunshine round here,' Rory groaned. 'Talk about a ghoul.'

She managed a laugh. 'Someone's made an opening at the side of the cistern,' she went on, standing on tiptoe to try and make it out. 'As well as making the hole at the top bigger, I mean. The water tank and the hypocaust were originally quite separate of course, but it's been altered so you can get through from the shaft. There's air down here and look, there must have been a proper hatch above us, cast iron perhaps? You can see the ledges it rested on.' She was excited. 'I bet it's still in use; that temporary lid would disintegrate in no time. Thank goodness we haven't got the original one up there. They were obviously in too much of a hurry to get rid of us.'

She felt carefully round the brickwork, wrinkling her nose as she came to the badger's sett. 'And who knows? The Attlins could even have used it in the Civil War, to hide royalist soldiers from the Roundheads.'

'Harriet.' Rory's voice was harsh, his breathing ragged. 'Shut up a minute and look over here.'

While she was thinking aloud, he had wriggled over to the culvert, so she joined him, shining her phone alongside his torch, her eyes squinting along the finger of light that shone into the darkness. The smell was much worse here, and she gagged just as she caught up with Rory, who was staring at something. Just visible, secreted in a blind alley that was part of the ventilation system, the long body of a man lay very still, his hand flung clear of the rough covering of stones. Not a Roman, not a skeleton, it was a man whose modern, casual trousers and dark-grey jacket were only too visible.

'Stay there a minute, Harriet, there isn't room for both of us.' Rory shuffled painfully on his hands and knees to the opening of the cul-de-sac. He carefully shifted a few stones; there had been no attempt at complete concealment, just a cursory camouflage.

'Christ almighty!' He stared down at the earth-sprinkled hair, at the bruised, but unmistakably dead features of a man he recognized. 'He's been shot!'

Harriet could bear it no longer. 'Who is it?' She halted, horrified. 'But, but that's the vicar; that's John Forrester.'

'No, it's not,' he said quietly, shining the torch to show her the dead man's face. His voice shook as he retreated.

'Oh, my God.' Harriet peered over his shoulder. 'I thought the smell was the badgers but . . . ' she gulped, her hand to her mouth, 'it's Mike Goldstein. But I thought it was Mike out there with Brendan. It was Mike who hit you, wasn't it? I was sure it was Mike.'

Her stomach heaved and she broke off abruptly, crawling aside just in time before she was violently sick. As she heaved, she was aware of Rory retching and taking deep breaths.

She rocked back on her heels, wiping her mouth on her sleeve, as they stared at the body of Mike Goldstein who so manifestly had *not* been digging in the Burial Field; Mike, who could not possibly have hit Rory;

Mike, who was so very clearly dead.

It was time to face facts.

'There's only one explanation; it has to have been John Forrester all along,' she said flatly, almost in disbelief. 'The vicar and Brendan Whittaker. All that stuff about oil exploration was just a smokescreen.'

It took them a good ten minutes to calm down. Rory was shivering, a hangover from the fever he'd caught in that Far Eastern jail, and for once Harriet was feeling her age and more.

'Here.' She found a packet of mints in her pocket. 'Very soothing to the frayed nerves, peppermint.' Habit helped her to summon up some self-control. She put an arm round Rory's shoulders and hugged him, but there was a treacherous wobble in her voice as she tried to joke, 'Bit more than you bargained for, isn't it? Me too. I promised Sam I wouldn't play at being Miss Marple but this is — ' She swallowed, unable to continue.

She shook herself, unable to leave it. 'You said Mike was at the party so he can't have been here . . . Oh, for goodness' sake.' She managed at last to shy away from the thought of the dead man. 'This place is depressing in its own right, a bit like a coffin, this tank. Sorry,' she grimaced. 'Not a helpful thing to say. Still, as long as I'm being macabre, it's a pretty crowded coffin. I'm going to wriggle along the way the cat came, and see if I can find out how he got in.'

Rory started to protest.

'Don't be stupid,' she retorted. 'I may not be thinner than you, but your shoulders are a lot broader than mine and you've just been beaten up. My concussion is on the mend and besides, I'm probably fitter than you anyway, even if I am thirty-odd years older, so stay put. I'll make marks so I don't get lost.'

Giving him no time to argue, Harriet set off, accompanied by the cat, whose curiosity was plainly roused. Glad of the company, she gave him an encouraging stroke. 'Where are the *Famous Five*, or a St Bernard, when you need them,' she grunted, speaking out loud to scare away the shadows. 'But you'll do, old moggie. Just remember to pack a small keg of spirits, whisky for choice, in future. You go in front and show me the way you came in, though I suspect it'll be too narrow for the likes of us humans. Let's take a look.' She shone the torch into the darkness.

'You know we could see that someone's shored up the outer wall of the hypocaust?' she called out to Rory. 'Even though the hypocaust has collapsed in on itself, a kind of tunnel's been pushed through, so a man could just about wriggle through. Just as well neither of us is exactly chubby but I'm quite sure we'd never squeeze through the hypocaust itself. This has been done properly, and not recently either. I think it could have been done in Tudor times as a hiding place for Catholic priests, even an escape route.'

She called back over her shoulder to report her findings. 'I can see that someone's been in here much more recently, clearing out muck and debris. There's not hundreds of years' worth of tree roots and rubbish in this passageway, not by a long chalk.'

With a lot of grunting and occasional cursing, Harriet slithered forward for some time in the wake of the cat. Toby pottered purposefully along, turning into a marginally larger space, with an enquiring look over his shoulder to see if she was still playing this interesting game with him.

'Just as well I don't suffer from claustrophobia,' she muttered. 'Oops, now what?' As she caught up with the cat she found herself facing a wall of tree roots and disturbed earth. All around she could see evidence of generations of animal occupation, small bones that could indicate that foxes had once been in residence. And then she saw it: filtering in from outside was a faint, greyish light, the welcome dawn approaching.

Her shoulder was hurting like mad. Bother

that bathroom ceiling, she muttered. Decorating in the spring had led to a frozen shoulder and although it was gradually improving, the pain was sometimes agonizing. Concussion and a frozen shoulder, what a state to go on a treasure hunt in. Miss Marple would have had a lot more sense. She gave a final massage to the afflicted shoulder then, following her marks, she wriggled back to where Rory was champing at the bit.

'I think we can just about squeeze out,' she told him as she led him back into the tunnels. 'This enlarged passageway ends in what looks like another entrance to the badgers' sett — they usually have several. You often get foxes moving in when the badgers leave and I could definitely see traces of a fox's earth. That must be how the cat got in and I'm fairly sure we can scrape at it till we can clamber out. It's the most terrific discovery; Cousin Walter shouldn't have any trouble getting people interested, grants, and so forth. *Time Team*, even.'

Harriet set out again, averting her eyes from Mike Goldstein's out-flung hand. Strange how pathetic it looked, she shivered, wondering about his death. And wondering even more who had killed him. And why.

Rory slithered after her, his broader shoulders making his passage through even the widened narrow flue more difficult. He gritted his teeth against the pain of his cracked rib, damaged knee and extensive bruises and when he caught up with her, he shone the torch back the way they had come. What he saw made him whistle.

'What is it?' Harriet was fearful now, the nightmare thought beginning to surface. 'It's not, not another body . . . ? Oh God, it's not Colin Price?'

'Not a body — but that's a thought, he could be down here, couldn't he? No, it's not a body, but look, there's something.' He hooked a long arm into a shallow alcove she had missed in her earlier exploration, and fished out a plastic document folder.

'Well,' Harriet burst out. *'That's* definitely not Roman.'

'There's something in here, a piece of paper, I think. Proves someone's been down here recently, doesn't it?' Rory fished it out and squinted at it. 'This isn't Roman either,' he said, disappointment in his voice as he handed it to her.

'Well, you're right, it's certainly not Roman,' Harriet said slowly, holding it up to her eyes as she tried to make it out. 'But modern is a relative term. It's old, though, but I'd have said eighteenth century, rather than much earlier. The writing's faded but it's in readable English.'

She spread the paper out and read the short message: 'Dame Margery keeps the secret of Aelfryth's Tears,' followed by an illegible signature. Harriet turned the paper over, fruitlessly looking for further illumination. 'That's all there is.'

Rory shoved it down the front of his sweatshirt. 'We'd better get a move on. Where's this fox's earth you want me to scramble through? I tell you, Harriet, you're not like any teacher I ever had; your classes must have been lively.'

'Fool.' She headed towards the increasingly bright light. 'Here, I think we can just about wriggle through here.' She heaved a sigh and peered at her watch. 'I wonder if Sam's picked up my text yet?'

'Sam? Text? What are you on about?'

'Sorry, didn't I tell you?' She blinked in surprise. 'Good Lord, I completely forgot to mention it. I sent Sam a text before we left the house, to tell him there was something going on in the Burial Field and we were going to take a look. As soon as he picks it up Sam will be galloping over the hill with the Seventh Cavalry to the rescue.'

'You could have told me,' Rory said, sounding aggrieved. 'No wonder you weren't in a state of total panic at being trapped underground. I've been in awe, thinking how brave you were.'

'That's boarding school. We were taught to be strong, capable women, not spineless jellyfish. It was the ethos of the school along with cold baths and lots of exercise. Mind you, I think we've both been pretty brave,' she reproved him, though he saw a twinkle in her blue eyes. 'But anyway, I also took the precaution of leaving a note in my bedroom, for Edith or Sam, whoever got there first. I just said there was someone digging around the old stone and it looked like Brendan and Mike Goldstein. And that I thought they were looking for the remains of the original villa, on the hunt for treasure.'

She shot him a disarming grin. 'I'm sorry you were worried. And it would have given Sam or Edith a pretty horrible ten minutes or so, wondering if we were still alive under there. However,' she squared her shoulders with a groan, 'let's get a move on and make our way above ground, because after that comes the difficult bit.'

'And that is?'

'Finding out where John Forrester and Brendan have gone.' She made a face as she added, 'And what they're up to.'

13

As they made their cautious way across the fields, Harriet cocked an eye at her companion. He was looking a lot better, she decided, in spite of his extremely disturbed night. Happier too.

'Are you getting on better with Edith?' she asked tentatively and hid a smile as he reddened.

'She's suddenly stopped treating me as though I'm something the cat dragged in,' he confided. 'In fact, she ... ' He halted, embarrassed, and Harriet tactfully turned to admire the sunrise.

'You know why she was treating you like a leper?' she asked casually.

'No idea,' he said. 'Whatever the reason, she's given up on it now.'

'It was because Lara Dean told her or rather, hinted, that you were brother and sister.'

'What?' He was so astonished that he stopped in his tracks.

'Shh.' She frowned at him. 'Keep moving and don't make so much noise. We've no idea where Brendan and the vicar went.' She glanced round fearfully, but the fields were empty of human life.

'Yes, anyway; I dragged it out of Edith tonight, no it's yesterday now, anyway, it was in the evening when she looked in on me. We had a very instructive ten minutes or so. She told me about poor old Oliver Sutherland and I knew there'd been something bugging her that was making you both uncomfortable. Apparently Lara saw an old documentary about heroes from Hampshire, including Major Richard Attlin, billed as the late son of a well-known local family, a bomb disposal expert who eventually died of wounds sustained years earlier.

'They showed a picture of Richard and Lara was struck by the likeness when she met you. She put two and two together and made far too many; then, out of spite, she told Edith, who hadn't got the sense she was born with, and half-believed it.'

At the gate to the kitchen garden Harriet paused. 'I'm going to ring the police now,' she said. 'I know we've no idea where Brendan and the vicar have gone, and I also know we're going to have the Devil's own job convincing anyone that the vicar is a murderer, but there's a dead man in those ruins and he needs justice.'

Looking stern, she called in, spoke urgently

to whoever was on duty, was transferred to someone else, and finally caught up with an officer who not only knew her but also took her seriously. 'He's sending a car right away,' she said, with grim satisfaction. 'And he also said we're to keep out of trouble.'

'Fair enough,' Rory shrugged. 'All I want to do is have a bath and go to sleep, but first of all, a coffee. Come on, I'll put the kettle on.'

Harriet nodded. 'Tea for me, please. No sign of Karen and Elveece? What happened to them?'

'He had a late-night gig in Portsmouth. The party here was very sedate and finished by nine o'clock, so Karen went with him. They're staying overnight with one of his mates so they've got today off.' He spooned coffee into a mug for himself and found a tea bag for Harriet. 'Let's have another look at that note.' He pulled the plastic wallet out from under his sweatshirt and they studied the document once more. It still made no sense to either of them.

'Oh well, let's leave it till tomorrow. That's the best cup of tea I've had in years,' she told him. 'I'm feeling much better already.'

'Me too.' He finished the slice of cake she'd cut and stood up. 'I'm not tired any more, still pumping adrenaline. Are you doing okay? So how about we go up and check out the picture gallery while we're still wired? I'd like to take another look at a couple of paintings — I think they could be very special.'

'Fine.' She drained her mug and followed him out of the kitchen. 'Edith told me you'd been dropping hints, but she was a bit put out that you wouldn't go into any detail.'

'No chance,' he grinned as they crossed the hall. 'You know what she's like, she'd be up there with the Fairy Liquid, trying to clean off the grime of centuries, hoping to find a Leonardo.'

Harriet was struck by his air of excitement. 'A Leonardo?'

'Maybe,' he said, with a tantalizing smile. 'It's no use teasing, Harriet, I'm not saying another word till we've got an expert in.'

As they passed Rory's door, Harriet was surprised to see him hesitate and glance anxiously round. He said nothing. They were heading up the back stairs, Harriet in the lead, when her heart almost stopped. Just above them, in the gallery, she could hear cautious footsteps on the old polished boards.

Too late to retreat, her abrupt halt made Rory walk into her and his ensuing grunt was loud enough to wake the dead. Damn, she thought, her heart thudding now, I really wish I hadn't had that particular thought. The door stood half open and she froze, panic rising like bile. What are we to do? There's a murderer in there. She reached a hand back behind her and was relieved to feel Rory's firm, warm clasp. Did he hear us? Can we get away downstairs?

'Oh, for God's sake.' John Forrester stood in the doorway, a look of mild exasperation in his eyes. 'I thought you two were out of the picture. Oh well, you'd better come in.'

The gun in his hand made the argument persuasive and they followed him into the room. Harriet gave a little gasp when she spotted Brendan Whittaker lying unconscious on the floor, and she shot Rory a warning look. The vicar was a very dangerous man, there was no question.

'Quite,' he said, evidently picking up on her thought. 'Sensible, Miss Quigley. Keep it like that.'

He looked at them and, to her astonishment, he smiled at her. 'For heaven's sake, sit down, Dr Attlin,' he said, pointing to a chair. Rory staggered across the room and sat down, unable, Harriet realized, to do more than obey. The boy was clearly exhausted almost beyond bearing and might be close to collapse. She turned back and caught the vicar watching her.

'You sit down too, Miss Q,' he said, pushing another chair in her direction. 'And maybe you can suggest what on earth I'm supposed to do with you both?' He shrugged. 'I should have made sure of you, I knew it at the time, but Brendan interfered. Oh well.' He nodded to her and she was suddenly chilled by the familiarity of his charming smile. 'Maybe you can assist me in my enquiries, as they say. You know a lot about the Attlins, don't you, being one of the family yourself.'

Harriet nodded silently, glancing covertly at the silent form of Brendan Whittaker. Was he unconscious, or — worse? John Forrester was still watching her and he followed her gaze. 'Yes, well, sometimes people get in the way.'

He said nothing more but she felt herself recoil. So it was true; and if Brendan had got in the way, what of Rory and Harriet?

'What have you got there?' He tweaked the plastic folder out of Harriet's hand and frowned. 'Something else I ought to have destroyed, or at least taken with me,' he said fretfully. 'I should have checked what Brendan had done with it, he was quite careless. Another minus point to chalk up to working with other people.

'I don't know.' He paced to and fro across the gallery, always watchful, looking first at the exhausted Rory, slumped in his chair, looking only half-conscious, and then at Harriet, with a calculating expression.

'Maybe we should pool information?' he began. 'I know your cousin, Canon Hathaway, was poking his nose into my affairs. I suppose he told you everything he discovered?'

She shook her head, feeling hopeless. It was ten, fifteen minutes ago that she had spoken to the inspector. How long would they take? Any time now, if he had despatched someone at once, but who knew? She shivered. John Forrester was surprisingly cool for now, but that surely couldn't last.

'I'll tell you what I've been researching,' he said. 'Then maybe you can come up with some answers, you never know. I'm aware that you're well up with the family legends, so you may know something I've missed.' He sat down and chewed at his thumbnail.

'It all started,' he said, 'when I was at Cambridge and there was a little local difficulty with a girl. I paid her off and it was over as far as I was concerned. I graduated, went to theological college, was ordained and started climbing the ladder to fame and fortune — in so far as it's possible in the Church of England.' He grinned at her. 'And it is possible, you know, if you're good-looking, can turn on the charm and have plenty of money, which I have, courtesy of my wife, who, sadly, turned out to be a drag on my ambitions and not the stepping stone I'd bargained for. Still, more of that later.

'Last summer I was having a drink in the Wykeham Arms when that little tick, Colin Price, tapped me on the arm and said, 'Remember me?' How could I forget? He'd been at Cambridge with me; he was a fresher when I was in my final year. He knew all about the wretched girl so of course he thought it would be worth my while to keep his mouth shut. It wasn't actually too bad; he was working in the Stanton Resingham archive and one evening when he'd had too much to drink, he bragged about the valuable stuff there was, that nobody had a clue about. So we did a deal. I financed his trips abroad and we split the proceeds fifty-fifty, with him always insisting on cash payment from the auctioneers or buyers. That went straight into two European bank accounts, under assumed names, of course.'

Harriet listened in silence, no need to feign interest, it was fascinating. And utterly terrifying. Besides — she nourished a faint hope — the longer she kept him talking, the sooner the police ought to arrive.

'One of the letters Colin found mentioned something called 'Aelfryth's Tears', which was said to contain tears shed by the Virgin Mary. Soon afterwards a couple of other references turned up. We narrowed it down to King Alfred's time; I used to nip into the archive room and work with Colin; nobody ever bothered me. Another clue led me to Alfred's mistress, and all the indications are that it was a fabulous piece of jewellery, along the lines of the famous Anglo-Saxon Jewel, or the Middleham one.'

Harriet glanced furtively at Rory and for a moment thought he had passed out but he caught her eye and gave the ghost of a wink. She breathed again, just in time as John Forrester gave him a pitying look and continued his story.

'I went into the business of selling archive items because Gillian was being very difficult about money at that time. Up until her breakdown she was always very generous, proud of her high-flying husband and looking to be an archdeacon's wife within a few years, but suddenly she turned very tight-fisted and tried to limit my allowance. I decided it would look good if I took a year out, to try to cope with my poor, neurotic wife; you wouldn't believe the outpouring of sympathy I got about it. So I put in my request for a country parish. It suited me very well, less scrutiny, lots of 'Ah, poor dear vicar', while my wife's health worsened visibly. It didn't take long for people to realize Gillian was an addict and the levels of sympathy rose even higher, encouraged by a few manly tears, judiciously rationed. Oh yes, nobody would be surprised if the poor, addled creature had an accident.'

Harriet caught her breath but she continued to sit in silence, nervously watching his every move with narrowed eyes.

'Where was I? Oh, yes, Colin Price. I had no idea the jewel was said to be connected with the farm here until he spotted a letter stuffed into the spine of some account books, dating back to Queen Anne's time. It referred to a hiding place, known only to the Attlin family, where they always stashed their treasures in times of trouble. The letter was written in 1642 and was obviously overlooked when the ledgers found their way into the Resingham collection. That's the last page you had there.' He waved a hand at the plastic wallet. His face darkened. 'It should still be safely in my study, but I suspect Brendan's been doing a spot of breaking and entering on his own account.'

His expression lightened and as he strolled over to peer at Dame Margery's portrait, looking so normal and conversational, Harriet had to remind herself that it was a real gun that dangled so negligently from his hand.

'Things suddenly fell into place,' he went on, with a pleased laugh. 'I wound up here, which was almost enough to restore my faith in miracles. There was no mention anywhere on the Web of the Attlins having a fabulous jewel in their possession so it didn't take a lot of guesswork to decide that any hiding place the Attlin family had might be connected with the legendary Roman villa, the ruins of which were known to be undisturbed. I set about establishing to all and sundry that I was burningly interested in the late Romano-British period and that I liked nothing better than pottering about Roman ruins.

'I was planning on suggesting to Mr Attlin that he should let me finance and oversee a small, exploratory dig when two things happened. The first was that just before Christmas old Misselbrook, the Attlins' tenant farmer, thought he was dying and sent for me. I let him talk and he told me that he'd found a way down into the ruins: 'I know you likes them old things, Vicar.' He'd been getting rid of badgers illegally, using snares and poison and so forth, and when he was digging out one of the setts he spotted that the badgers had broken through over the centuries into a brick-lined chimney, or so he thought. He didn't venture down there — too old and rheumaticky — but he told me he was sure it led to the ruins of the villa that his 'old dad' had told him about.'

John shrugged. 'He was a cantankerous old devil, and when he didn't die after all, he took to avoiding me, though he needn't have worried; I couldn't have cared less about his badger-killing exploits. I was just wondering what to do about this new bit of information, when I fell foul of Brendan Whittaker.'

The pleasant expression vanished for a moment and Harriet shivered. A glance across the room showed that Rory was still lying doggo; at least, she hoped that was it. Brendan, on the other hand . . .

'He found out something, guessed rather, about my private life. Something I really didn't want anyone to know.' The light, pleasant voice had an edge to it now. 'So, to get him off my back, and at the same time to make use of him for manual labour, I told him I was trying to locate the Attlin treasure. Spun him some rigmarole of a letter found in the vicarage, not the archives, and filled him with tales of golden guineas, Saxon torcs, Civil War silver and so forth. He wasn't very bright and he quite enjoyed a break from his job with Gordon Dean — all this oil business, which Brendan knew a lot more about than he ever let on. Gordon, on the other hand, had no idea about Brendan's treasure-hunting activities; no way he'd let his boss in on the act. Then, would you believe it? Mike Goldstein blundered in on us one night last week.' He shook his head. 'Mike saw Brendan drive at old Attlin, so he had to be brought in on it, of course. Bloody stupid thing to do, but that was Brendan all over.'

'I think the family always knew there was a hiding place,' Harriet ventured, pale at the casual mention of the attack on Walter, but too scared to react. 'The present-day family, I mean; it was just that the location was lost somehow. I remember my father telling me about it; his mother was some kind of cousin on Walter's father's side. If it was written down, there must have been a reason: perhaps the heir was too young to be told? But whatever happened, the secret was lost.' She hesitated, unwilling to trigger his anger. 'Have you considered that the same thing might have happened with this jewel? That Aelfryth's Tears might have been lost hundreds of years ago? Maybe spirited away, either by the family or by some other agency?'

'Of course I have,' he nodded impatiently. 'If I can't find it, obviously I'll have to give up on it. I'd expected to have a lot more time to search the ruins anyway, and if nothing turned up there I had in mind a back-up plan involving Edith.' He glanced over as Rory grunted. 'Back in the land of the living, are we? Oh yes, marrying Edith was to be my last-ditch solution, but that's not an option now, not after tonight's little performance. Still.' He looked pleased with himself.

'I've systematically transferred money into several overseas accounts, as well as setting up a few more around this country, under a variety of aliases and, of course, Colin had no idea I knew his account number and PIN. What with that and the Attlin plate . . . ' At Harriet's gasp he nodded smugly and reached out a foot to the large holdall beside him. 'Oh yes, that really was down in the Roman ruin in a rotten leather bag. Mike found it this evening. I couldn't let him go free, knowing that little secret; this isn't just silver, you know, some of it is silver-gilt. Collectors all over the world and no questions asked. I'd have liked more time to explore down there, but there it is.'

His audience sat spellbound, not daring to move. Harriet slid a sidelong glance at Rory and shook her head very slightly. No point trying to rush John, not in their present state of physical exhaustion, and not with that gun, still held lightly in his hand.

'You're a rare kind of woman, Miss Quigley, or may I call you Harriet?' John suddenly broke out. 'They talk about you in the village you know, a mixture of respect and awe: '*A good, strong woman, that Harriet, a sharp tongue on her but kind as kind if you need a helping hand. But certainly she'd have been drowned as a witch in times gone by,*' that's what they say.' He looked at her, a puzzled expression in his light-brown eyes. 'Tough as old boots, is another one and by God, after today, I can believe it. I know you're the sort that believes in a stiff upper lip, but to go on as though nothing had happened . . . ' He turned to look at Rory, 'She does know, doesn't she? About her cousin? You did tell her?'

Harriet stared at him, fear beginning to dawn in her eyes.

'They did tell you Canon Hathaway died yesterday afternoon, didn't they?'

14

'S-S-Sam?' His name hung in the air as Harriet's world trembled on the brink of destruction. Pain; she hunched over, feeling the pain, like a burning in her stomach, rising to her throat, as a scream of denial gathered. Then Rory, ignoring the gun, staggered over and put his arms round her.

'Shh, Harriet, it's not true.' He held her tightly, whispering urgently in her ear. 'He means Dr Sutherland — he thinks it was Sam.' She was shuddering now and he whispered again, 'Sam rang me last night, about half past ten. He's safe, Harriet, he's safe. Believe me.'

John Forrester had delivered his bombshell, and was now strolling along the gallery, peering at the portraits. He seemed unconcerned that Rory was no longer semi-conscious or that Harriet, though still grey with shock, had subsided quivering in her chair. 'You're sure?' she breathed and sighed with relief at Rory's surreptitious nod.

She was too shaken at first, the imagined loss of Sam, dearest friend, most beloved companion, making her weak and hollow.

Out of John's eyeline, Rory gave an infinitesimal nod and held his finger to his lips. 'Don't let him know,' he breathed, then, as John sauntered back towards them, Rory slumped on the floor beside Harriet, apparently close to collapse.

'I was sorry about Canon Hathaway.' Speaking in a conversational tone, John nodded towards Harriet. 'I hardly knew him but he didn't like me much, which did rather make him stand out.' His eyes gleamed. 'I'm used to people thinking I'm a pretty straight kind of guy. Didn't bother me too much, though, his not taking to me, but when he started asking questions recently, I had to take notice. He was such a dogged old devil too, and clever with it, asking the right questions of the right people. Very inconvenient for me.'

He shrugged as he looked over at Harriet. 'And then when I realized he'd got you at it as well, playing detectives, that was the last straw. Meant I had to take steps to stop him.'

For a moment Harriet felt indignant at the assumption that Sam had been encouraging her, when it had been all her own idea, then the sinister implications of what John had said struck her. She shivered and sat back quietly, not daring to meet his eyes.

'What, what did you do?' That was Rory, half whispering.

'Mmm? Oh, it was simple enough and quite painless, I do assure you, Harriet. I got Mike Goldstein to keep an eye on your cousin for me. We had a little transaction to carry out so I'd chosen the cathedral as our meeting place, nice and anonymous, you see. The other two, Mike and Brendan, knew I was getting irritated by Sam Hathaway, so when Mike spotted him on the High Street, he texted me and followed him at a discreet distance. I kept a lookout and spotted him, fast asleep, dozing under that ridiculous panama hat that all the locals know by sight. He didn't notice me when I sat down beside him and neither did anyone else. We were just two of several devout worshippers.'

He let out a short, mirthless laugh.

'An injection of potassium solution brings about a quick death with all the appearance of a heart attack and of course it has the advantage of being undetectable at a post mortem, or so I understand. He'd even got a couple of scratches on his wrist and I injected into one of them so there'd be no puncture mark. I had the hypodermic ready in my pocket — it was left over from when Gillian . . . I had to be incredibly quick, in and out of the chapel in less than three minutes. I assure you, Harriet, he didn't feel a thing, barely stirred when I did it because he was so sound asleep.'

Harriet gritted her teeth and raised a hand to her eyes. Let him think this was grief, anything but the incandescent rage that was bubbling up inside her at his casual dismissal of a valuable life. She kept her cool, though; the vicar's mental balance seemed less stable somehow, now he believed he was on the brink of finding the fabled jewel. Rory clearly felt the same, because he spoke nervously but calmly.

'What had Canon Hathaway discovered that was so important to you that you had to — to silence him?'

John's brow furrowed and he looked increasingly irritated. 'He'd been poking about in the archives, asking questions about Colin Price, and I couldn't have that. Besides that, he'd been asking questions about Gillian, about her health. And her death.'

'Why did that matter?' Harriet was very impressed by Rory. His quiet voice and calm, non-threatening manner, were just right. He was trying to keep things evenly balanced and not give a loaded significance to any question. Poor lad, she thought, he learned diplomacy in a hard school in that prison.

The vicar's assurance that he didn't want to hurt them began increasingly to ring hollow, she realized with a shiver, in view of the confidences that were beginning to spill out.

'Did it matter what Sam found out?' Rory repeated the question evenly. 'You don't mean Gillian really did kill herself, do you? That she jumped?'

John Forrester stared at him in astonishment then threw back his head and laughed out loud in what appeared to be genuine amusement.

'Jump? Gillian? Of course she didn't jump. I pushed her!'

'You — you *pushed* her?' Harriet's head came up with a jerk as she choked out the question. John gazed at her, looking mildly surprised.

'Of course, didn't you realize? Oh dear, you disappoint me, Harriet. I thought you were clever. Oh yes, all that distraught husband business, I did do it well, didn't I? I was a distraught husband all right, but that was before she died, when she decided to stop my allowance and started threatening to alter her will. Plus, she found out about my handy little arrangement with Colin Price, among other things. Besides . . . '

He paused, staring at the wall, a frown furrowing his brow.

'She was viciously possessive. She bought me with the promise of keeping me in decent

280

comfort and ultimately leaving me her money and she never let me forget it. But as I said, when she started talking about changing her will, I knew I had to do something. It wasn't hard to get drugs and I took it steadily at first, so that her behaviour became erratic, particularly when we were out, at dinners or public events. Just enough for people to start to wonder. Was she menopausal? A drunk? Was it drugs?

'I played the anxious, supportive husband to the hilt, in denial when anyone broached the difficult subject, but soon it was common knowledge: Gillian Forrester was an addict and her poor husband such a kind, patient man.'

Harriet was still sitting quietly, Rory the same, she noticed, anxious not to disturb John's train of thought or provoke any violent reaction. Memory surfaced as she recalled a teacher at her previous school, whose short-lived appointment had made life extremely difficult for the staff. At first sight the woman had been charming, an inspirational teacher, warm and friendly, but gradually it was borne in on Harriet and her senior staff that Miss Crawford was a liar of a high order.

Avril, Sam's wife, had been alive then, head of the English department. Harriet recalled her bursting into the staffroom one morning. *'I've been doing some research,'* she'd exulted. *'There's something called a charismatic psychopath, just listen to the symptoms: charming, attractive liars, usually gifted and manipulative. Often leaders of religious cults, they can be irresistible and surrounded by friends, talking their way out of difficulties and taking as their due the praise of others.'*

Harriet's eyes widened and she slid a speculative glance at the vicar, remembering how struck she and the rest of the staff had been by this. Avril had continued reading from her notes: *'There's no empathy, they don't feel sorry for anyone or anything and when they've got what they want, they move on to another victim.'*

Was this John? It certainly sounded like him and it had fitted that long-ago member of staff. In that case though, the woman had moved on after only two terms, blithely accepting a more enticing offer and not caring twopence for the inconvenience this might have caused. As it was they heaved a collective sigh of relief and Harriet made a note to take more care in future. Now, today, at this moment, things were a good deal more complicated.

Oblivious to Harriet's train of thought, the vicar was reminiscing, looking very pleased with himself and, Harriet noted with a nod to the memory she'd dredged up, with not a trace of remorse or sorrow.

'It was simple,' he said, with a complacent smile. 'New Year's Eve, lots going on, plenty of to-ing and fro-ing around the village. I'd been invited to join the bell-ringers for the last hour, to bless the bells and so forth, as they rang in the New Year, and to join them at the end for a celebratory pint.' He shrugged his shoulders. 'Dear God, I should have got an Oscar for that night's performance. In turns I was the solemn parish priest on duty, the good bloke sharing a joke and a drink, but all the time letting the anxious, harassed husband peek out from behind the mask. I tell you, I had them in the palm of my hand and I even managed a tear, or at least the impression of one, when I rang home to check on Gillian. There was no answer, of course, but I sighed and smiled and said, with a slight choke in my voice, that she must be asleep and I wouldn't disturb her. There wasn't one person in the belfry who didn't understand that I meant she was stoned out of her mind and that I was covering up for her — as always.

'Anyway, I rang again and when there was no reply, I did my saintly husband thing and told them I'd better go and check. It was

283

quite difficult stopping one or two of them who wanted to go with me, but I choked them off. I couldn't have timed it better.' His brown eyes gleamed. 'Gill was just staggering out of the bathroom when I got in, so I nipped upstairs, twirled her round and gave her a very gentle shove.'

Harriet schooled herself to receive this remarkable information without a blink, noting with approval that Rory too was absolutely deadpan. She had to grip her hands tightly, however, to hide the trembling.

'Enough of ancient history,' John said, almost gaily, as he started to circle the gallery once more. 'Time to have a go at this panelling again. I'm convinced there's some kind of hiding place behind it, somewhere near the portrait of Dame Margery. That has to be what the piece of paper refers to, the one Brendan dropped. I checked out her tomb in the church but it would take a block and tackle to shift, not to mention the attention it would attract. I just hope the portrait's not another blind alley, but in it Dame Margery's definitely wearing a jewel, which may be a reliquary, and I'm sure there's no other mention of Aelfryth's Tears. It would be considered a national treasure, from the scraps of information I've come across, and it's inconceivable that if it had been found it would have remained in obscurity. The Attlins would probably have done something noble but stupid, like donating it to the British Museum. At the very least they'd have lent it to some prestigious institution.'

Evidently tiring of conversation, the vicar went back to tapping industriously at the panelling, centring his attentions on the area round the Tudor portrait of Dame Margery. Rory caught Harriet's eye and indicated the gun but it was clear that any attempt to jump John Forrester would end in disaster, so they let it alone.

To Harriet's astonishment, John suddenly let out a yelp of delight. 'I've got it!' After tapping and banging all over the ancient carving he had somehow managed to slide his penknife into an almost invisible crack. A moment or two later he had the catch undone and with a protesting creak of rusty hinges, the panel swung outwards, showing another small door three feet away through the thickness of the wall. It must lead to the roof, Harriet supposed, keeping a wary eye on their captor.

Into her mind slid a dangerous thought: Would John begin to wonder, as she was herself, how the occupants of such an old house had missed this particular door? For instance, Walter had told her once that much of the roof had been replaced back in the 1920s and it was beyond belief that then, even if not before, the little outer door should not have been discovered. Time enough to consider this when they were out of this pickle, she decided, directing a ferocious frown at Rory who responded with an almost invisible nod.

'Oh *yes.*' It was a cry of triumph. John had reached into the gap where a tiny hatch was let into the brickwork. Almost sobbing with delight, he managed to wrench it open and reach into the cavity for a box of blackened and tarnished metal, measuring about four inches long by three deep and only about two inches to the top of its domed lid.

He drew it carefully out into the open, sighing with pleasure. 'This looks like silver,' he remarked in a conversational tone, huffing on the metal and rubbing it with his sleeve. 'Yes, see how it's polishing up?'

Delicately, infinitely slowly, savouring the moment, he negotiated the catch on the front of the little coffer. There was no key and he lifted the tiny latch. Inside, wrapped in faded silk, lay a small, jewelled object, the gold untarnished by the centuries.

Rory and Harriet forgot, for a moment, their predicament, and craned their necks to look at the treasure. Harriet frowned but stayed silent. Rory stared at it, puzzled. It was clearly the jewel in the portrait, the knotwork casing that held the large garnet, surmounted by small pearls, but why did he feel cheated? To his dismay he realized he was not the only one to feel that way.

'What the hell is this?' It was a howl of rage from John Forrester. 'This isn't Aelfryth's Tears, this is a copy.'

Furiously disappointed he flung the little silver chest with its bejewelled contents onto a small table and turned on Harriet and Rory. 'Don't you see?' he demanded. 'Look at the workmanship. Oh, I grant you it's not bad, in fact it could be considered very good, of its kind. Of its kind, though . . . I couldn't say offhand what date it is, but I don't even know that it's real gold, could be pinchbeck, and they've just made random marks instead of the correct runic inscription. It should read, *'Joy, Prosperity and Fruitfulness'*. And as for the pearl . . . '

It was almost a wail of fury and despair. 'I don't know about the garnet, could be glass and the pearls don't look right either. At a guess I'd say it's an eighteenth- or early nineteenth-century fake.' He picked it up again and fiddled with it. 'Could be earlier, I suppose, parts of it recycled, perhaps.'

His probing brought results at last and the garnet in its basketwork casing swung back on a minute hinge, revealing a cavity the size of a hazelnut. 'See? In the real jewel, this compartment would be smooth and polished. This isn't bad, but it's not the quality you'd expect. The real one ought to have a glass inner seal too because of the Virgin's tears inside.'

He fidgeted for a few minutes, eyeing up the aperture behind the panelling, then he turned to them with narrowed eyes. 'I'm going to try and get through there,' he said, glancing at the gun. 'You'll stay here and not try anything clever. I'd rather not shoot you, the noise will draw unwelcome attention, but it won't bother me if I have to.'

Rory was surely looking more grey and weary than just now. Harriet slid a sidelong look at him, her own head throbbing badly. She turned away and nodded slightly in response to a lifted eyebrow from the vicar, watching as he wrestled with the outer door, a struggle in the cramped space as he wrenched at the ancient, rusted bolts. At last he succeeded and the door creaked open, revealing a minute platform on the leads and slates of the roof; probably an access door for maintenance, Harriet supposed, but not in use for a very long time now. It was bolted on the inside, she noted, so maybe those workmen on the roof, back in the twenties, could just have assumed it was sealed up and disused.

As John scrambled back down into the gallery, Harriet checked her watch. Oh God, what if the cavalry turned up now? She ventured a question.

'What will you do now?' she asked. 'Join Colin Price wherever he's hiding out? You won't get away with it, you know.'

She was fleetingly aware of Rory's consternation and realized he had, like Harriet herself, begun to formulate a theory about the missing man's disappearance and was afraid lest she remind John of any of his previous opponents. However, John merely smiled at Harriet with the patronizing air he reserved for most women and she was close enough to Rory to catch his sigh of relief. He clearly understood now that she was trying to distract the other man. Perhaps — perhaps it would turn out all right.

'I mean, did he go abroad as the police have suggested?' she persisted. 'Did you help him to go away?'

He laughed at her this time. 'Oh yes, I helped him to go away. You could say that.'

His meaning was unmistakable, even to Harriet's reluctant ears, but she couldn't restrain herself. 'You're a man of the cloth,' she whispered and he looked amused, relishing her naivety.

'But — how did you manage it?' She was stammering slightly now, praying that she could keep John's attention long enough for the police to arrive. Where the hell were they? She didn't dare sidle over to the window to look. 'I mean, the police checked his room and he'd paid his rent in full, they said. And taken a bag of clothes. His passport was gone and he had money, so he could just disappear.'

'Well, of course.' He was still mildly amused by her, still instructive. 'That's just what I'd told him to do. I met him, you see, the day before Gillian's funeral. It was just a casual encounter and he offered his condolences.'

He smiled with remembered satisfaction. 'It was all beautifully planned. Gillian was becoming impossible and Colin was getting greedy, demanding a bigger cut. He said he had to take all the risks, set up the deals, see the contacts and that was worth more money. He did a lot of sailing, you see, so he took care of that side of the operation in Jersey and across the Channel. I wondered if I could get rid of the pair of them at the same time and for a while I toyed with the idea of the poor, tormented vicar suffering the ultimate humiliation of having his wife decamp with a toy boy, but I decided it was a bit contrived. It was easy to work out what to do about Gillian, but solving the problem of Colin's 'disappearance' took more thought.

'I thought about scuttling his boat with him aboard, somewhere mid-Channel, but the practicalities were against it. How could I have got back myself, for a start? I could have staged an 'accident' and been washed up, but it was too risky and I didn't want anyone to sniff out a connection between us.' He frowned suddenly. 'I was quite keen on the idea of disposing of him at the pig farm just up the road, but again it simply wasn't practical. I made some enquiries when I was away from home, but although pigs are omnivorous, you'd actually need to dismember a body before getting it into the mincer and I'm much too squeamish, I'm afraid. No, the solution I came up with was absolutely foolproof.'

He was rummaging around in the cavity, reaching right back into the little wall safe. 'Ha! What's this?' It was a small wallet of rotted leather and when he gently pulled it apart a tiny bundle wrapped in waxed silk was revealed. Delicately inserting his knife he sliced through the covering and a ring tumbled out. It was the ring Dame Margery was wearing in her portrait.

He stared down at it with surprise and pleasure and glanced across at the picture. 'Oh well, not all a waste of time, then.' Looking at Harriet, he stuffed the ring in his pocket and smiled ruefully. 'Where was I? Bit of a classic, this, isn't it? The murderer's confession; but luckily for me, you're no Miss Marple. Oh yes, once I'd decided how Gillian was to meet her end it was beautiful, I could kill two birds with one stone.'

He started to prowl round the gallery again, restlessly fingering the little emerald ring, the gun swinging nonchalantly from his fingers. Harriet moved slightly so that she was still in his line of sight; Rory leaned back in his chair looking exhausted but not, she narrowed her eyes, not quite as ill as he had appeared ten minutes or so ago. They were both carefully avoiding the window.

'It was brilliant, you know, bloody brilliant.' The carefree laugh rang out, striking chill into his listeners' bones, and reminding Harriet once more of Avril and her list of characteristics of a charismatic psychopath. You got it right, Avvie, she thought with a sigh. No mistake about this one.

'I played the grieving widower to the hilt and alternately wept manly tears or displayed an even more heroic stiff upper lip, according to my audience or comforter. Then, as a way of paying my last respects, I insisted on having her coffin at home the night before the funeral. Oh, they argued against it, said it would be too upsetting, but no-one could quite bring themselves to say outright that it was morbid, and not one of them felt able to deny a grieving husband, and him a clergyman, the privilege of a last vigil. It made it so easy.'

He hugged his memory to himself exultantly, straying perilously near to the window. Harriet moved casually in the other direction and, as she had hoped, his eyes followed her, anxious to tell her how clever he had been. It made frightening listening; this detailed confession didn't bode well for herself and Rory for surely there was only one conclusion to draw when John had told them everything.

'Our unexpected meeting was a blessing,' he continued, still in that cheerful, conversational manner. 'There were a few errands I had to do in Winchester and while I'd planned to ring him, it was safer this way. I told him I'd had a tip-off that Interpol were onto him and he was to get over to Locksley so I could help him get away. He was agreeable, a new start suited him and he'd no family and no real friends, only pub

293

acquaintances, so I told him to wait in the church till the old biddies had stopped turning up at my door with their quiches and cakes and casseroles. There's a path between the vestry door and the back door to the vicarage, so he slipped in unnoticed as I was seeing off the last couple of sympathizers. I'd told them I wanted to be quite alone, you see, and they were all pussy-footing around, respecting my grief.'

With no idea what, if anything, might be happening outside, Harriet prayed desperately that John Forrester's vanity would keep him in confessional mood.

'I got Colin drunk,' he was saying. 'I waited till he passed out on the sofa and used the syringe on him. I just used the same method again yesterday in the cathedral. Why change the plot?' He didn't even notice their involuntary gasps, Harriet realized, he was so deeply absorbed in his story. 'I unscrewed Gillian's coffin, ripped out the padding and lining, and managed to squash him down on top of her. He wasn't a big guy but though it was a tight squeeze, I managed it in the end.' There it was again, that light, amused laugh. 'It was quite funny, really. I ended up having to sit on the coffin to get the lid screwed on, like a slapstick comedy, sitting on a bulging suitcase. Next day was the funeral and the coffin never left my sight, not for a moment. I even insisted on following it through at the crematorium and watching it as it was consigned to the flames. One of the perks of office,' he chuckled. 'Even though they all clearly decided I'd flipped by then, but I wasn't risking some fly operator doing a last-minute sweep for jewellery, or running a used-coffin racket.'

'That took some nerve,' Harriet ventured, trying to keep him pleasant, to show appreciation of his cleverness. It seemed to work.

'Didn't it just?' he agreed. 'The next day I had a bonfire of Gillian's oldest clothes. I'd helpfully insisted on packing all the decent stuff into her suitcases and asked various village ladies to take them to charity. Poor dear vicar.' He grinned at her, inviting her complicity. A tremulous half-smile, which was all she could summon up, seemed to do the trick.

'It was easy to slip Colin's bag and the coffin lining into the flames and I dug the ashes into the garden, round the roses, with a generous helping of bone meal and chemical fertilizer mixed in with compost, just to make sure it couldn't be traced. The urn, containing the ashes of the dear departed, I scattered at sea in an ostentatious service of commemoration. No forensics there, you see, and it made such a good impression on the village worthies, stiff upper lip, heroic tears hastily mopped.'

He took another turn round the gallery while Harriet braved a swift glance in Rory's direction. Oh dear, he was looking even worse now, sweat beading on his forehead, his hand clutching at his damaged ribs and his left eye beginning to look discoloured from one of John's earlier blows. Harriet's own head was throbbing so badly it was almost blinding and she was only too aware that a badly injured Rory, along with a woman over sixty with an outsize in headaches, was no match for a fit man in his prime. She could only pray for deliverance.

'All those detective stories,' he suddenly surprised her, 'where the murderer has to boast about what he's done ... I never believed that, it seemed plain stupid, but would you believe it? Old Agatha was right. I've been longing to tell someone. It's amazing, like the best sex ever and you can't tell, but lucky me, here you are and now you both know. I'll let you go — maybe.' His glance flickered away from Harriet and she felt a chill of despair. 'By the time you've told everyone else, I'll be reading all about it in the papers in some unnamed foreign refuge.'

He straightened up and Harriet's despair deepened as she registered his cold, practical expression. Without taking his eyes off them he reached into his bag and pulled out a pair of handcuffs, flourishing them at her with a brief return of his charming smile.

'Astonishing what you can find in an English vicarage,' he remarked lightly. 'These came down the dining room chimney with a load of soot when I had the sweep in. Whatever do you suppose my predecessor did with them? Here.' He snapped them on Rory's wrists and shoved a cloth into the younger man's mouth. 'That ought to keep you out of trouble. Get on your feet.'

Harriet felt her stomach churn. This was it. John Forrester beckoned her to him. 'Give him a hand up onto the roof,' he ordered. 'I'm not risking gunshots, the sound carries, and I left the syringe at home. You go first.' He shoved Harriet unceremoniously up through the narrow door in the wall and manhandled the now shackled and gagged Rory after her so that Harriet, breathing an incoherent prayer, had no option but to reach back and grab Rory's shoulders. The vicar scrambled after them and up on the leads Rory shot a frantic, wide-eyed stare at her. Harriet grabbed at him, terrified he might slip and take them both down; she had a poor head for heights at the best of times and this wasn't one of them. *The best of times, the worst of times,* the words rang foolishly in her head as she clung grimly to a railing.

Then it happened.

'What the . . . ' Harriet looked up as John let out a strangled gasp. 'But — but he was *dead.*' John Forrester was losing it now. His eyes bulged in appalled surprise as he stared down into the stable yard. 'He was dead, I know he was. I killed him.'

She had time — a few seconds only, of complete and utter anguish — to stare down at her cousin Sam who was innocently riding an ancient bicycle across the cobbles before John Forrester whirled round to scream at her and Rory.

'You bastards!' There was a cold fury in his face as he turned on them, all his precarious mental harmony destroyed in a moment. 'You've been stringing me along.'

He reached for the gun and fired downwards, again and again, more and more wildly, his control lost, and his captives sagged in horror as Sam Hathaway crashed into the doorway of the stable. As Harriet, completely distraught, opened her mouth to scream and scream there was a loud beating sound immediately above them. A huge shape, silhouetted dark against the bright sunrise and with outspread wings flapping, flew out of nowhere straight towards the vicar of Locksley. Harriet, beside herself with grief, goggled in terror as Rory, who was shaking almost uncontrollably, managed to summon the last dregs of strength. He landed a lucky kick on the other man's shin.

With a scream, first of rage and then increasing terror, John Forrester lost his balance and slipped, bouncing on the slates and then, to their impotent horror, plummeting to the cobbled surface of the stable yard while the great winged creature whirled away.

15

Sam and Harriet stood a little to one side, watching the Attlins — Walter, Edith and Rory — as they clustered round the short, plump, fair-haired man who was closely examining one of the portraits, that of the sixteenth-century Richard Attlin, reluctant father-in-law to the nun, Margery. Professor David Porter, Rory's boss, was almost crooning with delight as he turned the portrait this way and that, tossing his coat onto a chair and even taking off his steel-rimmed glasses to peer at a detail.

'I think you could be right, Rory,' he said in a stunned voice. 'I honestly think you could be right.' His eyes were shining as he turned to them.

Penelope Attlin had stayed downstairs. 'I'll go up in my own good time,' she said firmly, so Walter, Edith and Rory had escorted the expert up to the gallery, with Harriet and Sam in tow, determined not to miss a thing.

Harriet was heavy-eyed and drawn, haunted during the day and in her fitful sleep by the memory of those long, agonizing minutes when she believed Sam was dead. Even now, two days later, she had to clutch at him frequently, tears springing to her eyes with no warning.

He put an arm round her now, and hugged her. Undemonstrative as they were by nature, both cousins were shaken to the core and Harriet thought she would never hear a sound more welcome than Sam's voice yelling up at her from the stable yard. She shivered and he tightened his embrace.

'It's only . . . ' she murmured, leaning her head on his shoulder for a moment. 'Oh, Sam . . . '

'Shh.' He too was speaking quietly, so as not to disturb the discussion on art history. 'I've told you, several times, when the first bullet hit the bike I had no idea what it was, only that I had to shift myself pretty damn quick. Good job I'm still pretty fit and knew enough to roll out of harm's way.' He hestitated, then gave her a gentle shake. 'The sight of you trapped up there with that madman . . . well, I can only thank God it ended the way it did.'

She pulled herself together. 'Oh well, we'd better catch up with Walter and the kids.' Her tone was matter of fact but the affection in her eyes was heartfelt.

'Mr Attlin.' The others were hanging on the expert's words as David Porter addressed his host. 'At this stage I can only offer conjecture, and there'll have to be extensive tests, of course, but I can say that I think — only *think*, mind — that this portrait, of a sixteenth-century Richard Attlin, could be an early Holbein, probably painted before he became court painter to Henry VIII, and as such it should be in the National Portrait Gallery. It's a very significant find, if I'm right, and I'm pretty certain I am.'

He smiled at his open-mouthed audience. 'It's not one of his best and looks as though it was dashed off in a hurry to make the rent money, possibly with several other people giving a hand, but even so, if I'm correct, we could be talking about some very serious money indeed. Here, take a look.' He pulled out his BlackBerry and showed them some images.

His explanation of style, brushwork, colour, all went over their heads. With the exception of Rory they were all stunned. Even Edith, who had joked about a Leonardo in the attic, was silenced; this was beyond her wildest conjectures.

'Would you like me to get in touch with the appropriate people?' David raised the matter with Walter Attlin who beckoned Sam to his side to support him. 'I realize it's Rory's discovery and naturally he'll get full credit, but this is a bit out of our league.'

'What about security?' wondered Sam. 'It's been perfectly safe here getting on for five hundred years. Another night or two won't hurt, will it?'

They settled that the professor should take charge and Edith was about to suggest a drink downstairs to celebrate, when David Porter took another turn round the gallery, stopping now and then to inspect a portrait.

'Rory? Any views on this lady here?' He was standing in front of Dame Margery whose painted eyes gazed serenely at him.

'I did wonder,' Rory joined him, followed by the rest. 'I just wondered about Lavina Teerlinc,' he suggested, looking diffident.

'Oh-ho, that was my first thought.' To everyone's annoyance the two artists said no more as they took a closer look. Edith tugged at Rory's sleeve and David Porter turned to her, looking apologetic.

'What? Oh yes, sorry. Levina Teerlinc was a Flemish artist, very distinguished family. Hang on, I'll look her up.' He flashed some more images under their noses. 'Yes, here we are. She's known to have painted a few miniatures of Queen Elizabeth I and she was even employed as court painter early in Elizabeth's reign. There's something about this picture that recalls her style and the dates would fit. Margery would be around fifty by then so it could be an early Teerlinc.'

Walter Attlin looked at his ancestress and smiled. 'I don't think I even need to consult Edith on this one,' he remarked. 'We couldn't possibly allow Margery to leave the farm, however valuable her painting turns out to be.'

Edith slipped an arm through his and gave him an affectionate hug, nodding agreement.

'The other portrait, though,' Walter continued, 'I'm more than happy to have you investigate that. If it turns out to be genuine I wouldn't want it to be sold abroad so maybe we could come to some kind of agreement about that. As long as we have enough to secure the fabric of the building for the future and maintain what land we have left, as far as is humanly possible, that would be an enormous relief. Other than that, we'll see. But Dame Margery — no, she stays here.' He exchanged glances with the lady and gave a short, embarrassed laugh. 'I saw her, you know, when I was young. Just the once but she was quite clear.'

Rory turned startled eyes upon Edith. 'But I thought . . . a side effect of the medication I'm on is known to be hallucinations. You really . . . ?' He faltered into silence and Edith left her grandfather's side to give Rory's arm a squeeze.

Professor Porter had been talking to Harriet, asking questions and now he spoke to Walter. 'This jewel, Mr Attlin,' he said. 'Would it be possible for me to take a look at the replica of Aelfryth's Tears? I'm no expert on antique jewellery but it sounds a fascinating piece. What a pity the original is lost.'

As Rory went downstairs to fetch the small silver box Harriet became aware of an extraordinary expression on her cousin Walter's face. Amusement, guilt and mischief mingled as he stood back and allowed Rory to show off the copy.

'What is it, Grandpa?' Edith had noticed it too. 'Why are you grinning like that?'

Everyone turned to stare at him as he fished in the pocket of his old tweed jacket and pulled out a soft leather pouch. 'I hadn't thought of this for years,' he said, with maddening deliberation, as he extracted a small, silk-wrapped object. 'I dug it out this morning to show you, and then forgot all about it. This was a fob on my grandfather's watch chain.'

On the palm of his hand lay Aelfryth's Tears, unmistakable as he set it down beside the copy. The original workmanship was superior in every line, the gold knotwork immaculately done, the pearls and the great garnet glowing at its heart and the runic symbols, although they couldn't read them, were not the random markings of the copy. He touched the spring and there was the rock crystal that covered the recess containing the drops from the Virgin's eyes.

'It was always known that there was a copy,' he said. 'But they thought this was it. I'm certain nobody for generations ever realized there was that secret store behind the panelling and it was supposed that the door on the roof had been long out of use, particularly as it was sealed up.'

Edith spoke into the awed silence. 'You mean this has been knocking around for years, in all that junk of your father's that you keep in your bureau?'

He nodded, looking very like a naughty schoolboy. 'I've been meaning to sort that out for years,' he confessed. 'It was always too big, far too ornate for Father, but my grandfather was a flamboyant old Edwardian and liked a bit of glitz.'

'But — it's priceless, Grandpa.' Edith was still struggling with the idea. 'Harriet, you're the historian, tell them what we found out.'

'Edith and I googled Saxon jewellery,' Harriet told them. 'And came up with the Middleham Jewel that was found some years ago. It was sold privately at first and then there was a public subscription to keep it in the country, to the tune of more than two million pounds. And that was a while back, so heaven knows what prices have done since.'

★   ★   ★

Harriet and Karen were in the Great Hall, which Walter Attlin had decreed was the proper place for a celebratory lunch. As Karen straightened place mats and cutlery, Harriet eyed her keenly.

'Don't overdo things, will you, Karen? There'll be a lot going on in the next few months and I rather think you'll be busy. Just take care, that's all.'

'We always did say you were a witch, Harriet.' Karen stared at her former headmistress almost in awe. 'How on earth did you know? Nobody knows except my husband and Mr and Mrs Attlin.'

'Lucky guess,' Harriet grinned, looking smug. 'You've been looking a bit peaky lately and I did wonder about the sickness and migraines you suddenly seemed to be getting. Congratulations! Will you be staying on here?'

'I hope so,' Karen nodded. 'Mrs Attlin's had a brainwave and as long as Edith is happy about it, I'm sure we can sort things out.'

As they tucked into roast pork, bred on the farm, Edith had a sudden thought. 'Didn't you say you'd gone off bacon and pork, Rory?'

'I did.' He glanced down at his laden fork. 'When I was in prison I was very ill with food poisoning — some bad pork, they reckoned. Anyway, it put me off all things pig-related for a long time. But this,' he smacked his lips and raised his fork in a toast to Walter, 'this isn't just pork; it's the food of the gods. I guess I'm pretty much cured now.'

When they had finished lunch Walter Attlin called for silence. 'I won't stand up,' he said, 'Penny will kill me if I do. But I wanted to thank you all for your efforts over the last few days. I'm sorry Professor Porter couldn't stay but perhaps it's better to keep it in the family.'

He smiled round at them. 'I don't need to tell you all that it's driven me mad, having to stay in bed for the past couple of days, just because I had a bit of a dizzy spell.' He directed a frown at his wife, who smiled serenely. 'Missing all the drama probably set me back worse than ever, but all anyone would promise was that they'd 'tell me later'. Still,' he glanced at Rory, 'in the end I wasn't the only one packed off to bed. I gather Harriet insisted on going home when it was all over, only for the doctor to send her off to be tucked up and sedated, and then Rory followed suit by flaking out with exhaustion. So,' he held up his hands, 'here we all are. Let's have a brief rundown of what went on.' He nodded to Sam. 'If you hadn't managed to sneak in now and then for a chat, I'd have gone stir crazy.'

Sam took up the story. 'We all know now what happened on the roof, but I don't believe you've heard it from my angle. I couldn't get to sleep. My mind kept going over and over everything we'd discussed and I tossed and turned and dozed all night. It wasn't till I went downstairs at about five o'clock, to make a cup of tea, that I heard my mobile beeping with Harriet's text message.' He grinned at his cousin. 'I could have killed you, Harriet,' he said with a heartfelt scowl. 'Of all the stupid things . . . '

He waved aside her protest that she and Rory had, on the contrary, been extremely careful, and went on. 'Oh well, never mind. I was in a bit of a fix because my cam belt snapped on the way to the dinner last night and I hitched a lift back with a friend. Needless to say, I had no idea Harriet and Rory were in such danger. I hadn't liked to call Harriet back in case something was up but really I just thought you'd have done something sensible, like take photos and maybe go back to bed. At least,' he looked rueful, 'I *hoped* that was what you'd done.'

For once Harriet tightened her lips, merely looking at him reproachfully. Sam carried on, 'I knew there was an old bike in the shed, left behind by the previous owner, so I wheeled it out and belted off up to the farm. I had to decide whether to check out the fields first but in the end I thought I'd better see if you were back at the house. I hoped it was all a storm in a teacup.' He looked sternly over his glasses at his cousin, but his glance was affectionate.

'I was just about to park the bike round in the yard when all hell broke out and, as you know, I managed to throw myself off and into the open doorway.' He winced and made a face. 'I'm black and blue but that's a small price to pay.' His expression sobered suddenly. 'I'm never going to forget what I saw when I managed to peer round the door jamb. Harriet clinging to the roof and screaming like a demented banshee; Rory — even at that distance — looking like something the cat dragged in and John Forrester falling, his arms outstretched, almost flying, in a kind of horrible mimicry of the heron that distracted him. The police arrived about then, thank God.' He pulled out a handkerchief and wiped his brow. 'It goes against everything I believe in to rejoice at the death of a fellow human being,' he said gravely, 'but it's hard not to be grateful to that heron for startling the vicar as it did.'

Harriet looked up sharply and slid a questioning glance at Rory, who was also looking thoughtful. 'A heron?' he said slowly.

'I don't remember seeing one so close to a house with those huge wings flapping like that,' Sam went on. 'But I don't know, you might call it providential, I suppose. It gave John Forrester a way out, and saved everyone a lot of unpleasantness.'

They digested this in silence, then Edith spoke up. 'I'm not sure I'll ever forgive any of you for leaving me to sleep through it all,' she pouted. 'The first I knew about it all was when I ambled down to breakfast and found the place crawling with police, Grandpa packed off to bed with Gran playing Florence Nightingale, and Rory and Harriet, both bandaged and bruised, also shipped off to rest for twenty-four hours.' She was sitting next to Rory and with a shiver she reached out to take his hand. Harriet, observing, was pleased to note that their misunderstanding seemed to have been cleared up.

'I can understand, in a way, why John did the things he did.' Edith frowned as she spoke. 'At least, I kind-of understand. He wanted money and there's a certain logic in his actions — if you haven't a conscience, that is. First ransacking the archive, then getting rid of his wife because divorce would be a death knell to his ambitions in the Church. And I can see where Harriet's idea might be true, about him being a psychopath. But I do wonder what dirt Brendan Whittaker had on him.'

'Probably saw him sneaking out of somebody's wife's bedroom,' interposed Sam to everyone's surprise. 'It wasn't till I started investigating last week that I learned that Forrester was known to have a mistress, the wife of a big name at Westminster with a country place north of here. And no, I'm not telling you who, Harriet; very risky business altogether but it didn't seem to have any relevance to the matter in hand so I kept quiet. Would have scuppered his chances anyway as it was known in high places and didn't go down at all well. Her Majesty prefers her bishops to have at least some notion of morality.'

'Hmm.' Edith's face was burning as she remembered John's sincere brown eyes gazing into hers. 'All right, but what about you, Harriet? Who do you think pushed you into the quarry?'

Harriet took a deep breath and felt a spasm of shame. She was enjoying this too much, she told herself, being placed centre stage. 'Your news about the vicar's lady friend, Sam, makes me wonder if he nipped out to see her after dropping Edith off at the farm that night. I'm pretty certain it was John Forrester who hit me. I had an impression of a long, low-shaped car, which fitted with his. It might have been Brendan's, of course, but I believe the police have run checks and that night his car was up on ramps in the repair shop having some work done on the sump. The garage people will swear to it that they were actually working on it late that night.'

Walter looked grave. 'That does rather narrow it down,' he agreed. 'But what about the American chap? Did he have a hire car?'

'He did,' Harriet nodded. 'But it was a red Mazda from Hertz, wrong shape altogether. I don't know why John did it. Serendipity, probably. He must have been coming south down the Stockbridge Road and recognized the Mini when I turned off across the fields. I suspect he just took a chance and made certain I wouldn't recognize him because he switched off his lights. I bullied my mole at the police station about it and he rang this morning.' She grinned. 'It's always *who* you know.' There were flakes of paint from the

Mini embedded in the wing of John's car.'

Walter Attlin began to rise to his feet but, obedient to a stern shake of the head from his wife, sat down again.

'I begin to be grateful that I did miss everything,' he smiled ruefully. 'It's exhausting just hearing about it. However, I just want to say something. I won't dwell on the danger that Harriet and Rory found themselves in, or on the fact that it was only by a fluke that Sam wasn't murdered in the cathedral. It will all be rehashed at the inquests and until then I suggest we let it lie. Time enough to think about it when it can't be helped. But I am most sincerely grateful that you are all sitting safely at my table today, and I thank you.'

There was a murmur of assent and, looking slightly sheepish, they raised their glasses to each other.

'It was odd, wasn't it,' suggested Rory a few minutes later, 'that the rumours about looking for oil turned out to be true.'

Edith shot a slightly disapproving look at her grandfather. 'Yes, you've been a bit sneaky about that, haven't you, Grandpa?'

The old man nodded. 'Maybe. The only person I've discussed it with, apart from your grandmother, is Sam. I needed to toss ideas about with someone sensible and discreet and Sam fitted the bill perfectly.' Sam made a mock bow, and Walter continued. 'I wasn't going to broadcast the possibility of a mineral water supply on our land — and that reminds me — negotiations are still going on about that, so please keep it under wraps. They believe there's still a market for a superior brand and that our water is particularly pure, so they want to sink an exploratory bore hole.

'I imagine some inkling of that business got out and that was the foundation for the local gossip. The fact that Gordon Dean or, as we are led to believe, his henchman, was in fact pussyfooting around checking out the oil options, seems to be a complete coincidence, though it could simply be that he got wind of the water deal, which might have set him (or them) thinking. We'll never know. In any case, I suspect he would have drawn a blank on that option; my contacts in the mineral water company were very sceptical about the suggestion of oil deposits here when I brought up the subject.

'Which reminds me,' he looked over in Sam's direction, 'any news on our erstwhile neighbour?'

'Gone to London,' Sam told him. 'I hear the house is going on the market, though rumour has it that he's squeaky clean. But who knows? Word is that his daughter's taken herself off back to New York, so I imagine the police have nothing on her.'

Karen brought in more tea and coffee and when they were settled, Walter Attlin called his audience to attention once more. 'Something else to discuss,' he said. 'Penny and I have been thinking for a long time that we ought to move downstairs. The stairs are getting too much and my accident has made the decision for us. Our plan is that we turn the downstairs rooms into a flat for ourselves, leaving Karen and Elveece where they are, which they're happy about. There's plenty of space, we don't need more than a couple of rooms as long as we can squeeze in a bathroom somewhere. There are a couple of small rooms that will do for that, and a tiny kitchen — just a kettle and a microwave, really, for snacks, as Karen will continue as housekeeper.'

Edith was looking thoughtful and her grandfather smiled across at her. 'I know Gran's already floated the idea by you, so what's your verdict? We thought you could take over the upstairs,' he said. 'I think the gallery will have to be accessible, possibly to the public if we go down that route, but in any case there will certainly be a procession of experts tramping up and down.

'However, there's plenty of room for you to tuck in a kitchen of your own, along with another bathroom or two, and Rory can stay on as your lodger if he'd like to. I know his original plan was to look for a place of his own and of course we'll give him every assistance if that's what he wants, but I'd just like to say that we'd be only too happy to have him stay on at the farm.' He hid a smile as Edith shot a startled glance at Rory and blushed. 'I propose we give it a try at any rate, for a year, say. Karen's going to be pretty busy — I'm giving away a secret here — but she insists she can manage with the catering if we all muck in. In a few months I think we'll insist on getting some help for her, but she won't hear of it just now.'

Afterwards, when the plan had been discussed and approved, Harriet noticed that the old man was looking weary and his wife anxious. 'One more thing,' he said, 'It's all right, Harriet, I know when I'm defeated — but before I'm bullied into going for a nap in a minute, I'll hand over to Sam to tell you what we've been discussing.'

'You might not all know,' Sam began, 'but I've been thinking of a change of direction for some time now. My office job is coming to an end; I've been co-ordinating a three-year project, and it seems a good time to reassess my options. I don't feel called to take on another parish so I'm going to continue as a kind of trouble-shooter, parachuted into parishes short-term, where the incumbent is ill or incapacitated; I also like being on call to conduct funerals at the crematorium. Not everyone's cup of tea but I enjoy the human contact.

'So, while I'm not ready to hang up my dog collar yet, I've been looking for a challenge to replace the office, something where I can be of use. Walter has now suggested I help him out with the admin, and so forth, attached to these new developments. I can deal with the tax ramifications regarding the potential sale of the portrait, look into grants that might be available and co-ordinate the investigations into the Roman ruins, among other things.'

'As you know,' put in Walter, 'they had to call in an archaeologist from the university when they pulled that poor young American out from the hypocaust and Sam's going to oversee their further efforts down there, which will be a load off my mind. I gather there'll be a great influx of experts descending on us anytime now.'

'Then they'll have to compete for space with the reporters already swarming round the front door,' commented Mrs Attlin in a dry voice. 'Dear Sam.' She turned to him with a warm smile. 'It will be quite wonderful to have you take charge of all these developments, and living on our doorstep too. I'm so glad.'

* * *

After lunch Sam went into a huddle with Walter and started sketching out ideas, until his host held up his hands.

'I'm pooped, Sam,' he confessed. 'Penny's got her eagle eye on me and I have to admit I can't get through the day without a nap these days, specially after a feast like the one Karen just served up. I'll be happy to go along with pretty much everything you've come up with so far. Why don't you get it all down on paper, then I can go over it in my own time. Meanwhile I'm off to have a snooze.'

Edith and Rory wandered out into the garden.

'What do you think?' She sounded diffident. 'This plan of theirs?'

'It's a great idea from their point of view,' he nodded. 'No stairs for them and much easier for Karen to manage. But what about you? If you're worried about me, I can always go back to plan A and look for somewhere in town.'

'I'm not, not worried, exactly.' She was looking shy. 'I think it could work out okay, provided we don't — '

'Don't take things too fast?' His voice was gentle and she nodded. 'Fine by me. I'm not really in a fit state yet for romantic moments, so let's just be friends and family? To start with?'

He dawdled along the gravel path and stopped to look up at the roof. 'I promised myself I'd come here one day,' he remarked. 'The day before my dad was killed he was telling me about the family, or at least as much as he knew, which wasn't a lot. Just that they lived near Winchester in a very old farmhouse and that there'd been a quarrel. He said we'd have a trip in the school holidays and introduce ourselves. Trouble was,' his voice was sad, 'he never came home again. There was a motorway pile-up, some moron driving like a maniac in fog, and Dad's car caught fire.'

Edith reached out and clasped his hand in silent sympathy.

'It wasn't till Mum died too that I thought about mending fences with the only family I had left, but . . . other things got in the way.'

'That'll be why Gran's been looking sad,' Edith realized. 'Both of them, your dad and mine, dying so horribly. That, combined with the family likeness, would have brought it all back to her. Still,' she tucked a friendly hand in his and grinned at him, 'things can only get better.'

★ ★ ★

Harriet and Penelope Attlin sauntered out into the sunshine.

'Come and admire my roses,' offered Penelope. 'We can compare notes and later perhaps we'll go and look at the old greenhouses. Elveece has very shyly suggested that we look into hydroponics — you know, growing salad plants in water. Apparently he has a friend who knows all about it and wants to get him here to check it out. Can you manage that tray with your stiff shoulder?'

The sun was beating down but Harriet set the coffee cups down on the garden table and pulled a couple of chairs into the shade of a parasol.

'Well?' Penelope looked at her.

'Very well, I suspect,' Harriet nodded agreement. 'Rory is looking a lot more relaxed than when he first arrived last week. Edith seems to have no regrets about leaving the States and is ready to plunge into working here full-time. Lots of plans in the pipeline. Let them get on with it; at least they'll be company for each other.

'And if you meant me, well I'll be fine too.

321

I'm limping from all the bruises, my shoulder is giving me gyp and I don't know when I'll manage a whole night's drug-free sleep without waking up with the screaming habdabs, but I'll get there, don't worry. Sam being next door will be a huge help. How about you, Penny?'

'Much the same. It's such a bonus to have Edith come home to live. It's put new life into Walter. And Rory is the icing on the cake. Even if they don't make a go of it, we're so happy to have the old quarrel mended.'

Penelope looked pensively at a rabbit that had sneaked in under the fence and was heading across the garden to the vegetable patch round the corner. 'Shhh, let's not frighten him off. But Elveece will be cross — his vegetables are his pride and joy! That's another blessing, Elveece and Karen. How can we be so lucky? Such a delightful couple and soon a baby about the place.' Penelope shot an involuntary look over at Edith, who was in earnest consultation with Sam, while Rory looked on, then she smiled fondly at Harriet, and settled back to doze in the sunshine.

Rory ambled over to join Harriet when she got up to lean over the garden wall, surveying the fields.

'They'll be at it all night,' he grinned,

nodding to Edith who had now produced her tablet and was making notes as she and Sam brainstormed. 'She just rang the agricultural college at Sparsholt, up the road, to make an appointment for someone to come over and give advice, and then she invited the new manager over to join their discussions, you know, the guy who takes over in September, because he's keen to get things on the move. The plans they've got . . . ' His mouth twisted in a wry smile. 'Art shows in the barn — that's apparently going to be my pigeon; weddings and mediaeval banquets in the Great Hall; an official dig with Roman history displays, of course, and the stables turned into holiday lets and God knows what else. They won't be happy till they open the Locksley Hilton.'

Harriet laughed out loud at the prospect. 'Did you know Walter is after a new tenant for the vacant farm?' she asked. 'He'd like to go in for some rare breeds and make the farm accessible to people, school visits and projects and so forth. It'll be a major undertaking but with the prospect of money from the paintings, he'll be able to think about it seriously. Old Misselbrook's house needs gutting from top to toe but it could be a really decent family home for the right people.' She gazed over the fields again, basking in the warmth of the sun. 'I believe there's even talk of looking into planning permission for a farm shop over there, as there's road access.'

'You're glad about Sam taking on the job of helping here, aren't you?' Rory asked. 'He'll be a godsend to Cousin Walter; there'll be a shedload of paperwork. I'll help where I can but I'll be pretty occupied once term begins.'

'It's a godsend to Sam too,' she smiled. 'He's really interested and I've not seen him this animated since Avril died. Moving to Locksley will be good for him, though I'm not so sure about his plan for our joint attic.'

Rory cocked his head.

'It was all one house once,' she went on, turning away from the fence and heading back towards the house. 'Sam's planning to open up the connecting door on the landing and the one downstairs too, which is fine by me, but he also wants to turn the attic into one enormous layout for his model railway. All kinds of plans on the cards, apparently.'

'Harriet . . . ' Rory changed the subject so abruptly that she halted in her tracks and stared at him. 'What Sam was saying, about when we were up on the roof . . . when the vicar fell, did *you* think it was a heron that flew at him?'

'No,' she said quietly, glancing upward with a shudder. 'For one insane moment — and

324

you have to remember I really *was* almost insane with grief and rage having just seen Sam shot dead, as I supposed — if you must know, I thought it was the angel, the one that appeared to the Roman, come to rescue its own.'

Rory's sigh of satisfaction confirmed her suspicions and he ducked his head away from her penetrating gaze.

'You too?' she shrugged. 'Hmm, yes, somehow I think we'll keep that to ourselves, shall we? I don't mind being thought eccentric but that might be a step too far.'

We do hope that you have enjoyed reading this large print book.

Did you know that all of our titles are available for purchase?

We publish a wide range of high quality large print books including:
Romances, Mysteries, Classics
General Fiction
Non Fiction and Westerns

Special interest titles available in large print are:
The Little Oxford Dictionary
Music Book
Song Book
Hymn Book
Service Book

Also available from us courtesy of Oxford University Press:
Young Readers' Dictionary
(large print edition)
Young Readers' Thesaurus
(large print edition)

For further information or a free brochure, please contact us at:
Ulverscroft Large Print Books Ltd.,
The Green, Bradgate Road, Anstey,
Leicester, LE7 7FU, England.
Tel: (00 44) 0116 236 4325
Fax: (00 44) 0116 234 0205

Other titles published by
The House of Ulverscroft:

THE ANNALS OF SHERLOCK HOLMES

Paul D. Gilbert

This sparkling collection of three new Sherlock Holmes stories draw on details and hints from the pages of Conan Doyle's classic works. From the pen of the acclaimed Doctor John Watson we are introduced to previously unsolved mysteries as referenced in many of the original stories.

THE DOLL PRINCESS

Tom Benn

Manchester, July 1996, the month after the IRA bomb. The *Evening News* reports two murders. On the front page is a photograph of an heiress to an oil fortune, her body discovered in the basement of a block of flats . . . Buried in the later pages there's a fifty-word piece on the murder of a young prostitute. For Bane, it's the latter that hits hardest. Determined to find out what happened to his childhood sweetheart, it soon becomes clear that the two stories belong on the same page, as Bane immerses himself in a world of drugs, gun arsenals, human trafficking and a Manchester in decay . . .

SLEEPING DOGS

Fay Cunningham

Gina Cross is a forensic artist for the police. She teams up with Adam Shaw, an investigative journalist, to find Nathan Fox, a school caretaker, involved in the mystery of a child's death twenty years ago. Fox had found something that incriminated three of the students, but then he'd disappeared. The students are now grown up: one is a renowned plastic surgeon, one a politician and the third is a lawyer. But now Fox is back, and no one is safe — and she's not the only one hunting Fox. When Gina's friend is kidnapped and held hostage, anything, including murder, is on the cards.

SAN CARLOS

Neil Forsyth

It's 1989. The Witness Protection Scheme pays you £180.75 a week. You're living a life that isn't working, under a name that isn't yours, and Ibiza offers an escape. But there you meet a woman with a story — and along comes your past . . .

OUT OF THE NIGHT

Dan Latus

One headless body, on the beach near Frank Doy's home on the Cleveland coast, was regrettable, two more were disturbing. But when an uncommunicative woman arrives at his house in the dead of night, only to disappear again, Doy is involved in something worrying. His search for her uncovers a mysterious man with a private art collection and some Russian émigrés. Led deeper into the strange events occurring in Port Holland and nearby Meridion House, Frank tries to unearth the secrets surrounding him and save the life of his desperate female visitor . . .

BLOOD ON THE MARSH

Peter Tickler

When an old woman dies in a care home, it should be a gentle return to duty for DI Holden. However, there is evidence of drugs misuse and Holden's examination reveals cracks appearing in the emotional fabric of Sunnymede Care Home. As staff, doctors and family fall under the glare of investigation, Holden finds her own stress levels rising. Then another death follows, this time, unequivocally, murder. Holden and her team must race to prevent further bloodshed as a killer runs amok in the grimy backstreets of Oxford.